The Hidden Adventures of Sherlock Holmes

By

Alan Dimes

Sixteen Stories combining two collections

The Book of Lucifer and Other New Sherlock Holmes Stories

The Most Terrible Murderer and Other New Sherlock Holmes Stories

Edited by David Marcum

First edition published in 2025

Hardcover ISBN 978-1-80424-722-8

Published by MX Publishing
335 Princess Park Manor, Royal Drive,
London, N11 3GX
www.mxpublishing.com

Cover design by Awan

To the memory of my father James William Dimes (1921-2011) and of my mother, Doris Eva Dimes (1923-2013)

Contents

The Book of Lucifer

My readers may remember the sensational trial of The Legion of Lucifer, some years ago, which resulted in the execution of the leader and several members of that repellant organization. It may also be recalled that the judge praised the efforts of those Scotland Yard officials who had been instrumental in bringing the culprits to justice. What went unsaid, as is so frequently the case, was the aid given them by my friend and colleague, Mr. Sherlock Holmes. It is true that the matter did not afford him much opportunity to exercise his outstanding powers of logic and deduction, but it is equally true that, without his knowledge and insight, the official force would have had little to work with. On this basis, and considering the intrinsic interest of the case, I have decided, with Holmes's consent, to lay the full story of his involvement before the reading public.

During his three-year absence from London, there had been, as he pointed out to Inspector Lestrade upon his return in 1894, three unsolved murders.

"Perhaps you'd like to take a look at them, Mr. Holmes," the inspector remarked when he called on us one evening a few days later, "and see if you can make anything of them."

Holmes agreed, with the proviso that he would naturally give priority to any current case of interest or importance on which he was consulted. He was given access to the Scotland Yard files, from which I am not permitted to quote, but after Holmes's supposed death I had maintained a keen interest in crime and kept a scrapbook of newspaper clippings concerning those I considered of most importance. I draw on these to provide a brief outline of each case as it was seen by the public.

John Cooper Whitney was regarded by all who knew him as an upstanding member of society. A lifelong Liberal and a personal friend of Lord Bellinger, he was also a member of the Methodist Church and an early and active supporter of the National Temperance Foundation. His large personal fortune came from his ownership of several cotton mills in the north of England, where his teetotal principles were strictly adhered to – any worker who was found drinking at work was summarily dismissed, and any worker who brought alcohol onto the premises was fined, and suspended from work for a period of two weeks. Any worker who was found guilty of offences involving alcohol outside the factory gates was also subject to dismissal, even though he had already been fined by the authorities.

Whitney had a large house in Rochdale, but spent most of his time at his spacious flat in Victoria Street, which he preferred for its proximity to the Houses of Parliament. He was unmarried and lived alone. He had three servants, a cook, butler, and maid who did not live in, but were employed under the same conditions as his mill hands, and liable to be out of their situation if they were caught drinking or in possession of alcohol. On the morning of April 27th, 1893, his current servants arrived at the flat to find their employer lying dead on the carpet of his living room, clad only in his nightshirt. His throat had been cut. The servants immediately went out into the street to find a constable, and within an hour two detectives and the medical examiner were present. There were no signs of a forced entry.

The murder was, of course, reported in the newspapers, and while he was well known within his own circles, there can be no doubt that, in the south of England at least, he became better known in death than he had been in life. As his life came under public scrutiny, it became clear that opinion on John Cooper Whitney was sharply divided. For every person who had come to the conclusion that he was a man of steely principle who had worked hard to rescue the labouring classes from the evils of drink, there was another who thought he was a damned interfering busybody who had no right to attempt to deprive the workers of one of the few pleasures they could afford. But could someone who held the latter view have hated him enough, or thought him enough of a threat to personal freedom, to have somehow entered – or been let into – his house to kill him?

With the assistance of the Lancashire police, Scotland Yard attempted to draw up a list of everyone who might have had a grudge against Whitney. I use the word "attempted" because he had been in charge of the family mills for forty-five years, and the number of people who had been fired because of his draconian attitudes ran into the hundreds. He had owned the flat in Westminster for twenty years, and in that time he had dismissed four cooks, three maids, and five butlers for alcoholic offences. The two police forces visited as many people on their list as they could, but found no one who didn't have an alibi, or was dead or had left the country. The three servants, and especially the butler, Lawson, fell under suspicion. The butler because he, other than Whitney himself, alone had a key to the flat, so he could have arrived earlier than usual and surprised his master in bed. Both cook and maid testified that he had in fact arrived last that morning, and that they had had to wait to be let in. Perhaps all three had conspired to kill him?

Witnesses came forward who had seen all the servants riding on the bus or underground after the time which the medical examiner determined to be that of Whitney's death. The suggestion was made in one of the more sensational newspapers that he had been done away with by someone hired by a cabal of disgruntled brewers whose livelihood he threatened.

"Despite the high profile of the National Temperance Foundation," said Holmes as we discussed the case one afternoon, "it is doubtful that their influence, and especially that of one member, would be strong enough to spread fear amongst the brewers and distillers, nor that they would have resorted to murder had it been so. There are adherents of temperance in Parliament who would surely have been a more important target for an alcohol advocating assassin. You realize, of course, Watson, that despite the evidence of the other servants, and those who saw him on public transport, the butler is not exonerated."

"Why do you say so?"

"He held one of the two keys, and keys can be copied. While it seems unlikely that he struck the blow himself, he may have facilitated the entry of the person who did. I shall recommend to Lestrade that he question Lawson further."

During the summer months, it was common for Martin Eastwick and his wife Joan to cross the small stretch of Hampstead Heath that separated their house in Spaniards Road from the Vale of Health, where Mrs. Eastwick's parents, Michael and Susannah Pope, lived, and, after their visit, return home by the same route. On June 22nd, 1893, Mrs. Eastwick made the short journey on her own as her husband was away on a business trip. According to Mr. and Mrs. Pope, their daughter stayed rather later than usual. She refused their offer of her old room and set off for her home in the dark.

An elderly gentleman who was out on his morning constitutional found her body at seven a.m. the next day. She had been strangled. As her rings, necklace, earrings, and purse were missing, the police concluded that robbery had been the motive. The value of the jewellery and money amounted to about forty-five pounds, a sum for which someone living rough on the heath (of whom there were several) might be prepared to kill. All the tramps known to be sleeping on the heath were rounded up and subjected to intense interrogation, but none confessed.

"Really, Watson, if you were homeless and sleeping on the heath, would you stay there after you had killed a woman and stolen forty-five pounds?"

"What should Lestrade have done, then?"

"He should have asked all the other tramps on the heath if one of their number was missing, and if so, whether they knew his name."

"Such people tend not to stay in one place for long," I said, "so it's unlikely that they are still all there to question."

"True. But then he should have gone to all the hotels and boarding houses in the immediate vicinity to see if any had rented a room to a obvious tramp with the unexpected ability to pay for it. That avenue of enquiry still remains."

"Supposing someone had another motive for killing the woman, and a tramp merely found her and took the money from her dead body?"

"That is a definite possibility, yet you will agree that in either case, a tramp must at least be looked for. Another possibility of course is that, as you say, someone had a motive other than theft, but took the money and jewelry to make it seem the work of a thief. There are certainly

difficulties there. Mr. and Mrs. Eastwick, and Mrs. Eastwick's parents, all appear to be upstanding citizens with no enemies in the world."

Since the death of his only child, his son David, Abraham Weston, a widower, had become increasingly reclusive, until he took this tendency to an extreme, selling his house in Camberwell and moving to a lonely little cottage on a remote promontory on the west coast of Scotland. His only human contact was with a middle-aged lady, Mrs. Laurie, who cycled to his home from the nearest village once a week, bringing him groceries and staying to clean the cottage. Every other week she took his laundry and returned it the following week. She testified that while he paid her generously for these services, he spoke to her very little during her visits, preferring either to closet himself in his study with his books or go for a walk across the windswept terrain while she attended to the housework.

She arrived at about half-past-ten on the morning of July 24th that same year and found Weston in his study, dead from a single gunshot wound to the head. A sturdy, sensible woman, Mrs. Laurie didn't succumb to hysteria, but immediately jumped on her bicycle and pedalled swiftly home and reported the death to the village constable, who then sent a message to the authorities in Lillapool. From there, the responsibility for investigation was handed over to the police in Edinburgh, and then to the Scotland Yarders, who in truth stood little better chance of finding the culprit. They questioned the folk in the village to see if any strangers had been seen in the area at the time, but none had. No one amongst the villagers had any motive, and indeed, the only item in the cottage of any obvious value, a silver teapot, hadn't been removed. The detectives then switched their inquiries to Camberwell, where their efforts proved equally fruitless.

"The fact that no one in the village saw any strangers hardly proves anything," said Holmes. "According to the medical report, the murder must have taken place in the hours of darkness. When we combine this with the fact that Weston's house was on a promontory, we can at least surmise that the killer arrived at night in a boat, committed the deed, then left by the way he came."

Holmes looked at the cases from time to time when the steady stream of new clients which attended his return to active practice permitted, but in the end was forced to confess that while he could get a little further than the official force, he was still unable to produce anything conclusive.

The situation would have remained thus, had it not been for the occurrence of five more murders which were equally baffling and seemingly insoluble . . . .

"Ali Ben Abou" was the stage name of Norman Waters, the forty-two-year-old son of a lighterman from Bermondsey, who had been an entertainer in the music halls, in various capacities, after starting as a stagehand at the age of fifteen. By the time he was twenty-nine, he had established himself as a magician.

At the climax of his act, a marked bullet appeared to be placed in a gun and fired at Ali, who seemed to catch it in his teeth. A member of the audience was called up on stage to mark the bullet, fire the gun, and identify the bullet when the magician removed it from his mouth. Despite the loud report and the large puff of smoke, it was of course a blank that was fired. The conjuror palmed the marked bullet, held his hand up to his teeth and produced it as if he had caught it in them. On this occasion, however, the young woman Ali called to assist him was horrified when she fired the gun and he fell forward with a cry, shot through the heart. As the blood spread across the front of his silken tunic, his unwitting killer fainted. The audience sat in stunned silence for a few moments. Then there was uproar.

The curtain was dropped, and a minute or two later the manager came from behind it to assure the crowd that an ambulance had been called, and under the circumstances could the auditorium please be cleared.

Waters' dressing room was locked, and when the police arrived they insisted that it be unlocked. The master key was obtained from the theatre's doorkeeper and entry effected. There, on the dressing table, they found an open box of blanks, or at any rate, a box proclaiming itself to be such. In fact, it contained real live bullets. The murderer must have emptied the box and made the substitution.

Waters was a notorious womaniser, and had been married three times, on all three occasions to women working in his act, which he had been doing for thirteen years. Such was his easy charm that his two previous wives seemed to have accepted their situation with equanimity and bore him no malice, as far as one could tell. Indeed, one of them had carried on acting as one of his assistants even after she had been replaced in his affections. There was always a possibility that a jealous husband or fiancé or a slighted lover had killed him, and the police investigated that line thoroughly.

The obvious suspect, the only conspicuous enemy that Waters had, was another magician, "Mehemet the Magnificent", (born Alfred Leaman in Stockwell, 1853) who had been loud in his claims that Waters had stolen some of his tricks, and had based the Middle Eastern flavour of his identity on Leaman's act. On the night that Waters was killed, Leaman was himself on the stage, in the middle of his own act at the

Camden Palais. It was of course possible that he had hired someone to kill Waters. The police investigated this aspect and could find no evidence for it.

Waters' assistants, including his wife, were all questioned by the police, along with the magician's behind-the-scenes staff. The regular Empire stagehands could be ruled out because they weren't privy to the magician's secrets, and Ali was strict about keeping his dressing room door locked when he wasn't in it. A thorough investigation of Waters' employees revealed that none of them had anything against him. They had all been with him for years, and he was a fair and conscientious employer.

The doorkeeper was briefly suspected, as his master key gave him access to Waters' dressing room at all times, but he could account for all his movements on that last day of Waters' life and hadn't been out of anybody's sight long enough to effect the substitution. His wife confirmed that he had come home at the usual time the previous evening and had been at home the entire night.

Quentin Maltravers was in his seventieth year and had sat on the bench for twenty, after a successful career as a Q.C. During his time as a barrister he had specialized in prosecution, and so it came as little surprise that when he was elevated to the High Court, he quickly became noted for the severity of his judgements. In his personal life, he was a bachelor of ascetic tastes, whose principal vice appeared to be the occasional pinch of snuff. He belonged to only one club, the Solomon, whose membership was restricted to sitting and retired judges.

It came as a great surprise and shock, then, when this pillar of society was found beaten to death in one of the least salubrious back alleys in Whitechapel. Had he been a secret participant in the various forbidden pleasures afforded by London's East End? Whether that were true or not, there was no doubt that the number of people who had a motive for his murder ran into the hundreds.

When Lady Violet Cantwell, the youngest daughter of Lord Caithness, was presented at court, there had been general agreement that she was the most beautiful debutante of her season, and now, some fifteen years later, it couldn't be denied that maturity had only increased her charms. As well as her physical attractions, she had an open-hearted and forgiving nature, which won her friends of all religious and political persuasions.

In those days of her youth, there had been much competition for her hand. Eventually it seemed clear to all that John Allingham, a subaltern in the Household Cavalry and the only son and heir of Sir Walter Allingham, had won her heart, and that their marriage would soon be announced. There was much surprise, then, when she became the second wife of Lord Kilgarriff, a widower eighteen years her senior. In some quarters, there was speculation that she was marrying the wealthy aristocrat because Lord Caithness was deep in debt, and that she was sacrificing her own happiness to keep her parents from penury and disgrace.

Whatever the truth of the matter, it soon became obvious that the marriage was far from happy. After thirteen years, Lady Violet had failed to produce an heir, a fact which Kilgarriff continually threw in her face. He embarked on a series of liaisons with other women, and didn't attempt to conceal them from her.

John Allingham, now Sir John since the death of his father, had remained unmarried. Lady Violet at first sought him out as a friend, and a sympathetic ear for her troubles, but, inevitably, the passionate love which had once existed between them was rekindled. So deep was that love that it couldn't be hidden from society at large, and both Lady Violet and Sir John were prepared to face scandal and divorce if it meant that they could finally be together. Lord Kilgarriff refused to grant a divorce, and there the matter stood, until one morning the bodies of Sir John and Lady Violet were found floating in the Grand Union Canal.

Lord Kilgarriff was the most obvious suspect, but at the time their drowned corpses were discovered, he had been at his estate in the Scottish Highlands for ten days, in the company of a young local woman, and his staff could bear witness to the fact.

There was a suggestion that the lovers had had a mutual suicide pact due to the intractability of their situation, but friends of both denied that this could be so. The couple, they said, had been determined to live through the situation, come what might.

Giuseppe Parisi arrived in London from the seaport of Gioia Tauro in Calabria, in southern Italy, and went straight to that little triangle formed by Rosebery Avenue, Farringdon Road, and the Clerkenwell Road which is variously known as the Italian Quarter, Little Italy, or Italian Hill. Parisi had no marketable skills – at least, none that were legal, other than his great strength. He soon became known in the area as a man to go to when heavy lifting was needed, and this provided him with a reasonable income. He became engaged to one Theresa Prezzemoli, daughter of a local trader, and it must have seemed to him that he had an opportunity to lead an honest, safe, and productive life. Then, six months after his arrival, Theresa, worried that she hadn't seen her fiancé for three days, went to his landlady, Signora Barbieri, and asked her to unlock the door to Giuseppe's room. Inside, the two women were horrified to find him hanging upside down from a gas fitting on the ceiling, his body naked and his skin a ghastly white. His throat had been cut and he had been allowed to bleed to death like a slaughtered pig.

Theresa fell into uncontrollable hysteria. Signora Barbieri did her best to look after her and sent another of her lodgers, Franco Vitale, to fetch the police. It transpired that Franco and Guiseppe had become friends, and that one evening, after they had shared a bottle or two of wine, Giuseppe had told Franco the full story of his life – that he wasn't, as he told everybody, Guiseppe Parisi from Salerno, who had been a sailor all his life, but Guiseppe Baldini of Naples, bandit and assassin. He had sworn Vitale to secrecy, on pain of his life, but now, as Baldini could no longer harm him, nor be harmed by the disclosure, Vitale told the police all that he knew.

There was one thing about the crime that Vitale and all the Italian community knew, which was that hanging a man upside down after his death was a sign that he had been killed because he was a traitor. Had an avenger followed Baldini's trail, all the way from Calabria to Little Italy? It seemed the only solution, and yet extensive questioning of virtually everyone in the district yielded up no clues.

Like many young aristocrats of the time, the Honourable Harold Hamilton-Acott devoted most of his time to the pursuit of pleasure. He was a frequenter of the music hall and the racetrack, but was most often to be seen playing roulette at Porter's, his club in Pall Mall. Porter's facilities included bedrooms for those of its members who could not, or did not wish to travel home after a late night at the club. So great was Hamilton-Acott's devotion to the wheel that he sometimes spent an entire week there, remaining awake until three or four in the morning, repairing to an available bedroom and then emerging in time for a lavish meal before returning to the tables. According to fellow habitues, and the club's staff, he was merely a fair player, neither winning nor losing a great deal of money on most evenings. The family fortune was considerable, and the allowance supplied by his father, the sixth duke of Conway, was extremely generous, so he might have been a far worse player and still able to carry on with his obsession.

His lack of large wins meant that he made no enemies among his fellow players due to deprivation or envy. His erotic liaisons tended to be either paying encounters with high-class courtesans, or love affairs with unattached women of his own social circle who shared his easygoing attitude towards the whole business of *l'amour*. It was unlikely, therefore, that when he was fatally stabbed outside his rooms at the Albany, his murderer had been either another gambler or a jealous husband or fiancé. After several days at Porter's, Hamilton-Acott decided it was time to go home, because the next day was the Derby Stakes at Epsom and he wished to attend. He took a cab from Porter's at five in the morning and was found dead in the foyer about an hour later, with seven knife wounds in his back. None of the other occupants of the Albany heard anything suspicious.

Scotland Yard did not come to Sherlock Holmes with these matters. It was their belief that their usual methods – the application of more detectives to the case, and the extensive questioning of witnesses – would yield whatever solutions were possible.

Nevertheless, Holmes was deeply interested in them, and followed the progress of the investigations with avidity, returning to them whenever his current cases allowed. Then one morning as we sat reading the newspapers, he threw *The Daily Chronicle* down on the table with an exclamation of impatience.

"What is it?" I asked.

He made no reply, but reached over to his pipe rack and took out the cherry-wood. I remained silent, as I knew that this meant he was in a contentious mood. He stood and went over to the mantelpiece, where he filled the pipe from his Persian slipper, pressing tobacco into the bowl with his long thin fingers.

"Those murders are connected," he said, tossing his spent match into the grate.

"Which murders?"

"Why, man, the murders of Waters, Judge Maltravers, Giuseppe Baldini. Hamilton-Acott and Sir John Allingham and Lady Kilgarriff."

The notion seemed so absurd to me that although I had determined not to engage in conversation with him while he was in a disputatious frame of mind, I exclaimed, "Really, Holmes, how can they be? Waters was shot, Maltravers was beaten to death, Baldini's throat was cut, Hamilton-Acott was stabbed, and Sir John and Lady Violet were drowned. It isn't even sure if the last two really were murdered. Waters and Baldini came from a different social class. Surely all they have in common is that their killings are unsolved and, as far as I can see, likely to remain so."

"Nevertheless, I am convinced that there is a thread that binds them together."

"Until you can tell me what it is, you can hardly expect me to believe that. You have said yourself, there are unsolved crimes aplenty, and for all your powers, you are only one man."

"The knowledge is somewhere in my brain. I merely need to find it and bring it to bear. Will you give me your gift of silence for an hour or two?"

"Certainly. I'll do better than that: I shall go for a walk in the park."

When I returned at eleven o'clock, Holmes sprang from his armchair with a smile.

"You have found a connection then?"

"Yes, old friend. Does this mean anything to you?"

He handed me a piece of paper on which he had written:

John Cooper Whitney: Temperance
Joan Eastwick: The Female Pope
Abraham Weston: The Hermit
Norman Waters: The Magician
Quentin Maltravers: Judgement
Lady Kilgarriff and Sir John Allingham: The Lovers
Giuseppe Baldini: The Hanged Man
Harold Hamilton-Acott: The Wheel of Fortune

"The three previous murders are also part of this? I'm sorry, Holmes, but I am none the wiser. What does all this mean?"

"Have you heard of the Tarot?"

"Something to do with fortune telling, isn't it? Like tea leaves and palmistry. Stuff and nonsense. We are men of science, Holmes."

"Agreed, but as men of science, we must acknowledge the existence of other methods of thought and accept that there are those who follow them, no matter how unscientific they may seem to us. Such a system is the Tarot. You are correct in saying that it is often used as a device for fortune telling, but I suspect that our murderer thinks that he has found something more profound within it."

"Murderer? Singular? One man has perpetrated all these atrocities?"

"I think that one person is ultimately responsible for these crimes, though I don't doubt he has agents who do much of the work, the investigation . . . and sometimes the killing."

So saying, he reached into the pocket of his mouse-grey dressing gown and took out a deck of cards. He pulled out eight and placed them on the table between us. *Temperance*, *The Hermit*, *The Magician*, *Judgement*, *The Wheel of Fortune*, *The Hanged Man*, *The Lovers*, and *The High Priestess*. He pointed to the last.

"In most decks this card is known as The High Priestess, but it is sometimes called *La Papesse* – the female Pope, a reference to the mediaeval legend of Pope Joan, who supposedly reigned as pontiff from 855 to 857. You will recall that Mrs. Eastwick's maiden name was *Pope*."

"Joan Pope – Pope Joan. And for that fact alone she was killed? That's insane."

"These are eight of what are known as the *Major Arcana*. In all, there are twenty-two, so if nothing is done, we may expect fourteen more killings, each of them somehow reflecting one of the cards."

And he spread them out in front of me.

The Emperor, *The Hierophant*, *The Chariot*, *Strength*, *Death*, *The Devil*, *The Tower*, *The Star*, *The Moon*, *The Sun*, *Justice*, *The World*, *The Fool*, and *The Empress*.

I confess that my imagination ran riot, wondering who our mysterious antagonist might kill for each card. Strength – a circus strongman? The Fool – a clown, or a music hall comedian? Justice – a barrister? Someone else on the Bench? The Tower – would he have someone thrown from one, or destroy one, as in the picture on the card? Perhaps even The Tower of London itself? I shuddered as I looked at the picture of The Empress. Might he even attempt the assassination of Queen Victoria, the Empress of India?

As so often, Holmes, who knew me so well, divined my thought.

"We will stop him before he has time to perpetrate any more of the horrors these crude pictures may suggest, old friend."

"I certainly hope so. What is our first move?"

"We are going to visit a member of The Order of Thoth."

The Hermetic Order of Thoth, as my companion informed me en route, was founded in 1865 by three Freemasons called William Henry Archer, Hartley Frobisher, and Michael Drax-Morton. A number of celebrated names were involved, or alleged to be involved with the organization. The rituals of The Order were influenced by a mixture of so-called magical disciplines: The Hermetic *Qabbalah*, geomancy, alchemy, astrology, and the occult interpretation of the Tarot.

"How did you come to be interested in any of this?" I asked Holmes.

"It does seem a little out of character, does it not? I came to this knowledge by a circuitous route. As you know, before we began sharing rooms in Baker Street, I lodged for some time in Montague Street, near the British Museum. Pickings were thin, and it occurred to me that if I couldn't always use my abilities in the field, I might at least make a little money by writing monographs on subjects which were germane to the profession. I have mentioned before my studies of the different types of tobacco ash and the effect of different types of labour on the contours of the human hand. Both of these were produced doing this period. There were others which I started, but, for various reasons, did not complete.

"One of these was on the subject of the different methods of cheating at cards. There would be no point in finishing it now because Maskelyne has since written the definitive text on the subject. As to the

Tarot, I learned, while studying the history of cards in the Reading Room, that despite some claims that it has its origins back in the mists of antiquity, in actuality the deck can only be traced back with any certainty to mid-fifteenth century Italy. First known as '*Trionfo*', then '*Tarocchо*', the cards were used to play various games. The name *Tarot* comes from the French. It wasn't until about 1780 that it began to be used as cartomancy, using the fall of the cards to predict the future."

"And this fellow that we are going to see – ?"

"Is an expert on the Tarot. In fact, he has written a book on the subject. His name is Sebastian Childe."

"You don't think he is the author of these crimes?"

"I think it extremely unlikely, but he may be able to guide us to the person who is."

After Holmes rang the bell at 23 Holland Park Grove, the door was answered by Sebastian Childe himself. He was a tall, thin man of about thirty-five with a pale face, watery blue eyes, and light blond hair. Perhaps the most notable thing about him was his air of abstraction, which evoked the feeling that he wasn't entirely engaged with mundane reality, but lived half on another more-rarified plane of existence. I could agree with Holmes that he seemed unlikely to have anything to do with anything so base as murder.

"Yes?" he inquired in a reedy voice.

"Mr. Sebastian Childe?"

"I am he, and you are – ?"

"I am Sherlock Holmes, and this is Dr. John Watson, my colleague and friend."

An expression of pure joy spread across Childe's sharp features and he seized my companion's hand and shook it.

"Mr. Holmes! Why, this is indeed an honour!"

I hadn't expected a practitioner of the occult to be so pleased to meet the foremost practical logician of his day, but Childe continued, "A positive pleasure to meet another seeker after truth, for that is what we both are, in our own ways, though we travel to it via different paths. And Dr. Watson! I have read everything you have written, and with great enjoyment. Please, please, come in, and tell me how I may assist you."

Childe ushered us into his living room. Although it was still day, the gas lamps were lit, as the tall windows were masked by thick, colourful tapestries. A piece of some lightly scented incense was burning in a metal bowl set on a tripod in the corner. The walls were covered in bookshelves which were stacked with heavy old tomes, and here and there some obviously more recent publications, all doubtless concerned with mysticism and similar topics. On almost every other flat surface – the mantelpiece, the tables, and part of the floor – there were various artifacts which reflected the occupant's interests: A foot-high Buddha which appeared to have been carved from ebony, a bronze statuette of the goddess Kali, several African idols, a nine-inch replica of the Diana of the Ephesians, and, on a small metal stand, an icon of Isis, Osiris, and Horus. Amidst all this, only one modern thing stood out: A typewriter at a small desk, which Childe, or his secretary (if he had one), doubtless used to transcribe his various writings.

At his bidding, we sat down in two capacious armchairs opposite a chaise longue.

"Would you care for some tea?" he asked, ringing the bell. "I generally take some at this time. I trust oolong is to your taste?"

A neatly dressed, petite young maid brought the tea, and Childe said, as I took my first tentative sip, "So, how may I be of assistance to the Great Detective and his associate?"

"You are an acknowledged expert on the Tarot," Holmes began.

"Thank you. I take it you have read my book, *The Tarot Explained*?"

"Yes."

"Do you have a copy? You must let me give you a signed one before you leave, if you have not."

"That is gracious of you, but let me come straight to the point. Your interpretation of the deck is that it goes back to ancient Egypt, and that it is a guide to spiritual growth."

"Yes. I spent many years researching the subject before I first put pen to paper, and I am convinced that that interpretation is the only correct one."

"That may be so, but what other interpretations are you aware of? Are there any, for example, that might countenance or encourage the use of violence?"

"A strange question. Why do you ask?"

"You are unaware of the recent rash of murders?"

"I never read newspapers, Mr. Holmes. The mundane trivialities they deal in can only distract one from contemplation of the eternal verities. But since you ask, yes, I do know of one such. Have you heard of Valentine Athlone?"

"Never."

"The better for you. It is a lamentable aspect of occult groups that they are inclined to factionalism. Individuals will disagree over the meaning of texts, the correct conduct of this or that ritual, or the necessity of keeping the workings of the group a secret from outsiders. Fortunately, The Order of Thoth was free from such divisions – or, that is, it was until the coming of Valentine Athlone. My reading of the Tarot was accepted by most of the members of The Order, except him and a few others. It became clear that he was a Satanist, that he saw the Tarot as a guide to the liberation of Lucifer and his elevation to the Lord of the Universe. He was expelled from The Order and began his own group, The Legion of Lucifer. Our Order has a distinguished membership of artists, writers, and actors. He managed to convince a few of us, the weaker ones, the ones less sure in our truth, to join him, but for the most part his Legion is a cesspool of drug addicts and criminals. Let me show you a copy of his book, in which I believe he advocates human sacrifice."

He stood, went over to one of the crowded bookshelves, and took out a slim volume which bore the title *The Book of Lucifer*.

"It is an almost unreadable mixture of bad poetry, prose poems, and tortuous Satanic utterances, but look at this page."

He opened the book and handed it to Holmes. I leaned over to look. It read:

The Coming Age is The Age of Lucifer!
Tremble, O ye Christians, mired in repression and fear!
Tremble, O ye Muslims, in your base servitude!
Tremble, O ye Jews, in your temples of greed!
Tremble, O ye Hindus, in your dark and childish ways!
Tremble, O ye Atheists, deniers of His light!
For the Coming Age is The Age of Lucifer!
He rises once more from the ancient prison!
All earth shall bow to His thought!
Intellect shall rule over base emotion!
For His way is the way of the mind!
What must be done shall be done!
O, the Coming Age is The Age of Lucifer! "

On the Tarot

The ancient Tarot, first formed by the sages of Egypt and passed down the centuries to us, is more, has more power, than any other single talisman on earth. Some have called it a mere game, others a guidebook for the progress of the soul. I alone have uncovered its true secret. When the Catholic Church dubbed it the Devil's Picture Book, they were more correct than they knew. By the correct use of the Tarot, we can expedite the ascension of Lucifer to His rightful place on the glorious throne.

The way will be hard and bloody, and beset by the dull morality of the unbelievers. It will mean sacrifice for each of the twenty-two cards of the Major Arcana, *but when it is done and we are steeped in blood, then shall Lucifer return, for the Coming Age is The Age of Lucifer!*

The superior man shall rise, and the inferior man shall fall, for the Coming Age is The Age of Lucifer!

"These are the ravings of a madman!" I cried.

"Perhaps," said Holmes, "but there is nothing more dangerous than a madman who believes himself to be sane – saner, indeed, than all others. Mr. Childe, do you have Athlone's address?"

"You will find it in the book."

"May we take it?"

"Certainly, but – "

"I rather fear that Athlone has already begun his campaign of death. Come, Watson, there's no time to lose!"

"Your signed copy of my book – " Childe began.

"Send it to me. I think you know the address."

We rushed out into the street and hailed the first passing hansom.

"Scotland Yard!" cried Holmes as we clambered inside.

As may be imagined, the prosaic, stolid Scotland Yarders at first found it difficult to believe that the unprepossessing, badly printed little volume that Holmes presented to them could possibly contain the key to a series of unsolved murders. But during his long absence, it had become clear how valuable his methods were, and how keenly he was missed. His stock among the Force was high, and it wasn't long before a detective and two constables were dispatched to bring Valentine Athlone in for questioning. He proved to be a tall, dark-haired young man whose characteristic expression was a sneer of aristocratic disdain.

While he was being held at Bow Street Police Station, Inspectors Gregson and Lestrade acquired a warrant to search Athlone's house in Highgate. Holmes and I were permitted to accompany them, and there the four of us found ample evidence of Athlone's guilt.

The house, as well as having rooms adapted for various Satanic rituals, also contained information gathered by Athlone's Legion regarding the victims – newspaper clippings, transcriptions of gossip, names copied from electoral registers, dates and times, theatrical programmes, legal reports, and more. All evidence that the victims had been meticulously researched and chosen.

It was then that the diligence of the professionals came into play. By unstinting hard work, they eventually had the names and addresses of all the members of The Legion of Lucifer and a good grasp of the extent to which each one was involved in The Legion's terrible crimes. So the praise they received from the judge was well deserved, but as so often, without the help of Mr. Sherlock Holmes, they would have remained forever in the dark.

The Conk-Singleton Forgery

In her youth, Lady Lydia Conk-Singleton had been a noted beauty, and even now, well into her sixth decade, she was still an exceptionally handsome woman. Indeed, part of her attraction was that she had allowed herself to age naturally, without recourse to the dyes and heavy make-up so often resorted to by ladies of a certain age. Her hair was a little touched with grey, and her delicately featured face was pale. Nature had provided her with an erect carriage and a slim form, which she retained, despite having given birth to two children. Her husband, Lord Alfred Conk-Singleton, was some twenty years her senior. There were those who had expressed disbelief that he was finally giving up his bachelorhood, and presumed that he had married her because the necessity for an heir was pressing. Others found the match questionable, not only because of the difference in their ages, but also because Lydia Lilburn was the daughter of a northern industrialist rather than a product of the nobility.

But it wasn't long before all such doubts and reservations were summarily dispelled by the obvious and absolute devotion which existed between the couple. As well as serving as a shining example of marital harmony, their administration of the extensive Conk-Singleton estates was a model of aristocratic responsibility. They maintained the rents at a reasonable and affordable level and cared for their tenants, who knew that if they were in financial difficulties, or had other troubles, they could always look to the big house for help. In addition, the Conk-Singletons kept the parish church and the local school in good repair, despite the fact that there was no onus upon them to do so.

It was somewhat of a surprise, then, for both Sherlock Holmes and myself, when we received a telegram from the lady in question, informing us that she would call on us at eleven o'clock that morning on a matter of extreme delicacy and importance. What might have happened, we both wondered, to disturb the even tenor of their lives?

Lady Lydia entered our sitting room at exactly the stated time, clad in an elegant dove-grey ensemble. She took a seat opposite us and removed her kid gloves.

"Good morning, Lady Lydia," said Holmes. "You are most prompt. Would you care for some tea?"

"No, thank you, Mr. Holmes."

"You may go, Mrs. Hudson."

Having ushered the lady in, our housekeeper had hovered by the door in anticipation of Holmes's offer of refreshment.

"Now," said the detective as Mrs. Hudson's footsteps padded down the stairs, "how may Dr. Watson and I be of assistance to you?"

"Have you heard of Lord John Fleming?"

Holmes's thin lips pursed in distaste, and I fancy that my own expression must have displayed the extreme loathing that any decent person felt at the very mention of the fellow's name. An inveterate gambler and undoubtedly a cheat, married but an unscrupulous womanizer, he was one of the very worst men in London. He had investments in the Congo Free State and supported Leopold II's tyrannical regime in that unfortunate colony. There were even rumours, largely unsubstantiated, that he was a practising Satanist who carried out unspeakable rites of black magic at his crumbling ancestral manor in Cornwall.

"Oh, I have heard of him," said Holmes, "and considered it only a matter of time before our paths must cross. But what have you to do with such an arrant scoundrel?"

"In order to answer that question, I must go back some way into my husband's family history."

"Please proceed. I take it you will not object if Dr. Watson takes notes?"

"Not at all. It is common knowledge that the first Lord Singleton was given Hemsworth Hall, and all the lands that go with it, by Henry VII, as a reward for supporting the king at the Battle of Bosworth Field in 1485. The house was renamed Conk-Singleton Hall when the third Lord married the Duchess of Conques from southern France and combined their titles.

"In 1720, as a result of investing in the South Sea Company – which, as you may know, had a disastrous collapse – the tenth Lord Conk-Singleton's wealth was drastically reduced. In 1750, his grandson attempted to restore the family fortunes by sinking their remaining money into tea. By this time it had become the national drink, and clipper ships were making regular journeys between England and India and China. The twelfth Lord had purchased three such ships and, unfortunately they were several weeks overdue. They and their cargo were insured, but there must be definite report of their loss before the insurance company would pay up, and his creditors were becoming insistent.

"Alfred's ancestor borrowed a considerable amount to pay them off. But the man who supplied the money was one Lord Augustus Fleming, who up to that point Lord Conk-Singleton had considered a friend. Fleming took advantage of the twelfth Lord's fear of ruin and dishonour. He demanded the house and estates, which were worth at least ten times what was owed, as collateral against the debt. Should the clippers not return before a certain date, and bearing a cargo of sufficient value to cover the debt, Conk-Singleton Hall, and, as they say, 'all the lands appertaining thereto' would become the property of Lord Augustus Fleming."

"But clearly," I said, "that didn't happen."

"No. Lord Fleming disappeared shortly before the due date. Inevitably, some people claimed that Lord Conk-Singleton had murdered him, or had had him murdered. Fleming was addicted to gambling and brothels, so others thought he'd been killed in some vile den and his body tossed in the Thames."

"I have two questions," said Holmes. "First, was there any documentation, and does it survive? And second, Fleming must have had an heir – presumably Lord John's ancestor."

"I know of no surviving documentation, but Fleming claims to have a deed signed by the twelfth Lord acknowledging that he has failed to meet the conditions of the bond, and transferring ownership of the house and estate to Lord Augustus Fleming and his heirs in perpetuity. Signed by both parties. Alfred consulted his solicitor, and if genuine, it still has the force of law."

"There would have been a record at the Port Authority stating when the ships came in."

"Gone, though it isn't clear when. It doesn't seem to have occurred to Fleming's heir to try and track it down. He was Augustus Fleming's nephew, about seven years old when his uncle died, and living with his widowed mother, Fleming's sister-in-law, on a remote Scottish island. He was in his mid-twenties before he heard about any of this."

"There will still have to be civil proceedings before anything can be settled."

"I don't want that to happen, Mr. Holmes. I am here by myself because my husband is now seventy years old and in poor health. I'm not sure that his constitution could stand the strain of a public exposure of a stain on his ancestor's character. I dare not think what would follow if this document is upheld. We have said nothing to our children. How are we to tell them that they might lose their inheritance? And then there are our tenants. What will happen to them if the estate falls into Fleming's hands? I have no doubt that he will bleed them dry, raise the rents, and refuse to give them any assistance of any kind, whatever trouble they are in. The parish church is older than the Hall itself. Will a man like that do anything for its upkeep? You must help us, Mr. Holmes, Dr. Watson! You must! You must!"

Lady Lydia's aristocratic demeanour broke down in that instant, and tears welled in her eyes. I was about to go for my medical bag and obtain a sedative, but Holmes reached across to her, and she didn't demur as he took her hand in both of his and spoke in a soothing tone.

"Lady Conk-Singleton, you may rest assured that both my friend and I will do all we can to thwart this villain's plans. But what is there for us to do?"

The lady gently withdrew her hand and, after dabbing briefly at her eyes with a monogrammed white handkerchief, regained her composure.

"I apologise, gentlemen. There is one hope: We have the legal right to have the document examined by an independent agent, and as I have been informed that you have an expertise in these matters, I should like you, Mr. Holmes, to be that agent. Surely you can determine whether it is genuine or a forgery."

"I shall certainly do my utmost."

"We shall reward you handsomely, come what may."

"For the moment, I would merely ask you to defray any trifling expenses we may incur in the course of the investigation. Any additional payment you may care to make if the case is successfully concluded will be at your discretion. Now, I assume that this document is in the hands of Lord Fleming's solicitors. Their name and address?"

"Melmoth and Poole, 14 Old Fish Street, E.C. I shall arrange an appointment for you via my solicitors, Pettifer and Treadgold."

"We shall await your notification."

Lady Conk-Singleton rose.

"Thank you, gentlemen. I feel much better, knowing the matter is in your hands."

The head partner of Melmoth and Poole, Solicitors, of 14, Old Fish St, London E.C., was Sir Cecil Melmoth, a dry, cadaverous individual whose prevailing vice seemed to be the use of snuff. He sniffed a pinch of the powder into each flaring nostril of his hawk's bill of a nose and looked somewhat disdainfully across his desk at the three visitors whose arrival had upset the placid order of his morning. One of them he doubtless recognised as Donald Sedge, a junior partner in the firm of Pettifer and Treadgold.

"Sir Cecil," said Sedge, "allow me to introduce Mr. Sherlock Holmes and Dr. John H. Watson."

"Pleased to make your acquaintance, I'm sure."

"We understand that as you are Lord John Fleming's solicitors, he has left the document attesting to his ownership of Conk-Singleton Hall and its lands in your keeping."

"That is correct, Mr. Sedge."

"Mr. Holmes and Dr. Watson are here on behalf of Lord and Lady Conk-Singleton. You may have heard of them. They have assisted

Scotland Yard in the solution of crimes, and the apprehension of criminals."

"I'm sorry, the names mean nothing to me. Nor do I see how any assistance they may have given to the police has any bearing on a civil case."

"Sir Cecil," said Holmes, "I'm sure you would concede that in a case of this kind, the provenance of such a document is of the highest importance, especially when so much property is in question, and after such a long time. Where was the document found?"

"At Fleming House, in an old box in a drawer containing several other papers from the same period. The box was locked and had clearly lain unopened for many years."

"Were there any others present when the box was found?"

"Lord John's wife and brother. They were also present when it was opened."

"I see."

"I thought you had a request, rather than questions. What is it?"

"We wish, as legal agents for Lord and Lady Conk-Singleton, to examine the document to ascertain whether or not it is a forgery."

"Ah," said Sir Cecil, "Lord John suspected that someone acting on behalf of the Conk-Singletons would make such a request, and, under my advisement, he is prepared to allow it – provided some conditions are met."

"Which are?"

"Firstly, that the person making such examination must do so here in these offices, in the presence of two or more witnesses appointed by his legal representatives. In other words, by us."

"I acknowledge your right to make that condition," said Holmes.

"At no point is the document to leave the sight of said witnesses."

"Agreed."

"Only one agent of the Conk-Singletons is allowed to be here in our premises to examine said document. Given that this chap here seems incapable of speech – " He looked over at me contemptuously. " – I'm assuming that will be you – What was your name again?"

"Sherlock Holmes."

Donald Sedge departed to walk the short distance back to the offices of Pettifer and Treadgold and Holmes and I hailed a cab to Baker Street

"I am afraid that Sir Cecil Melmoth is well within the law in insisting on such conditions," said Holmes as our vehicle rattled through the cobbled streets of the City, "but you may rest assured that I shall give you a full report when I return from their offices tomorrow afternoon. Now, I don't know about you, but I suddenly feel a distinct need to drive the atmosphere of Number 14, Old Fish Street from my system. The Reichmann Quartet are playing in – " He consulted his pocket watch. " – twenty minutes, and I find that there is nothing like the sound of stringed instruments in harmony to sooth and invigorate the mind."

He raised his stick and thumped the roof of the vehicle.

"Cabby!"

"Yes, sir?"

"A change of destination. Wigmore Hall, and an extra five shillings for you if you can get us there before three o'clock."

Hans Reichmann and his three associates were indeed in fine form on that spring afternoon, and, as they embarked on the opening movement of Cherubini's *Second Quartet in C Major*, I turned to look at my friend as he sat, eyes closed and chin slightly lifted, totally absorbed in the performance. I marvelled, for perhaps the hundredth time, at the strange multiplicity of his nature. How, for example, the man who relentlessly pursued the criminal as the hunter pursued the beasts of the jungle might transform thence into the thinking machine whose keen logic saw through the machinations of lesser men, or into the being beside me, who could be transported to some other realm by the sublimity of music, and how, in some unfathomable fashion, each of these personae supported and strengthened the others.

The day continued in pleasant manner. We returned to our lodgings and had a splendid dinner, after which we sat and chatted in an aimless and desultory manner on various subjects – possible treatments for colour blindness, the early history of the papacy, the work of Joseph Bazalgette, and the poetry of Francois Villon – until, at about ten in the evening, Holmes stood up and glanced at the clock.

"I must bid you goodnight, Watson, for I suspect that tomorrow will tax my patience as well as my intellect, and I would be well rested."

As may be imagined, when Holmes returned late in the following afternoon, I was eager to learn what flaws he had found in the old document, and how the odious Fleming would be prevented from seizing the Conk-Singleton house and estates. But as he entered our living-room, it was immediately obvious that his examination hadn't been a successful one. I said nothing as he threw himself down into his customary armchair with a sigh and pulled his pipe from his pocket. I silently handed him his Persian slipper and waited as he filled the bowl and applied a match to it. The first few inhalations of smoke seemed to lighten his mood a little.

"Watson", he said, "what do you know about the falsification of documents?"

"Nothing at all," I replied. "You have yet to write a monograph on the subject."

"Don't pretend that you spend any time reading my little efforts. Do you remember what you said about *The Book of Life*, the first one you ever saw?"

"As I recall, I called it the product of an armchair lounger whose theories wouldn't stand up if he attempted to put them to practical use, or words to that effect. But we have both come a long way since then."

"Then you have read them?"

"Well, I've glanced at one or two."

I was pleased to hear Holmes give a short barking laugh.

"Ha! I've had a frustrating day, and part of my irritation was that my old friend wasn't there to provide me with a sounding-board."

"I'm here now, Holmes, and you were about to enlighten me regarding the forgery of documents."

"So I was. Firstly, there is the material upon which the document is written or printed. Old vellum which hasn't been written on isn't so easy to come by these days, and it is relatively simple to discern if something is a palimpsest – that is to say, a piece from which the top layer, and the writing on it, have been scraped away and replaced by a different text. Fresh vellum is too obviously new to serve the forger's turn. In any case, the document was written on paper. I should have liked to take a flake of the page and examine it under the microscope, but I wouldn't have been allowed to do so. The paper had no watermark by which it could be dated, but it appeared to be of genuine eighteenth-century manufacture.

"Then there is the writing itself. Everyone's handwriting is ultimately based on the way they were taught at school, and the script children were taught a century or two ago is different from that which you and I use. However, my examination revealed no significant variations from the standard style of the eighteenth century. Next comes the ink. The ink of the period was made of a few very simple ingredients. In fact, many people made their own. Again, if I could have examined it under a microscope, I would have seen whether or not it contained any modern elements.

"Staying with the writing, we must consider the spelling and the style. Once more, I found nothing to arouse my suspicions. Last of all, there are the signatures, purporting to be those of the twelfth Lord Conk-Singleton and Lord Augustus Fleming. If either one of those could be proved false, it would invalidate the entire document. But with only one example of each signature, how was I to prove either false?

"I received permission to make a copy of the document, which I have here."

He produced a folded sheet of paper from the inside pocket of his jacket.

"I made a particular effort to reproduce the signatures as accurately as possible, and I flatter myself I did a fine job of it. Do you know where I took it to find signatures with which to compare my copies?"

"Somerset House?"

"Not a bad guess, but no. Fleming and Conk-Singleton were both aristocrats, members of the House of Lords, and I felt there were bound to be examples of their signatures in the archives of the Houses of Parliament. Normally one would need an appointment, but fortunately Cavendish, the archivist, was indebted to me because I had once disproved an allegation of theft which was made against him."

"Cavendish? I don't recall the name."

"It was before your time. I was still in Montague Street. My surmise was correct. Lord Conk-Singleton's signature on the document didn't seem to be exactly the same as that on a memorandum in the archive.

Cavendish politely explained, however, that one's handwriting might change, temporarily or permanently, due to illness or old age. Were it not for the fact that he has been in Pentonville Prison for the last eight years, I might have thought it the work of our old friend Victor Lynch, had he decided to move from currency to documents. I am still convinced that it is a forgery. It would need an expert, or a team of experts, to carry it off, but it is far from impossible."

"How would it be done?"

"First you get an old, blank sheet of paper from the eighteenth century. There are plenty of them in existence. A page from the back of an old book, for example, where the text didn't run to the end of the section. Mix up a batch of ink using simple ingredients. Copy the script style and the writing style from books or magazines of the period – there are enough of those around, too. As to the difference between the two Conk-Singleton signatures, I can even explain that in another way to Cavendish. The signature on the document was shakier than the one in the archive. The document was written in 1752. Conk-Singleton was thirty-seven then, but his signature in the archive came from 1779, when he was sixty-four, and it was firm and clear. He died in 1792 at the age of seventy-seven. Yes, it's possible that he was ill when he signed the document, but supposing he wasn't?

"The main problem with forging signatures, or handwriting, is hesitation. It is difficult to produce something that flows in the way that the genuine article does. But this can be overcome, though the process is long and tedious. If you practice over and over again, eventually you will reach a point where you can produce a reasonable copy spontaneously. What's happened here, I think, is that the forger has done his practice, but the example he had to copy was from very late in Conk-Singleton's life, when his signature had become shaky."

"But we cannot prove any of this."

"No. But there must be something. I will re-examine this copy, and if I find nothing there, I will look at the original again tomorrow."

"Will Sir Cecil Melmoth let you?"

"Oh, I don't doubt he will puff and bluster, but the law is on my side. Remember, I am the Conk-Singletons' designated agent. I must have access to it until the civil case comes to court."

"Watson! Watson! Wake up, old chap!"

"What? What is it?"

Mrs. Hudson had cooked us a particularly fine dinner, accompanied by an excellent Chablis, and shortly after we had finished, I seem to have drifted into a light sleep.

I rubbed my eyes and saw Holmes standing before me, his face wreathed in a smile of triumph.

"Watson, luck has been on our side!"

"Luck? You have always said that a detective should never rely on luck."

"Nor should he, but when luck goes his way, he would be foolish not to take advantage of the fact."

"You've solved the secret of the forgery."

"I have indeed. I should have seen it from the very first."

"Are you going to tell me?"

Holmes's grin become positively impish.

"I think I shall take a hint from your fantastic little tales and leave the revelation until the *denouement.* In the meantime, here is my copy of the document. See what you can make of it."

"I don't need to look at the original?"

"No, no, the answer is there in front of you."

I looked at the sheet again and again but was unable to see what Holmes was driving at. After an hour, I gave up the attempt and took myself to bed.

The following afternoon found us once more at the offices of Messrs. Melmoth and Poole, nestled in one of the more archaic back streets of the City, where fish had once been on sale. Also present were Lady Conk-Singleton, Sir Cecil Melmoth, Donald Sedge, Lord John Fleming, his brother George, and his wife Lucy.

"I have complied with your wishes, Mr. Holmes, and with those of Lady Conk-Singleton," said Sir Cecil, "but this is very irregular."

"Irregular, but necessary," said Holmes. "I have irrefutable proof that the document Lord Fleming claims entitles him to the Conk-Singleton manor house and estates is nothing but a forgery."

"Impossible!" bellowed Fleming. He was a giant of a man with a heavy black beard and a red, choleric face. "The drawer containing that box with the document was opened for the first time in centuries, in front of witnesses."

"Witnesses? Your brother and your wife? Hardly impartial, or unimpeachable."

"You can't prove it's a fake, d--n you!"

"Meaning it is one?"

Sir Cecil Melmoth paused in the middle of taking a pinch of snuff.

"Lord John," he said wearily, "you are doing your case no good with these outbursts. And you, sir – Mr. Holmes – please come to the point."

"I shall very shortly, Sir Cecil, but first, I must ask your indulgence while I deliver a short history lecture. In October 1582, Pope Gregory XIII introduced the Gregorian calendar to replace the Julian calendar, which had miscalculated the length of the year by eleven minutes. Over the course of the centuries this had resulted in the date of the vernal equinox, which marked – "

"What the d----d Hell is this?" blustered Fleming. "The date of the document is *1752*, not *1582*!"

"As I said before, if you will please indulge me, the relevance will soon become clear."

Fleming's face flushed a brighter red and he sat back with a sour expression, but remained silent.

"Thank you, Lord John. Now, this error meant that the vernal equinox, which marked the first day of spring, was far too close to the traditional dates calculated for Easter. To correct this situation, Gregory excised eleven days from the month of October 1582. While this reform was accepted throughout the Catholic countries, the Protestant states rejected it, partly because it was a considered a Papist heresy and partly because it would create confusion over the correct time for the celebration of Christmas. But eventually, over one-hundred-fifty years later, Protestant countries began to accept it.

"Britain was almost the last to adopt the Gregorian system, and it is said that when the days were excised from the year, uneducated folk rioted, demanding, 'Give us back our eleven days!' This story is often told by those who love to depict the common man as irredeemably stupid, but if these riots did take place, it was probably because people were justifiably afraid that they would have to pay a full month's rent while only being paid for the smaller number of days they had worked that month. Now, Sir Cecil, I understand that the document has been placed once more in your safe. Would you do me the courtesy of removing it?"

The aged solicitor stood and went to the steel safe standing at the back of the room and opened it, carefully shielding the combination from everyone else.

He took out a manila folder and handed it to Holmes, who rose, turned back the flap, and passed it to Fleming.

"This is your document, sir?"

"You know damn well it is!"

"In that case, would you read out the date at the top, please."

"The eighth of September, 1752. What of it?"

"It may interest you to know that the year in which eleven days were finally excised from the British calendar was 1752. The month was September, the days in question being the 3rd to the 13th of that month. Could you explain to us all how this document came to be written and signed on a day that didn't exist?"

Fleming flung the paper to the floor with a snarl and rose from his chair, his face scarlet with anger, his powerful bulky body towering over Holmes.

"Well?" said the detective. "Can you?"

There was a firm knock at the door. I stood and opened it to reveal the familiar face of Inspector Lestrade, who was accompanied by two burly uniformed constables.

"Ah, good afternoon, Inspector. I trust you haven't been waiting long."

"Good to see you, Mr. Holmes. And you too, of course, Doctor. I got your note and came at once. Now, Lord John Fleming, I must ask you and your wife and brother to accompany myself and Constables Barnaby and Callaghan to Scotland Yard to be questioned on the matters of fraud and attempted extortion."

For a moment it seemed that Fleming was sizing up Barnaby and Callaghan to see if there was any chance that he could take them down and make his escape.

"Don't try it, Lord John," Lestrade said gently. "You wouldn't last two minutes. Come quietly. Cuff them, Barnaby."

Holmes bent down, picked up the document, and handed it to the Scotland Yarder.

"Evidence?" asked the inspector.

"Yes. It was evidence that Fleming thought would secure him a fortune, but now it's evidence that will send him to prison. His accomplices too, if you can find them."

Fleming lunged towards Holmes, but Callaghan and Barnaby seized an arm each and held him back.

"I'll break you, Holmes!" he screamed. "I'll snap you like a rotten twig!"

"So many have said so, but here I am, still unbroken."

"There's a Black Maria outside for you three," said Lestrade. "Let's not keep her waiting any longer."

Sir Cecil Melmoth reached into his waistcoat pocket and once more took out his little tin of snuff.

"Thank you for arranging this meeting at such short notice," said Holmes.

"You're welcome," said Sir Cecil, and sniffed up two pinches of the brown powder. "I underestimated you, Mr. Holmes, and for that I must apologise. There were a few other papers in that box of Sir John's. Might I ask you to take a look at them to check their authenticity? For your standard fee, of course."

"I would be happy to."

"Good. I shall send them 'round to you by courier tomorrow afternoon. Your address?"

"221b Baker Street."

It was pleasant to be outside once more in the spring sunshine.

Lady Lydia Conk-Singleton took the detective by the hand and said, "Thank you, thank you, Mr. Holmes! You have given our children back their future, saved our tenants, and lifted the clouds that loured upon our house. My husband can live out his remaining years in peace. All this is due to you, and here is a small token of my gratitude."

She reached inside her reticule and withdrew a folded cheque. Holmes opened it and said, "My Lady, this is most generous."

"'*The labourer is more than worthy of his hire*.' Now, here is my carriage. May I take you gentlemen back to Baker Street?"

The following day, Holmes was deeply involved in some abstruse chemical experiment when a thought struck me.

"Holmes?"

"What?"

"Something disturbing has occurred to me."

He swung round in his chair, a foaming beaker in his right hand.

"And what might that be?"

"There is no proof that the twelfth Lord Conk-Singleton's clippers actually *did* return to England in time for him to repay his debt."

"True enough."

"And for all we know, Conk-Singleton's ancestor may have actually had Lord Augustus Fleming killed."

"Again, that is undeniably possible, but what is your point?"

“Lord John Fleming’s claim to the manor and estates may have been justified.”

“Possibly, but would you have preferred that he had won the case?”

“Well, no, of course not.”

“Then I suggest that you do not let it trouble your conscience, as I certainly don’t intend to let it trouble mine. Do you know the philosophical conundrum of the drunkard with a hundred gold pieces?”

“I don’t believe so.”

“A drunkard has a hundred gold pieces, which he plans to spend on drink. Another man comes and steals his money, and distributes it to the poor. Who has the right of it?”

“Very well. I take your point.”

The Adventure of the Elfrincham Maze

The events surrounding the death of Edward Crawley in the hedge maze at Elfrincham, West Sussex, are no longer fresh in the public mind, and may therefore serve as the basis for the following narrative, which reveals, for the first time, the part played in the case by my friend, Mr. Sherlock Holmes, and, to a somewhat lesser degree, by myself.

It was a beautiful, sunny morning in late June. From the window of our sitting room in Baker Street, I looked down to see young couples stopping before the shop windows, the men dapper in their summer suits, the young women bright as new blooms in their gaily coloured dresses. No one abroad in the thoroughfare that day seemed to be in a hurry. The traffic was full but not heavy, and even the tradesmen in their carts seemed content to amble on at little more than a snail's pace. The sun beamed down on rich and poor alike, and while there was undoubtedly work to be done, its warm rays imparted a holiday atmosphere to the day's proceedings. In all, it seemed an improbable venue for the consideration of such things as murder, but having lodged with the world's first consulting detective for some years, I had become accustomed to the fact that violence and crime could rear their heads in the unlikeliest of circumstances.

The morning's glad sunshine was certainly no guarantee that all was right in the world.

Holmes was in the midst of composing a short, bright piece for violin. The mid-morning had been punctuated by little bursts of music, between which he wrote or crossed out notation on the sheet before him on his desk. I sat in my usual armchair and picked up one of H. Rider Haggard's fine adventure stories set in the African veldt.

Mrs. Hudson entered with a telegram for Holmes, who seized it eagerly and, after running his eyes over it, gave a bark of satisfaction.

"Ha! Thank you, Mrs. Hudson."

As our landlady turned to go, Holmes smiled at me and said, "Well, Watson, it is as I expected," and passed me the message. I put my book down. The telegram read:

> *Elfrincham Maze case proving a puzzle. Would be grateful if you could come down to assist. Have booked rooms for you and Dr. Watson at Crown Hotel in High Street.*
>
> *Inspector Walcott*
> *West Sussex Constabulary*

"Walcott is a sound fellow, if a little slow," said Holmes. "You may recall, he brought us in over that business in Arundel Castle."

"The theft of the Gainsborough?"

"Exactly. Now, my friend, what do you know of this Elfrincham affair?"

"Only that Edward Crawley was found dead at the centre of the maze."

Holmes took a slim volume from his desk.

"I picked this up in Paternoster Row yesterday afternoon," he said, handing it to me. "It will provide you with all the information you need to understand the background to the case."

I looked at the spine. It read: *The Hedge Mazes of England* by H.R. Kitson.

“A train leaves from Victoria Station in – ” He glanced over at the clock on the mantelpiece. “ – forty minutes. I’m sure ten minutes will suffice for you to gather all the necessaries for our little trip, so I shall meet you downstairs at a quarter-past-eleven.”

Soon we were ensconced in a comfortable smoking carriage on the 11:45 to West Worthing. Holmes was immersed in the last two days’ newspapers, so I opened the little book by H.R. Kitson to the chapter on the Elfrincham Maze and read:

> *The hedge maze in the grounds of Elfrincham Manor in West Sussex has not achieved the same measure of fame as, for example, the celebrated maze at Hampton Court, despite its being the largest and most complex such maze in England. There are two probable reasons for this: Firstly, it was originally planted in 1594 but has not been in continuous existence since then, having been destroyed by fire in mysterious circumstances in 1726. It was replanted in 1797 in accordance with the original ground plan. Secondly, it has never been open to the general public.*
>
> *A tradition was established in 1810 whereby, on the weekend of or before each Midsummer’s Day, exactly forty guests are invited to stay at the manor, and from those forty, four men and four women are chosen by lot to enter the maze at sunset. The lots are kept in two large leather bags, one for the men and one for the women, which have been replaced a few times over the years, but the majority of the wooden lots date back at least as far as the replanting. They are simple wooden discs, and four in each bag have a star painted on*

them. First a man picks from their bag, and then one of the women from the other, until all eight starred discs have been taken out, and then they are paired off according to the order in which the discs were picked.

The maze has five entrances. One man and one woman go in at each of four of the entrances, and the first couple to emerge from the fifth, which faces the doors of the manor house, are proclaimed King and Queen of the Maze for that year. Famous past winners include Lord Byron in 1813 (accompanied by Lady Anthea Brigstock), and Lord Balmoral and the Duchess of Abergavenny in 1865. The tradition has continued to this day, despite the purchase of Elfrincham Manor by Lord and Lady Caerphilly from its original owners, the FitzAlwyn family, in 1871.

The rest of the chapter went on at some length about the exact species of hedge used in the planting and replanting of the maze, and the similarities and differences between the Elfrincham Maze and others in England and on the Continent, in terms of the difficulty of their solutions and the nature of the patterns they formed. Before I had reached the end of this discussion I closed the book, as I deemed that such facts were unlikely to have any bearing on the solution of the case. It was enough that I had learned that since it had been Midsummer's Day the previous weekend, Edward Crawley must have been participating in the contest of the maze when he was killed.

Holmes had dispatched a telegram to Inspector Walcott just before we had left, so when we arrived at West Worthing he was waiting for us with a dogcart. Walcott was a tall, beefy man, slow of speech, with an amiable, open expression on his broad, rubicund face. He shook us both warmly by the hand and thanked us for coming. He was, as Holmes had said, a sound fellow, but while I had no doubt that his solid physique was an asset when it came to dealing with the type of criminal he was most likely to encounter, I recalled from the Arundel Castle case that he was a little lacking in that faculty of imagination that Holmes considered an essential factor in the art of detection.

"Elfrincham isn't too far from here," Walcott said as we climbed into the cart. "About fifteen minutes, and then only about another five to the manor."

"I should like to examine the scene as soon as possible," said Holmes.

"Begging your pardon, Mr. Holmes, but the young woman who found the body is also staying at The Crown. She has to leave later today, as she's taking ship to America tomorrow. I was sure you'd want to speak to her."

"I would. Is she leaving for good?"

"No, she's visiting relatives in New York. She's given me a signed affidavit. And don't worry, I've made sure the scene remains undisturbed."

Holmes looked in my direction with a rueful little smile. I knew he had little faith in the ability of the police to leave the location of a crime untouched, but at the same time he didn't wish to malign the well-meaning Walcott.

A few minutes later we arrived at The Crown, a rather more impressive establishment than one would expect, considering the size of the village and, after depositing our luggage in our respective rooms, we were taken by Walcott to see Victoria Pryce-Jones.

She was a slim, pretty young woman with an abundance of thick, wavy brown hair braided into a long plait which hung over her left shoulder. I sensed that she possessed a natural vivacity which was still somewhat suppressed by the shock she had sustained a couple of days before. It is no small thing to be in the presence of a dead body, especially when one is aware that a life has left its mortal shell as a result of violence.

"Mr. Holmes! Dr. Watson!" she exclaimed. "I am so glad that you have come! Inspector Walcott told me you would be here. If anyone can solve this terrible crime, it is surely you. I am ready to answer any and all of your questions."

Holmes nodded. "My first question must be: Why are you staying at this hotel? Surely, as a participant in the maze game, you could be at the manor house. It has fifty guest rooms, or so I read, and the players traditionally stay for a few days after the King and Queen of the Maze have been honoured."

"That is so, but I could stay there no longer, Mr. Holmes. To awake every morning and see the maze – to be reminded of the horror I found there – was more than I could bear."

"I see. Now, Miss Pryce-Jones, I have some of the facts, but I would be obliged if you could take us through the events of that evening. Pray give us as many of the details as you can, then we'll trouble you no longer and you can prepare for your journey."

We sat on the four chairs in Miss Pryce-Jones' hotel room, and the mid-afternoon sun illumined her face as she began.

"As you may know, the game begins when the sun goes down. Eight people are chosen by lot, and I was one of them. The other seven were Johnny Faulconbridge – that is, Lord Faulconbridge – Lady Vanessa Hart, Sir Michael Rutledge, Katie, the Duchess of Belminster, Max Chesterfield, Helena Broughton, and, of course, poor Edward. That's how we were paired: Johnny and myself, Vanessa and Michael, Katie and Max, and Edward and Helena. At the centre of the maze there is a circular space about fifteen feet in diameter, and of course, as soon as you reach it, *if* you reach it, you know that you're about halfway through, which gives you some idea of how long it should take you to finish. Of course, there's no guarantee that you're the first couple to reach it, or that you'll be King and Queen."

"What happens if you meet another couple at the centre?" I asked.

"Well then, there are two other openings on the other side of the centre, and each pair goes into one. I suppose it's possible that three or even all of the couples could get to the centre at the same time, but as far as I know it's never happened. Johnny and I reached the centre pretty quickly, and we were about to congratulate ourselves on how well we were doing, when I heard a sort of low moan. Johnny had heard it too. We moved further into the center and found Edward and Helena. The maze is well lit. We saw Edward lying on his back, his shirtfront was covered in blood, and – and – " She wiped away a sudden tear with the back of her hand. "His eyes were staring upward and he had a ghastly look on his face."

Her voice became quieter. "I don't think I'll ever, ever forget that look."

"Are you all right, Miss Pryce-Jones?" I asked. "We could ring for someone to bring you a coffee, or something stronger, if you'd prefer."

"No, I – Yes, please, I'd like some water. There's a glass and a carafe by the bedside."

Walcott went over and poured her a glass. She accepted it gratefully and drank half of the contents before continuing.

"Helena was lying beside him, and there was blood on the front of her dress. She was face down, and on the back of her head you could see through her hair that there was a huge, discoloured swelling. The low moan had come from her, so we knew that she at least was alive. Max and I discussed what we should do and decided that since I was younger and fitter than him, I should run through the other half of the maze as quickly as I could and alert everyone waiting at the entrance. Max would stay in the centre to look after Helena if she woke up and tell the others what had happened when they reached the centre.

"The next twenty minutes were a nightmare. I made two or three wrong turns. and my heart was pounding so hard that I thought every minute it would burst, but eventually I made my way out. Between the entrance to the maze and the doors of the manor house, a marquee had been set up. The other thirty-two guests were sitting, drinking at little tables. As I emerged, a band struck up and, at a signal from Lord Caerphilly, the night sky was suddenly full of exploding fireworks. Even the servants were all there to see the display. I had to walk the twenty yards to where Lord and Lady Caerphilly sat, but by the time I was ten yards away he saw the expression on my face, and realizing something must be wrong, sent one of his men to tell the orchestra to stop, and that there must be no more fireworks. After I gave him the terrible news, he sent another servant to Elfrincham Village for the local doctor. All the guests and the staff went back inside the house."

"How many people know the layout of the maze?" asked Holmes.

"I imagine Lord Caerphilly must have a plan of it, but I doubt he knows it without that. Of course, the maze has to be maintained, and the gardeners who do that must know the simplest way to get through it. In fact, when the doctor arrived, Lord Caerphilly sent one of them with him, to take him through – and help the other six players out."

"Have these gardeners been questioned?" asked Holmes.

"No," said Walcott.

"Whyever not? Surely it is clear that whoever committed this crime must have known how to negotiate the maze. What was to prevent one of them from entering after the game had begun?"

"That isn't possible," said Miss Pryce-Jones.

"Why do you say so?" demanded Holmes.

"About twenty years ago, there was a suspicion that the King and Queen had won by cheating – that they had come out of the maze, gone round to the front entrance and waited until they could slip forward and appear to have come through it. Nothing was ever proven, but since then a servant has been posted at the other four entrances to make sure that the players go in and do not come out again by any of them."

"That's one thing that wasn't in Kitson's *The Hedge Mazes of England*," I couldn't help remarking.

"It was written more than twenty years ago," retorted Holmes. He returned his attention to Miss Pryce-Jones. "Do you know of anyone else who would know the plan of the maze?"

Miss Pryce-Jones hesitated, then said, "Yes, there is one other person who would know. Margaret – Margaret FitzAlwyn."

"The daughter of the previous owner," Walcott informed us.

"Was she there on the night in question?"

"Yes, Mr. Holmes," said the young woman. "The Caerphillys broke a little with strict tradition by inviting her, as it meant there were forty-one guests instead of forty, but it was a courtesy to her, done out of kindness and consideration of the circumstances in which the FitzAlwyns had had to let go of the manor. Margaret's father had made some bad investments, and the family fortunes were in serious decline. Eventually, he came to the conclusion that the only way to pay off his debts and save the family from disgrace was to sell Elfrincham Manor. It was a terrible wrench, because the family connection to the Manor went back to the Thirteenth Century. Margaret was an only child, and she'd played in the maze when she was a little girl."

"By herself?"

"As far as I know. She did play with the village children, I think, but never with them in the maze. Her parents probably brought her up to respect its secret. So obviously, she didn't take part in the drawing of lots."

"Did she know Edward Crawley?"

Again, she hesitated.

"Yes, yes, she did," she replied, and drank the remainder of her glass of water.

"How well?"

"Mr. Holmes, Margaret FitzAlwyn is my friend. We were at school together . . . ."

"I'm afraid, Miss Pryce-Jones, that your duty to the truth must override your loyalty to your friend. I repeat: How well did she know him?"

"They were once engaged to be married."

"Since Edward Crawley has, or rather, had a wife, the engagement must have been broken."

"Margaret's parents had lived a very simple life after the sale of the manor. They managed to save enough for her to live fairly comfortably, and even take the occasional holiday now and then. It was on holiday, about six or seven months after her parents' death, that she met Edward Crawley. Now it seems she'd never really had a beau, even though she was a perfectly presentable girl. She fell for Crawley totally, and there seemed to be every indication that he felt exactly the same toward her. Within a few weeks, they were engaged and planning to be married in late spring. By this time, she was living in a small apartment in London.

Then one day, Margaret came down with a bad case of flu and was unable to go to a gallery opening in Bond Street that they'd both planned to attend. He offered to come over and sit at her bedside, but she insisted that he go along and enjoy himself.

"At the opening, he met one of the artists, Julia Bramwell. In many ways she seems to have been the polar opposite of Margaret – confident, sophisticated, outgoing – and Crawley found himself falling in love with her almost immediately, and Julia returned the feeling. He really did try not to hurt Margaret, and struggled to control his passion, but in the end he couldn't stand it any longer, and three months before their scheduled wedding, he told Margaret that he couldn't marry her. Four months later he married Julia. Margaret was devastated. For about a year, she was walking around like a ghost, but then she recovered and entered society once more.

"Mr. Holmes, I can understand how you might suspect her of killing Edward, but I swear to you that that is impossible."

"How can you make that statement with such confidence?"

"I was sitting next to Margaret at one of the tables when the lots were drawn. She had complained of a headache and, just as I stood up to join Johnny and take my position at one of the entrances, she told me she was going back into the house to lie down in her room. I saw her walk away in the direction of the doors."

"Miss Pryce-Jones," said Holmes, rising, "I see no reason to detain you further. Thank you for your co-operation, and I wish you a safe and pleasant journey."

"I suppose," the young woman said a little bitterly, "that I am now Queen of the Maze, but as Juliet says, '*It is an honour I dream not of.*' Good day, gentlemen."

"Inspector Walcott, we have a few hours before sunset and, you may recall, I should like to examine the maze."

As the inspector had said, it was but a few minutes' drive to Elfrincham Manor. Holmes hefted one of the great brass knockers on the double doors and we were ushered into the drawing room and the presence of Lord and Lady Caerphilly by a tall, lugubrious butler.

"Good afternoon, my Lord, my lady," said Walcott with the characteristic deference of the policeman toward the aristocracy. "This is Mr. Sherlock Holmes and his colleague, Dr. Watson. I've asked them to help us out in this terrible business of the maze murder."

The Lord and Lady were in late middle age, both elegantly dressed in country clothes, and possessed of an amiable disposition.

"Holmes, eh?" said the Lord. "You're the fella who helped out the Conk-Singletons with that forgery business, right? And that spot of trouble Backwater had a number of years ago."

"Correct, sir. Now, as we need to inspect the actual site of the murder, we shall need a guide to take us to the heart of the maze."

"Of course."

He rose from his chair and tugged at the bell-pull. The long-faced butler reappeared.

"Pearson, I believe Anderson is in the back orchard. Go and fetch him for us."

"Yes, my Lord."

"First rate fella, Anderson," the Lord continued when the butler had left. "Came with the house. Must have worked here for – Oh, what, thirty years?"

"I believe so, dear," said Lady Caerphilly.

"Ah, there you are, my good man," her husband said when Pearson reappeared a few minutes later with a short, sinewy man with iron-grey hair and a face as brown as a nut, dressed in plain work clothes. "Take these gentlemen to the centre of the maze."

"Right you are, sir."

The Elfrincham Maze was, indeed, an impressive sight. As Kitson's book had said, it was larger and more impressive than even its great counterpart in the grounds of Hampton Court. At seven feet in height, its green "walls" were taller than most men, and rising even higher was a ring of electric lamps on metal poles that served to illuminate it by night. The comparative gentleness of the curve that the front of the maze presented to us hinted at its great circumference. According to Kitson, its diameter was an impressive one-hundred-fifty yards.

"Were you here last night?" Holmes asked Anderson as we entered.

"That I was, sir," the gardener replied. "It was me as led the doctor to the centre of the maze. Horrible it was. Mr. Crawley lying there dead, blood all over his front, and that poor girl with a lump on the back of her head the size of a goose egg."

"What about before you took the doctor through? Were all the other maze gardeners there?"

"Oh yes, sir. All the servants were given the evening off. There was no one in the house. Me and the other mazers, we were at a table together, drinking from a barrel or two his Lordship had kindly given us."

I didn't take note of how long it took us to make our way through the maze, but I must confess that by the time we reached the centre, the narrow pathways threading backward and forward, the occasional unexpected curve and the towering green hedges were beginning to make me feel a little nauseous, and I was glad when we reached the open space. Holmes, as was his wont, seemed unaffected by the oddity of his surroundings.

"As I said, Mr. Holmes, no one has been here since poor Mr. Crawley's body was removed."

Holmes pressed a finger against his lips, silencing the policeman, and gestured to the three of us that we should remain where we were. For the next few minutes, he made a thorough examination of the space, at first stepping carefully, then going on his knees, and finally lying down full length. Eventually he stood and brushed down his clothes.

"Thank you, Anderson. I observed from the noticeboard at The Crown that dinner will be served at half-past seven. If you will take us to the local doctor now, Inspector Walcott, we should have ample time to question him and then get back to the hotel, to rest a little from our exertions and change for our meal."

The return journey through the maze was a little less onerous, but I hoped that our investigations wouldn't require us to enter there a second time.

It transpired that the surgery of Dr. Thomas Pocock was on a side-turning off the High Street, and thus only a few minutes' walk from The Crown. After giving us such simple directions as were necessary, Inspector Walcott departed for home with a promise that he would meet us the following morning after breakfast.

Dr. Pocock was a tall man in his late thirties with thick-lensed glasses, a full, neatly-trimmed beard, and a head of dark blond hair. His accent was, naturally, that of an educated man, but I fancied that I caught a hint of the familiar Sussex burr beneath his sophisticated tones, which suggested to me that he had returned to his home county to practice after he had completed his time at a teaching hospital.

He greeted us warmly.

"Inspector Walcott told me yesterday that I could expect a visit from you, gentlemen. I shall give you whatever assistance you need to find a solution to this ghastly business."

"If you could first tell us of the condition of Crawley's body as it was when you found it," said Holmes.

"I determined that the death had taken place about an hour or so before, The heart had been punctured several times by something long, thin, and pointed. Any one of these wounds would have been sufficient to bring about death by itself."

"And what of the Honourable Helena Broughton?"

"She was taken to the hospital in West Worthing. She was in a state of semi-consciousness, and from an examination of her head, I determined that she had probably been dealt a blow with a heavy blunt instrument at about the same time as Crawley was killed. I should say it will be a day or two before she can be questioned, and even then she may well be unable to remember any of the event."

I concurred.

"That is often the case in instances of concussion."

Holmes and I returned to the hotel and came down to dinner after a short rest in our separate rooms. The meal was doubly welcome. Neither of us had eaten since our breakfast in Baker Street that morning and, like the accommodation, it was of a higher standard than one would expect of such a rural establishment. Once the first course had taken the edge from my hunger, I was keen to hear what conclusions Holmes might have reached, but as there were several other diners present, he kept his own counsel, and our conversation was restricted to trivialities.

The hotel smoking room, however, was empty of fellow-guests, and as soon as we sat down to smoke our after-dinner cigars, Holmes spoke of the matter in hand.

"I learned little from the scene and, in truth, I didn't expect to glean much. Including Anderson and Dr. Pocock, no less than eight people had tramped all over it. What do you make of it thus far?"

"Well," I said tentatively after a pull at my cigar, "I agree that whoever the culprit is, he must know how to negotiate the maze. He managed to commit his crime and escape without encountering the other six people who were in there at the time. I think he must have gone into the maze before the contest began, and thus before the guards were placed. Is it not also possible that he remained in the maze until after Crawley's body and Helena Broughton were removed? The guards would be gone, and he could escape under cover of darkness."

"A credible scenario, but do you have any ideas as to the identity of the culprit?"

"We know that Margaret FitzAlwyn was present at the drawing of the lots, and also that she returned to the house, so we can eliminate her. The maze gardeners were all together at their table, but supposing an enemy of Crawley, whoever he was – "

"Yes," interjected Holmes. "If Mrs. Crawley is still at the castle, we should question her on that point."

"This enemy bribes one of the gardeners to reveal the secret, perhaps getting him to draw up a plan, and then, as I said, goes in before the contest begins and leaves after the victims have been found and taken out."

"Again, that is possible, although if Anderson is typical of the 'mazers', as he called them, it becomes less plausible. Such men as he usually place their loyalty to their masters above mere monetary gain, but it may be prudent to meet them all and see if we can assess their individual characters, And there are one or two other factors to be considered."

"Which are?"

"Even a single blow to the heart with such an instrument as Dr. Pocock described would produce a considerable amount of blood, would it not? More than had soaked into Crawley's shirt front – and there were several such blows. Yet there was no blood on the ground. That is one fact I did derive from my examination. The only other blood was on the front of Helena Broughton's dress, and it must have been Crawley's, because her wound was on the back of her head. Had it bled, we would expect the blood to be on the back of her dress. Does this suggest anything to you?"

"That Crawley's body was moved!"

"And the unconscious Miss Broughton must also have been moved, since the pair were walking the maze together. That might explain the blood on her dress. Now, to my second point: Dr. Pocock described the murder weapon as 'long, thin, and pointed'. What could that be?"

"A stiletto!"

"Watson, you scintillate this evening! But I think it unlikely that we would find an Italian instrument of assassination in a village in the Home Counties. A far more common object fits the description equally well: A hatpin. And while I would agree that it isn't wholly conclusive, it indicates that our killer may well have been a woman."

"Holmes! Supposing it was one of the other three women who went into the maze that evening? In fact, Victoria Pryce-Jones is a friend of Margaret FitzAlwyn. She may have hated Crawley for the emotional pain he had caused her, and killed him for that reason. She claimed to be going to America to visit relatives, but perhaps she has fled, never to return."

The detective gave a deep sigh.

"Ah, Watson! You were doing so well, but this theory flies in the face of the facts."

"Why? Margaret FitzAlwyn could have given her a plan of the maze, or they may even have gone into it together when they were friends at school."

"Perhaps, but that isn't the issue. Have you forgotten that the participants are chosen at random, by the picking of lots? It is beyond the bounds of probability that both the murderer and the intended victim would be picked, and even further beyond those bounds that the murderer's partner would be an accomplice to the crime, as he would have to be if the deed were to go unpunished. Remember that the players stayed in their pairs."

"Yes, of course. My apologies."

"Don't reproach yourself. Many would have done worse, and not all your ideas were without merit. Now, I am off to bed. We shall visit the manor house again tomorrow."

As he had promised, Walcott met us again the following morning with his dogcart, and we set out once more for Elfrincham Manor. *En route*, Holmes questioned the inspector about the "mazers" and received the following answer: "I've known all of them all the years I've been in the constabulary, and I'd vouch for the honesty and loyalty of all of them."

"None of them have been in any kind of financial difficulty?"

"When you're in their position, in this kind of area, you can't keep that sort of thing hidden, and I've never heard of any of them having anything of the kind."

"Could any of them had had any kind of grudge against Edward Grawley?"

"Well, Mr. Holmes, once the players have gone through the maze at Midsummer, they're never asked back. So every year there are at least eight new guests, and this year Mr. Crawley was one of 'em, so I don't think any of the 'mazers' even knew him."

At the manor, we briefly paid our respects to the Lord and Lady and inquired as to whether Crawley's widow was still in one of the guest rooms.

"Yes," replied Lord Caerphilly. "She's staying for the inquest, which is being held tomorrow afternoon, and then I understand the body will be taken to London for burial alongside his parents in Brompton Cemetery."

"And Margaret FitzAlwyn?"

"She was at breakfast. I believe she's still here."

We found Julia Crawley, *née* Bramwell, alone in her room, and in the course of a brief interview, she stated that her late husband had been well thought of by all who knew him and she was unaware of any enemies.

We returned to the Caerphilys' private apartments only to find them empty. Pearson the butler informed us that his master and mistress had gone out shooting with some of their guests and wouldn't be back for at least two hours.

"A pity," said Holmes. "I had hoped to act with their permission, but we cannot wait two hours. The solution to this mystery lies, I believe, below stairs."

"One of the servants?" asked Walcott, but Holmes didn't reply. Instead, he went back toward the main door and began to descend the stone steps to the kitchen, which were located near the bottom of the main staircase. Walcott and I exchanged puzzled glances, then followed him down.

In the kitchen, some of the servants, mostly female, were bustling about the room, busy preparing for the next meal. They stopped and turned their heads when we entered.

"Some of you know me," said the policeman. "I'm Inspector Walcott. "You may have heard of my friends here: Sherlock Holmes and Doctor Watson."

"You all know of the bad business in the maze," said Holmes. "We are helping Inspector Walcott with his investigation, and I need to ask you some questions. First, were all of you at the Midsummer celebrations?"

"None of us would miss that," said a matronly, middle-aged woman I took to be the cook. "One of the highlights of the year, that is."

There were nods of general agreement.

"We was all there – the kitchen staff, the mazers – yes, everybody. I don't recall anybody being missing."

"So, the manor house would have been completely empty."

"Well, yes."

"My second question: Has anything gone missing from here since the celebration?"

The cook spoke up again.

"Yes, one of the big food trolleys. But how did you know that?"

"My last question: What is the lowest point of the house?"

"That would be the cold room."

"Please direct us to it."

The cold room lay at the end of a corridor that sloped gently downward. Within, piles of various foodstuffs were neatly stacked against the right- and left-hand walls, but the back wall was clear. Holmes immediately went over to it, took his magnifying glass out, and began to examine the wall and the edges of the other walls where they met it. For two minutes we were all silent. Then Holmes gave a little cry of triumph, pressed one of the bricks on the left side, and stepped back. Before our eyes, the entire wall rotated through ninety degrees on a central pivot.

Holmes struck a match, and Walcott and I followed his light down a long stone corridor for about thirty yards until we reached a great circular hall supported by concrete pillars. At this point, Holmes's match died down. I reached into my own pocket for my box of vestas and struck one. By its light, we saw that as well as the pillars, there were four sets of spiraling stone steps that seemed to lead only to the ceiling. At the foot of one of them was what could only be the missing food trolley. Holmes climbed to the top, even as my match began to fizzle, and I saw him push upward with both hands. My vesta went out, but at the same moment a shaft of bright summer sunshine burst in upon us. Walcott and I followed Holmes up the steps, and found ourselves in the centre of the Elfrincham Maze.

Holmes pushed back the block he had removed and pointed at it.

"I saw this when we were in the maze yesterday," he said, "but I didn't make the connection. It looks as if a tree has been cut down and its trunk levelled without being uprooted, but it conceals this secret entrance, and I have no doubt one would find something similar at the other three."

"I begin to see that in some way this was how the murder was carried out," said Walcott, "but who is the culprit?"

"And what is the purpose of that underground chamber?" I asked. "I can't believe it was built to facilitate murder."

"No, indeed. If I am correct, it was constructed for the preservation of human lives, rather than their destruction. The FitzAlwyns became High Church Protestants during the reign of Charles I, but before that, they were one of the richest and most prominent Catholic families in England. In the sixteenth century they were recusants, refusing to attend Church of England services and remaining loyal to the Pope and to the 'Old Religion'.

"For some time, '*recusant*' was just a label, but in 1593, Elizabeth I passed a statute which gave the term a legal definition and made recusancy a crime. There were four basic forms of punishment: Fines, confiscation of property, imprisonment, and execution. You were fined if it could only be proven that you weren't attending Church of England services, but if it could be shown that you had attended a clandestine Roman Catholic service, your property would be confiscated, and if you went on attending, you would be imprisoned or possibly executed. Rich families like the FitzAlwyns, who could afford to pay the fines, went on not attending C. of E. services, but were very careful not to be found attending Catholic services. Instead, they had their own priests to cater to their spiritual needs. If this was discovered, both the priest and at least the head of the family were likely to be executed. So the priests were lodged in secret chambers known as 'priest-holes'.

"There was a Jesuit priest called Nicholas Owen who specialised in designing and building them until he was executed in The Tower of London in 1606. In 1594, he was arrested and heavily fined. A wealthy Catholic family paid the fine and he was released. He then disappeared for three years until he rescued the Jesuit John Gerard from The Tower in 1597. Now, there's no record of which family paid his fine, but it's a reasonable assumption that it was the FitzAlfreds, and that a little later he embarked on a special project for them."

"1594 – that's the year the maze was planted," I interjected. "Are you saying he designed the maze?"

"No. I believe that at first the maze was nothing more than a blind, an explanation as to why there were so many people coming and going on the Elfrincham estate. I suspect that the reason why it's so large and complicated was so that it would take a long time and continue to be a cover for what was really being done – the construction of the underground chamber beneath it, which would provide a safe haven for not one but many priests. The stairs and concealed openings which give access to the maze were probably placed there so that if the chamber were discovered, the priests would stand a chance of escaping. They were doubtless informed how to negotiate the maze so that they could hide there until there was a possibility of escape, or until whatever danger there was, was over.

"When the FitzAlwyns became Protestants, the underground chamber became redundant and was eventually forgotten – until, that is, someone discovered it, presumably by accident."

"This is all very interesting, Mr. Holmes, but who is there for me to arrest?"

"Margaret FitzAlwyn. Here is how I read it, and how I reached that conclusion: She heard Edward's name called out as one of the maze walkers, and within a few moments had formulated a plan. From the order in which the names of the walkers were called out, she knew which entrance they would use to enter the maze, and therefore which paths they would be using until, as was likely, they reached the centre. So she went into the house, down into the cold room, through the secret door, and into the underground chamber. Using one of the concealed entrances, she went up into the maze and hid until she saw Crawley and Helena Broughton.

"I don't know what she hit Miss Broughton with, though I expect we shall find it if we examine the chamber. Crawley was probably too surprised to defend himself, and we know the first blow was fatal. That she went on stabbing him testifies to her hatred of him. Then she dragged them back down into the chamber. But how had she transported Crawley's corpse, and the unconscious Helena, to the concealed entrance nearest the centre? No woman would be strong enough to drag two dead weights through the chamber. That was why she took the food trolley. She must have put Crawley and Helena next to each other on the trolley, which, incidentally, explains the bloodstains on Helena's dress, and pushed them through the chamber until she reached the concealed entrance nearest the centre. Now she did have to drag them, but it wasn't too far. She likely took them up the steps one at a time."

"But," I remarked, "from what you have said, it couldn't have been premeditated. How did she know to have the trolley ready?"

"No, she didn't premeditate it, but she was thinking and acting quickly. All the servants were at the ceremony, so the house would be empty. She went straight down into the kitchen and took the trolley along the corridors, and down into the cold room and through the secret door. After she'd committed the crime, she went back upstairs and probably went to bed. And now, let us return to the underground chamber, since that will get us out of here more quickly than going through the maze."

Margaret FitzAlwyn was formally charged with the murder of Edward Crawley when her luggage was searched and found to contain the dress she had worn on that fateful evening. It was covered with bloodstains which she could not explain, and on being questioned by Inspector Walcott, she confessed. Her mental health was examined by a board of doctors, who determined that she should be placed in an institution rather than executed. As usual, Holmes allowed the police officer to take the credit for solving the case.

A few days later we read in *The Daily Telegraph* that Lord and Lady Caerphilly had decided that the Elfrincham Maze, and that singular underground chamber, should at last be open to the public. Holmes turned his attention back to his musical composition and produced a gentle air which, to this day, I still enjoy hearing him perform.

The Taverne Emerald

Mr. Sherlock Holmes, the consulting detective of 221b Baker Street, seldom took a holiday. He was wont to say, not without a little vanity, but also with some justification, that during his absence the London criminal classes would become more active, and take more liberties, than they would when he was in his proper place in the metropolis. Moreover, there was also the possibility that while he was away, crimes would be committed whose urgent solution was beyond the abilities of Scotland Yard.

Nevertheless, in the late summer of 189-, I accompanied him on a short cruise to Portugal, Spain, and the western Mediterranean. Why this was necessary, and what befell during that brief period at sea, I shall now relate.

The early months of that year were marked by repeated absences on Holmes's part. He did not neglect those cases which came to him in the usual manner, but took every opportunity to be off on some mysterious business of his own which kept him away from our lodgings for increasingly longer and more frequent periods.

My feelings regarding the situation were mixed. Whatever he was involved in, it was clearly absorbing his attention, making it less likely that he would experience that stifling *ennui* which, after all these years, might still lead him back to the use of cocaine. On the other hand, I was a little piqued by the fact that he hadn't chosen to take me into his confidence. I was no stranger to his habit of squirreling away some vital fact or deduction until the right dramatic moment presented itself, but this was the longest he had kept me in the dark – at least while we were occupying the same apartments.

One evening in April, alone in our rooms, I was looking up at the clock and wondering whether to have an early night or spend an hour or two reading the latest issue of *The Lancet*, when I heard Mrs. Hudson's voice raised in protest and the clump of heavy footfalls on the stairs. The door to our sitting room was then flung open and a sinister figure stood on the threshold. Clad in threadbare dark clothes, he was tall and bulky, but his back was somewhat bowed. He had a head of thick wavy red hair, a set of yellowed teeth, and a scar along the length of his left cheek. He came into the centre of the room with a shambling gait.

"Are you Holmes?" he asked in a distinct Irish accent.

"I am Dr. Watson," I replied, standing up from my chair. "Can I be of help?"

"Nah, it's Holmes I need to see. When will he be here?"

"I couldn't say."

"Now that's a pity, so it is."

So intimidating was the fellow's manner and aspect that my sight stole over to the nearest object I might use as a weapon – a fire iron standing next to the grate, a couple of feet from where I stood.

The fellow must have followed my glance, for he said:

"Sure now, there's no need for that. I've come here to help Holmes. Got some information for him. Patrick O'Flynn's the name."

"Mr. Holmes isn't here and, as I said, I have no idea when he'll be back."

"He's back now," the man said in a familiar tone, and piece by piece, the elements of the disguise – the red wig, the false scar, the padding used to bulk out his wiry frame – were removed, to reveal the face and form of my fellow-lodger. With a quick movement, he pulled a handkerchief from his pocket before doffing the shabby topcoat and then rubbed the yellow tincture from his teeth, and the transformation was complete. While my features no doubt registered my surprise, any comment I might have made regarding the imposture seemed superfluous, so I remained silent as Holmes reached for his Persian slipper and his old clay pipe and sat down with a sigh of pleasure. "Ah, the comforts of home! You are aware, of course," he said, filling the bowl, "that the late unlamented Professor Moriarty had two brothers, one a Colonel and the other a station master in the West Country."

"Of course," I replied, resuming my chair. "It was in response to Colonel Moriarty's letters in *The Times* that I felt compelled to set down the true story of our dealings with the Professor."

"Well, I received word from Shinwell Johnson that a Moriarty was attempting to revive his brother's criminal organization. I thought it unlikely that it was the station master, but I investigated him thoroughly to be on the safe side. He is actually a half-brother to the other two, some twenty years younger than the Professor and sixteen years younger than the Colonel. Since both of those gentlemen left home when he was still a young boy, it is unlikely that they had any malign influence on him. There is no evidence that he is other than what he seems, a law-abiding citizen with a responsible job who has remained in his immediate environs for some years."

"And the Colonel?"

"He served in India alongside Sebastian Moran, and it may well have been he who brought Moran to the Professor's attention. While he did nothing criminal on his return to England, he displayed two dangerous traits: He idolized his older brother, and, unlike the Professor, he is reckless and hot-tempered. Consider, for example, how injudicious those letters to *The Times* were. He should have realised that the investigation and the subsequent trials left no doubt as to the Professor's criminality."

"But you completely destroyed Moriarty's organization."

"Yes, I did, with, you must concede, more than a little assistance from Scotland Yard – and you, Watson."

"Then how can his brother revive it?"

"My dear Doctor, all of the criminals in London didn't belong to the organization. Parker, the garrotter, for example, did not, but upon my return he was very quickly recruited by Moran. And, sad to say, a fresh generation of criminals has arisen since our friend the Professor went over the Reichenbach Falls."

"What will you do, then?"

"I shall continue to gather information, both with Johnson's help and in my guise as Patrick O'Flynn, the cracksman from the Emerald Isle. The Colonel is, of course, nowhere near as gifted or as astute as his late brother, and so the whole affair provides none of the intellectual challenges presented by the older Moriarty. It is simply hard work. If I have kept my recent doings from you, it isn't out of secretiveness, but because they contained little of interest, and certainly not anything that you could spin into one of your compact little narratives."

"But why that particular disguise?"

"I considered it vital that I present myself as a complete outsider. Had I adopted the persona of a London criminal, there might have been those who were suspicious of the fact that I was unknown to them and had never been heard of in the metropolis. So I concocted a story in which I had fled Dublin in haste because the police were finally closing in on me. Hence the poor condition of my clothes. I also dropped fairly obvious hints that 'Patrick O'Flynn' might not be my real name, just in case anyone made enquiries in Ireland. You will recall that I keep several rooms around the city where I can change my appearance, and since the majority of the recruitment is taking place in the East End, it is to my foxhole in Aldgate that I have had most frequent recourse."

By the beginning of July, Holmes had accumulated enough evidence to prosecute Colonel Moriarty on several counts of criminal conspiracy, which also implicated the members of the higher echelons of his organization, to say nothing of being responsible for the arrest of many lesser felons, some of whom had been reckless enough to boast of their criminal exploits to "Patrick O'Flynn". But all this came at a great personal cost to Holmes. On the evening on which he informed me that his labours in this matter were now at an *end*, I called his attention to the physical toll the case had taken on him. He was pale-faced and more gaunt than ever. There were dark circles below his eyes, and, although he said nothing of it, I recognized the symptoms of someone suffering from occipital headaches and nervous spasmodic cramps.

"You have perhaps the strongest constitution of any man I have ever known," I began, "but there are limits to even your powers of endurance. I speak as both your friend and your medical advisor when I say that you must take a holiday. If you do not, there may be serious consequences – to your health, your sanity, and even your life."

"I am afraid you exaggerate, Watson."

"You don't trust my judgment, then, or my medical skill?"

"On the contrary. I have the highest regard for both – except where I am concerned."

"And what do you mean by that?" I said with some asperity.

"A husband should never treat a wife, a parent, a child, nor a friend a friend. Your connection to me compromises your diagnosis."

"I see. Well then, if you will not accept my opinion, will you consent to see a specialist? Penrose Fisher or Sir Jasper Meek? Or Charles MacNaughtan?"

Holmes agreed to see Meek. I accompanied him to the consultation, and though I was not, of course, privy to their conversation, I deduced from Holmes's unaccustomed air of contrition when he emerged from the surgery that the well-known expert had confirmed my conclusions.

And so it was that less than a week later we found ourselves in adjoining cabins on the *S.S. Amphitrite*, calling at Lisbon, Cadiz, Tangier, Gibraltar, Alicante, and Algiers. I had taken the precaution of booking us on board under assumed names, to prevent any problems that might arise from Holmes's celebrity. I embarked as Dr. James Wilson, while my friend was to be known as Simon Holland, thus ensuring that the initials on our luggage didn't betray us. Our only confidant was the captain, one Hamish Robertson, a strongly built man of middle height with a black, spade-shaped beard and a light Edinburgh accent.

On the first Saturday evening aboard the *Amphitrite* a dinner and dance was scheduled to take place in the ship's great hall. Holmes and I were invited to dine at the captain's table. There were ten of us in all, and when everyone was seated Captain Robertson, clad in an immaculate white dress uniform, made the introductions. On his immediate left were Emily Audley and her husband, Ronald Audley, Liberal M.P. for Ceredigion. Audley was known as a fast-rising member of his party, and expected to achieve high office when the Liberals returned to power. A tall, well-built man who held himself as upright as a guardsman, he exuded self-confidence, while his wife, the younger daughter of the celebrated society portraitist Edmund Lowery, seemed quite a frail creature. Her hair was mousy, her face pale, and her manner ill-at-ease.

One had the impression that she couldn't easily keep up with her ambitious, energetic spouse.

Next to the Audleys was Lady Caroline Porter, a woman of unusual and striking beauty who was also an advocate of women's suffrage. Once known for the luxuriance of her chestnut hair, she now wore it in a short bob. She was outspoken in her views, and many young women were already adopting her distinctive style of dress, which was predicated on comfort and ease of movement rather than elegance. Sitting beside her was John Cardew, and beside him, opposite the captain, was Cardew's aunt, Lady Taverne.

The first thing that struck one about John Cardew was his remarkable good looks. He appeared to be as flawless as a Greek god: His hair was thick, black, and wavy. His skin was clear and without the slightest hint of a wrinkle, his eyebrows described two perfect narrow arches above his startlingly blue eyes, and below his straight nose, his regular teeth shone white behind his well-shaped lips. His manner was easy, and he spoke in an attractive light baritone.

Cardew's aunt, on the other hand, was remarkably plain. True, she must have been in her seventies, and thus well past the age by which most good looks have faded, but it was clear that even in her heyday she wouldn't have been pretty, let alone beautiful. Now her hair, well arranged though it might be, was clearly grey and wispy, her face and form almost painfully thin. A complex net of wrinkles had gathered around her eyes, which were the same colour as her nephew's, but lacked any trace of their clarity and sparkle. And yet, whatever she looked like now, or had looked like in her youth, at least one man had seen beyond the transient, superficial envelope of flesh to the good, kind heart that lay beneath, and had loved her. Sadly, he had died early, leaving her alone and childless, and it was obvious to the most casual observer that she now lavished all her affection on her favourite nephew.

I was sitting on Lady Taverne's left, next to the Dowager Duchess of Swanley. The Duchess must have been widowed early, as she appeared to be in her mid-forties. She was short, trim, and blonde, and wearing a pale green dress discreetly decorated with pearls. Next came Holmes, and sitting between him and the captain was Isobel Dewey, an American heiress and a veritable Gibson Girl: Tall, green-eyed, and full bosomed, with her thick blonde hair piled high upon her head.

"Excuse me, Lady Taverne," said Ronald Audley when the waiter had finished serving us all aperitifs, "but is that the famous Taverne Emerald you're wearing?"

Everyone else at the table looked over at the old lady and the great stone in its elaborate silver filigree setting that hung from a chain about her neck. "Why yes, Mr. Audley."

"I'm a little surprised," said the M.P. "I rather thought you'd keep in a safe or a strongbox somewhere."

"Well, I hope you'll forgive an old woman's vanity, but I enjoy wearing it, and I like having everyone else see it. Besides, I doubt very much if anyone here's going to try and steal it, if that's what you were thinking. And if they do," she concluded with a little laugh. "don't you know there's a curse on it?"

"A curse?" said the Duchess of Swanley.

"Yes."

"Oh, do tell us about it!"

Lady Taverne laid an affectionate hand upon the dark sleeve of her nephew's dress jacket.

"John can tell the story much better than I can. He knows all about it, don't you dear?"

"Is that all right with you, sir?" Cardew asked the captain.

"Oh, you go right ahead, laddie," said Robertson. "We've still got a few minutes before they serve dinner, and I'd like to hear the tale, too."

Cardew took out a silver case, lifted out a cigarette with an immaculately manicured finger and thumb, put it between his lips and, striking a vesta, applied the flame of the match to the end. He expelled a thin stream of smoke, blew out the match, and then, picking up his aperitif glass, he drained its contents and signalled to the waiter for a refill.

"Well then," he began, "according to the legend, there was a great temple in northern India, dedicated to the Hindu goddess, Parvati. On display in this temple, but closely guarded, was a small figurine of the goddess, carved from what was said to be the largest emerald ever mined in India at that point, sometime in the fourteenth century. For over two-hundred years, the statuette was safe. Then, in the middle of the sixteenth century, the temple was sacked by Pathan tribesmen who took the image as part of the loot."

"Ferocious warriors, the Pathans," I said. "I encountered them when I was serving in Afghanistan."

"Quite. Anyway, as Parvati's high priest lay dying from horrendous wounds, he put a curse on the Pathans and on any not of the Hindu faith who so much as touched the holy statue. The figurine was broken into four pieces."

"How did that happen?" asked Audley.

"That part isn't clear."

Cardew paused as the waiter refilled his glass.

"Thank you."

He took a sip of wine.

"As fanatical Muslims, the Pathans had no respect for anything the Hindus held sacred. Apart from despising what they saw as polytheism, they also believed that one shouldn't try to make pictures or statues of the divine. So perhaps they were simply destroying it as an image, or perhaps they were dividing it so that four deserving leaders could each have a piece. Whichever it was, those stones were eventually polished and recut and faceted so that no one might see the true nature of their origin, but the curse remained. The pieces went to four different destinations, and in time brought death and misfortune on whosoever had possession of them. I have to say, they must have passed through quite a few hands, but we only know about what happened to the famous ones."

He flicked the ash from his cigarette into the glass ashtray at the centre of the table.

"One found its way to the Ottoman emperor, Osman II, who was strangled at the age of eighteen in 1622 by one of his own Janissaries. It next turned up in Russia, where it is supposed to have caused the death of Czar Alexander II. Another piece was presented to the Mughal emperor, Dara Shukoh, who was assassinated by his younger brother Aurangzeb in 1659. The third piece wound up in Ethiopia. It fell into the hands of the Emperor Iyasu, who was murdered in 1706 at the order of his own son, Tekle Haymanot, who was apparently known as *Irgum*, which means '*the accursed*'. He outlived his father by less than two years, because he himself was killed by a rebel group of courtiers. What happened to those three pieces after that, no one seems to know."

"You see?" Lady Taverne said proudly. "He knows all about it. He even remembers the dates."

"As to the fourth piece," Cardew continued, "well, if you believe the story, that's what my aunt is wearing around her neck. Somehow, it reached England, where it caused the deposition and execution of

Charles I. After the Restoration, James II inherited it and he was deposed too, in the Glorious Revolution, though he managed to escape to France."

"So how did it come to be in your family?" asked Lady Caroline.

"Lord Taverne's ancestor was a devout Catholic, and one of James's most ardent followers. The stone was given to him in recognition of his devotion to the King's cause, and ever since then it's been known as the Taverne Emerald."

"You're very quiet, Mr. Holland," observed Lady Caroline.

"I've never had much time for such fairy tales," said Holmes. "There are much better explanations for murder and assassination. Greed and ambition are more common, and likelier, than curses."

"Ah," said the captain, dispelling the momentary mood induced by Holmes's somewhat dour pronouncement, "here comes the first course."

All discussion of the jewel was suspended while we all turned our attention to the Brown Windsor soup. This was followed by fried Dover sole, accompanied by boiled new potatoes, garden peas, and tomato compote. The meal concluded with chocolate mousse and fresh fruit salad. All was washed down with a couple of bottles of Muscadet from the captain's own stock. When everyone had finished eating, another bottle was brought. Lady Caroline was the only smoker amongst the women. She produced a small bag of tobacco and a packet of papers, rolled a cigarette, and took a light from Audley, who then lit a Sullivan's for himself.

Holmes accepted a panatela from Captain Robertson and Cardew offered me a cigarette from his silver case. As plumes of smoke rose into the air, the table split into smaller conversational groups. The captain turned to Emily Audley, who was sitting on his left, and with his calm and reassuring air coaxed her a little out of the shy silence she had displayed for most of the meal. Next to her, the lady's husband was speaking across the table and applying his considerable charm to the Duchess of Swanley, who was smiling rather coquettishly amid little bursts of laughter.

I turned my attention to Lady Taverne and her nephew.

"Mr. Cardew – " I began.

"Oh, call me John, please."

"Well then, John, I wanted to ask you a little more about the Taverne Emerald, if you don't mind."

"Not at all. Please do."

"You said about the other three pieces that only the stories about the famous people who were affected by it have survived. But the Taverne Emerald – there must be more known about it, surely. Is there any more evidence for the curse?"

"You don't believe in it?"

"No, of course not. I'm just wondering if there any events in the Taverne history that might encourage others to. Any mysterious deaths, murders, anything of that sort? I like a good story, and this has me intrigued."

"The Tavernes have always been a military family, so one would expect a certain number of early deaths in the ranks. One of them, Ernest I think, was killed in the Crimea in 1854 in the Charge of the Light Brigade, at the age of twenty-six or so. Oh, and before that, a Taverne died in the Black Hole of Calcutta, 1756. Then there was the terrible scandal of 1867 – "

"Do you have to bring that up, John?"

"Come on, Aunt Jane, don't be squeamish. I'm just trying to answer Dr. Wilson's question."

"Oh, very well."

"Charlotte Taverne was the sister of the then-current title holder, and in possession of the emerald. She was swept off her feet by a dashing young officer in the Buffs called Reginald Tremayne. After a short engagement, they married and went to live in Canterbury, where the Buffs were garrisoned. But it seems the old adage, 'Marry in haste, repent at leisure', applies here, because it wasn't too long before Charlotte discovered that Tremayne was a wastrel, an utter cad. He gambled, and womanised, and quickly got through even the generous dowry the Savernes had handed over. When Charlotte reproached him, he was violent towards her. She had to start wearing dresses with long sleeves and high collars, even in summer, to cover her bruises. She could only take this for so long. Finally the inevitable happened. She found someone else, an Italian music teacher. One evening Tremayne came home from a regimental dinner unexpectedly early and found them *in flagrante*. He took out a pocket pistol he always carried and shot them both. They died instantly. A maid who had heard the shots burst into the room and found Tremayne standing over the bodies with the gun still in his hand."

"Tragic," I said in a low voice.

"Well, yes," said Cardew. "Tragic enough, even though in some ways it's an old, old story. Charlotte's mother died not long after, and her brother, the fifteenth Lord Taverne, was a broken man for the rest of his days. I suppose some would attribute that to the curse. Oh, the orchestra's starting up! Excuse me – I promised the first dance to Miss Dewey."

The Audleys also got up and went onto the floor.

"Lady Taverne, would you care to dance with me?"

"Kind of you to ask, Captain Robertson, but my dancing days are long over. I'm sure the Duchess of Swanley would be pleased to accept your offer. And everyone – don't stay here on my account. Go off and enjoy yourselves."

"Are you sure you'll be all right on your own?" I asked.

"My dear boy, I'm used to being on my own. Now off you go."

Lady Caroline had stood and was waving to a friend at another table before going over to speak to her. Neither Holmes nor I had any taste for dancing, so we made our way over to the well-stocked bar just as the lights were being dimmed a little to provide a suitably romantic atmosphere.

"What do you make of John Cardew?" asked Holmes when we were both seated with a drink in hand.

"Well, he's a very handsome young man, well-mannered, and a fair storyteller."

"Ah, I should have known that that aspect of his personality would appeal to you."

"And he seems to be devoted to his aunt."

"She is unquestionably devoted to him, but I wonder how far that devotion is reciprocated. My suspicion is that he's taking advantage of her."

"You seem to know a lot about them."

"I know a little. She is in receipt of an allowance from her brother-in-law, which he isn't obliged to continue after he is married. And she can only use the title of Lady Taverne until then."

"Will she have to give up the emerald?"

"Yes, I believe so, and the probability is that he will marry soon. In the meantime, she appears to be lavishing most of her allowance on her nephew rather than herself. Her dress, for example, is quite old. It's been mended and redyed. Excellently done, but not well enough to fool a trained eye. You realize that Cardew has no blood connection to the Tavernes?"

"Really? He seems to know a lot about their family history."

"His mother was Lady Taverne's younger sister. She and her husband were killed in a train crash when Cardew was about thirteen. Lady Taverne was already a widow by then, and she took him in. When she dies, he'll be virtually penniless."

"What about Audley and his wife? They strike me as an ill-matched pair."

Holmes was about to reply when from the other side of the hall there arose an ear-piercing scream.

The orchestra fell silent.

"Oh my God! The curse of the emerald! Lady Taverne's dead!"

It was the Duchess of Swanley who spoke.

Then Captain Robertson cried, in a loud, commanding tone: "Please remain where you are, everyone. Stewards: Close the doors and windows. Lieutenant McAvoy, turn the lights up."

"Aye, aye, sir."

A tall young officer, clad in a similar white-dress uniform, left his table and hurried to comply with his captain's command. When the lights were up, Robertson went over to Lady Taverne and, kneeling down beside her where she lay, gave her a quick examination. Like all his officers, he had been trained in first aid.

"She isn't dead," he pronounced in a loud voice, and there was an immediate relaxation of the tension which had instantly pervaded the room.

"She seems to have fainted. McAvoy, fetch the nurse."

"Look! Look!"

It was the Duchess again.

"The Taverne Emerald! It's gone!"

"Everyone remain still. No cause for panic."

Robertson pushed Lady Taverne's chair, which had turned over, to one side and made a quick examination of the floor immediately around the fallen woman. There was no sign of the emerald. The only thing he found was her reticule, which he placed on the table. McAvoy returned with the nurse, who bent down and waved a small bottle of smelling salts under the old lady's nose. She came round quickly.

"It's gone! It's gone!" she cried in a shrill voice. The nurse, a brisk, efficient-looking woman in her early thirties, helped Lady Taverne to her feet, saying, in a lilting voice tinged with a Welsh accent, "Come with me, Lady Taverne. We'll keep you in the infirmary overnight, where we can take care of you. You've had a nasty shock. We'll see how you feel in the morning."

"Thank you," Lady Taverne said weakly, "but let me go to my cabin first. I want to get my nightdress, and some other things."

"All right, I'll take you there. How about that?"

"Don't forget this," said the captain, holding out the little purse. The old lady took it with a thin smile and then shuffled out of the room, the nurse's arm around her stooping shoulders, through a door held open by one of the stewards.

"I am afraid this isn't going to be very pleasant," the captain told us all. "The Taverne Emerald appears to have been stolen, and everyone will have to be thoroughly searched. Lieutenant McAvoy and I will search the gentlemen, and our two assistant nurses will deal with the ladies."

He looked over at another of the stewards.

"Tomlinson, fetch Miss Grierson and Mrs. Fitch."

"Aye, aye, sir."

Robertson came over to where Holmes and I were sitting and said, *sotto voce*, "It looks as if we may need your assistance, Mr. Holmes."

"Certainly not," I replied softly. "Mr. Holmes is on holiday, recovering from a long and exhausting investigation."

"I can speak for myself, Watson. Have everyone searched, and if there is no sign of the stone, I will give you what help I can. But on no account are you to reveal our identities."

I opened my mouth to protest, but then closed it without speaking. Holmes had set out his terms, and I knew from long experience that his resolve couldn't be shaken. The best I could do was to keep watch, and respond to any sign I might see that his health was endangered.

"I don't see John Cardew," said Holmes, looking around the room after the captain had gone about his business.

"Nor do I. Do you suspect him? After what you have told me, he seems a likely culprit."

Holmes glanced around once more.

"I don't see Isobel Dewey either. That settles it, I think."

In an hour or so, the long and somewhat embarrassing business of searching and being searched was concluded, without the emerald being discovered, and we were all permitted to go to our cabins for the night.

"Holmes," I said as we parted for our separate rooms, "you are still recuperating, and I am still your medical advisor. Don't stay up contemplating the solution to this case. Get a good night's sleep. Whoever the thief is, he or she cannot escape from a ship at sea. The mystery will still be there in the morning."

"As you wish. Goodnight, Watson."

When morning came, I was awakened by movement in my cabin, and opened my eyes to see Holmes standing before me.

“Good morning,” I said, stretching a little. “You’re up already.”

My companion appeared to in a rather cheerier mood that he had been of late.

“I’m not just ‘up’. I’ve already been for a little walk. You know – to stretch my legs, work up an appetite for breakfast, that sort of thing. And to confirm a suspicion I had. And would you credit it, I was right! Look!”

He reached into the pocket of his canvas jacket and pulled out a heavy object which dangled on the end of a silver chain. I jerked upright in bed.

“My God! The emerald! You’ve found it! The Taverne Emerald!”

“I didn’t so much find it as steal it.”

“Steal it? What are on earth do you mean?”

“Well, not last night. This morning. Technically it was theft, because I picked the lock and broke into the temporary dwelling of the person it belongs to, and took it from there without their knowledge or permission.”

“The person it belongs to? You mean Lady Taverne? How could it possibly be in her cabin? It was stolen.”

Holmes gave an enigmatic smile.

“Now, get up and get dressed, please, as we have something to do before breakfast, which is at eight. It is now a quarter-past-seven.”

Five minutes later, we were strolling along the deserted decks under a brilliant, cloudless blue sky.

“You still haven’t told me where we’re going,” I said.

“The infirmary, to speak to Lady Taverne.”

“Are you sure that’s wise? She had a terrible shock last night.”

“Oh, don’t trouble yourself on that account.”

As we turned the corner to the infirmary, we found Captain Robertson waiting for us at the door, dressed in his dark blue peaked cap and working uniform.

"I got your note, Mr. Holmes," he said. "You'd better be right about this, is all I can say."

"If I'm not, then there will be a blot on my reputation, but no disgrace to the Attic Line, or to the captain of the *S.S. Amphitrite*. In any event, I've recovered the jewel, which is surely the most important thing. Shall we?"

The head nurse greeted us as we entered the hushed, slightly darkened rooms.

"Good morning, Mrs. Davies," said the captain. "We've come to see Lady Taverne. Is she awake?"

"Yes, sir, and she seems well enough to get up and have breakfast in the dining hall."

"Is anyone else here at the moment?" asked Holmes.

"No, sir."

"Good. Let us proceed."

Lady Taverne, who was sitting up in bed, looked rather surprised to see three people enter her room, but before she could speak, Captain Robertson said, "Excellent news, my Lady. The best possible. The jewel is recovered."

Holmes once more pulled the Taverne Emerald from his jacket pocket, but instead of the old lady's face suffusing with joy, it turned deathly pale.

"Lady Taverne," said the detective gently, "you would have made a fine actress, but a very poor criminal. I know you acted out of love, but having deduced your intentions, I'm afraid my conscience will not allow you to carry out your plan."

Lady Taverne broke into racking sobs. I instantly sat in the chair beside the bed and took her pulse. It was regular. Her hands were perhaps a little cold, which might well be attributable to her advanced age. At the same time, I doubted that she should be subjected to an interrogation, and shot a warning glance at Holmes.

He moved closer and said in a still gentler tone, "No true criminal would have tried to steal so conspicuous an object in such a crowded space, however dim the lights. Who is the only person who is never searched when such a crime takes place? The victim, of course. Your scream, your fainting fit, they were performed to make sure that everyone present was convinced that that was what you were. You were very lucky that no one saw you undo the clasp and slip the emerald into your reticule."

"How do you know that?" said Lady Taverne, the tears streaming down her wrinkled cheeks.

"Because that's where I found it when I went into your cabin, less than an hour ago. You insisted on returning there last night – not because you wanted to pick up your nightdress, but because you wanted to leave the reticule there, behind a locked door where there was no chance that its contents might somehow be revealed. And you did all this, you broke a lifetime's habit of honesty, all for your nephew, John."

"Yes, yes, for my lovely Johnny. When I die, he will have nothing. What could I do?"

"So the jewel was 'stolen' in front of a huge number of witnesses, and couldn't be found. You had it heavily insured, I think, and would put in your claim when you returned to England. In the meantime, you could sell the jewel at one of the ports we are calling at in the course of the cruise. There are plenty of places where no questions would be asked.

The emerald could be broken up into smaller stones and those sold, and no one would be the wiser. That was it, wasn't it?"

"Yes, it was."

"Is John Cardew really worthy of such love as yours?" I asked.

"I know what he's like – what he is – if that's what you mean. Have you ever loved, Dr. Wilson?"

"Yes, yes I have."

"Then perhaps you will agree that if love was only given to those who are worthy of it, then very few of us would be loved. And now, could all three of you please leave me in peace?"

The cruise liner *S.S. Amphitrite* continued to make its leisurely way round the western Mediterranean, stopping at Tangier, Gibraltar, Alicante, and Algiers. The next Saturday there was a dinner and dance, and John Cardew danced each dance with Isobel Dewey. Lady Taverne had her meals brought to her cabin, which she never left for the rest of the cruise. As for Holmes, to my great relief he relaxed and seemed to enjoy the remainder of the holiday. One afternoon, we were standing at the ship's rail in the bright sunshine and gazing out over the blue-green ocean.

"There's one thing I don't understand," I began.

"What's that?"

"On the night of the 'theft', when you couldn't see either Cardew or Isobel Dewey, you said, 'That settles it.' What did it settle?"

"Well, like you, I at first considered Cardew the likeliest culprit. But he and Isobel Dewey were clearly taken with each other. I was sitting next to her, you may recall, and she never took her eyes from him. They had danced together, and then left the hall, no doubt for a little privacy. When, then, had he a chance to steal the emerald, even assuming he could somehow have lifted it from his aunt's neck without her knowledge? And however strong the attraction between them, Miss Dewey's complicity on such short acquaintance was unlikely."

A few weeks after the end of the cruise, Holmes and I were having breakfast in Baker Street when Mrs. Hudson came up with the morning papers. I selected *The Daily Telegraph* and, having already finished my boiled egg and toast, turned the pages, taking occasional sips from my cup of coffee.

"Dear me," I exclaimed.

"What's that?" asked Holmes, looking up from the Clarion.

"Lady Taverne's dead. Died in her sleep. They found her yesterday morning."

"It's on this page too," Holmes replied. "Births, marriages, and deaths. But listen to this: '*The engagement is announced today of Mr. John Cardew of 34 Tranmere Square, London S.W., to Miss Isobel Dewey of Baltimore, Maryland.*'"

"The American heiress. So 'lovely Johnny' has actually fallen on his feet . . . ."

"Quite so, but I haven't finished. '*On Saturday, 24th August, the marriage of Michael, Lord Taverne, to Gwendolyn Ruddick will be solemnized at St. Stephen's Chapel Westminster.*'"

"It's rare to find life being neater than fiction," I noted. "All the ends tied up in one day."

"Poor Lady Taverne. You know, sometimes I wonder if that curse isn't still at work, only in less obvious ways."

"Come, Holmes, you don't believe in curses any more than I do."

"A good woman very nearly became a bad one," observed Holmes. "A subtler horror than mere death."

"The key words in that sentence are 'very nearly'. That didn't happen, because you were there to stop it happening. And you wouldn't have been if I hadn't forced you into taking that cruise."

"*Touché*, Watson. No, it was love that created the situation. Love. The greatest curse of them all."

"For some. For others, the greatest blessing."

"As so often, old friend, we must agree to disagree."

Dinner at St. Luke's

My readers will perhaps recall that in 1895, Holmes and I visited one of our great university towns, where my friend carried out researches into early English charters. These researches were interrupted by the case which I have related in "The Three Students", but we were presented shortly after with another problem, the details of which I have refrained from making public. This was at the explicit request of Mr. Hilton Soames, who was still in a state of nervous agitation after the successful conclusion of the affair.

Despite the fact that Holmes's investigations entirely exonerated the College of St. Luke's and all its academic staff from any involvement in the death of Marcus Cullingford, lecturer in Ancient History, there was still gossip in the town concerning the nature of his demise. I assured Soames that if I chose to record either of the events which we had investigated, I would change the names of all those involved, and omit any details which would enable the reader to identify the college. He consented to my telling the tale of Bannister and Gilchrist, but baulked at the idea that I should turn Cullingford's death into a story for public consumption.

Now, however, many years have passed, and as I am maintaining the incognito of the college and its members, I feel that there is nothing to be achieved by suppressing the facts any longer.

Holmes returned to his researches in the university libraries on the day following the business of the unseen translation, while I took a morning walk through the town, had a pleasant lunch in a little pub by the river, and then returned to our lodgings to resume reading a yellow-backed novel I had brought with me.

At three o'clock there was a knock on my door, and I opened it to see before me the tall, spare figure of Hilton Soames.

"My dear Dr. Watson," he exclaimed with a smile. "It's all prepared. All settled. I have spoken to the other dons, and they are all agreed."

"One moment, sir. What is prepared? What is settled? And what have the dons agreed to?"

"That in consideration of the service you and Mr. Holmes have done the whole college in averting a scandal, we should like you to come to dinner at the High Table tomorrow evening. I assure you, our head cook is a virtuoso and the wines will be of the finest vintage."

"I will inform Mr. Holmes of your invitation."

"Splendid. We shall expect you at seven-thirty."

Holmes came back at a little after four, in a remarkably good mood. He strode into my room without knocking, a sheaf of notes clutched in one hand.

"I've done it, Watson!" he exclaimed. "I've established beyond question that the charter supposedly granting land to the Bishopric of Athelney in 705 was in fact a forgery, made a hundred years later. Don't you see what that means?"

"I'm afraid I don't."

"Why, man, it means that all the rents and land taxes imposed by successive Bishops over the intervening centuries were essentially illegal. It makes the land common property. The Church may even have to reimburse the current tenants for the rents they've paid."

"That sounds as if it's going to have some serious consequences."

"Justice sometimes does, but it is justice, nevertheless."

He brandished the handful of papers.

"It's all here, and cannot be denied. I confess, Doctor, I feel like celebrating. A good meal and a bottle or two of fine wine, I think. What say you?"

The mention of food and drink reminded, me of the invitation to the High Table, so I informed Holmes of Soames" visit.

"You didn't accept?" he said with a groan. "You know how I feel about social gatherings of that kind."

"No, I merely said I would tell you that we had been invited. But I have to say, I think it would be churlish of you to refuse."

"Oh, you do?"

"Yes, Holmes, I do. You have done these fellows a great favour. Allow them to thank you in the best way they know how. If you don't, they will feel dishonoured."

Holmes gave a deep sigh.

"Very well. I suppose it is a small price to pay for the interesting little problem with which Soames presented us."

The following evening found us in St. Luke's dining hall at the designated hour. We were greeted effusively by the company and, when the first glasses of wine were poured, Hilton Soames led a toast in our honour. As he had promised, the food and the wine were both excellent. The first course was pea-and-ham soup, followed by crab flakes in a shrimp sauce with mayonnaise and Dijon mustard. The main part of the meal consisted of shoulder of mutton in gravy accompanied by boiled new potatoes, green beans, and broccoli. The dessert was hot apple pie with Devonshire clotted cream. All this was washed down with a fine Bordeaux.

I confess that I do not remember the names of those at table as well as I recall the repast. Whatever they might be like when encountered individually, collectively their demeanour had that combination of the schoolboy and the monk which frequently marks those men who have had no significant contact with women of their own class since leaving their mothers to go to one of the public schools. Their conversation consisted mainly of gossip about academics from the other colleges, little jokes at each others' expense, and observations related to their own individual disciplines. One man who did stand out, however, was Marcus Cullingford, and this was not solely because this was fated to be the last night of his life. To judge from the greetings he received when he took his seat – "Didn't expect to see you here, Cullingford" and "Finally decided to dine with us, eh?" and the like – I assumed that his presence at such gatherings was a rare event. Another thing which made him worthy of note was that he was the youngest of the company, with a full head of dark hair in contrast to the bald pates or white hair of the majority of the dons. He said little, but consumed rather more wine than the others.

Holmes had also remained largely silent throughout the meal, which he had clearly enjoyed, but was subject to a little ragging when brandy and cigars were served.

"University man, Holmes?"

"Yes, though not, I regret to say, at this estimable establishment."

"Detective, eh? Bit of a rum sort of profession, what? Sneaking around and digging out people's secrets."

"It provides me with my bread and cheese and, as Watson here can tell you, once or twice we've been able to serve our country by 'sneaking around and digging out people's secrets'."

"Is that so?"

"Please remember that Mr. Holmes and Dr. Watson are our guests of honour," interjected Hilton Soames.

"Perhaps you could tell us a little about some of your other exploits," suggested another of the dons.

"Ah, storytelling is Watson's department," said Holmes.

I then regaled the company with the case of the Bogus Laundry, which had the advantages of being relatively short and easy to relate, while demonstrating both Holmes's powers and his patriotism.

"You didn't do much in that, Watson," observed Cullingford, who was now beginning to look somewhat inebriated.

"My friend is a modest fellow," said Holmes, "and he continually underplays those personal characteristics which make him the perfect companion and helpmeet. And in a dangerous situation, there is no one I would rather have at my side."

"That's told you, Cullers!" chuckled a short, tubby don whose head was completely bald, apart from a circle of fluffy white hair at the back.

Cullingford did not reply, but gave the man a venomous look which seemed wildly out of proportion in response to that mild piece of badinage.

Holmes and I returned to our lodgings at about eleven o'clock.

"Admit it, Holmes," I said as we climbed the stairs. "You enjoyed the meal."

"Yes."

"Even if the company was a little lacking."

"The most interesting one was Cullingford. There's something eating away at that man, though as it is unlikely to be criminal, it does not come within our purview."

His words proved slightly prophetic, for an hour or so after we had our breakfast the following morning, there was a frantic knocking at the door of our lodgings. The landlady opened it to reveal the presence of

Hilton Soames, who looked straight past her to Holmes, just coming into the hall, and about to head off for another day's research at the university library.

"Mr. Holmes! Mr. Holmes! You've got to help us!

His voice was high with anxiety and a cold sweat was forming on his pale, broad forehead.

"Good Heavens, man! What is it?"

By this time I had heard the commotion and came to see what it portended.

"It's Marcus Cullingford! He's been murdered!"

"Murdered? How?"

"Has the university doctor been consulted?" I asked.

"Yes, and he thinks it's poison, though without an autopsy he can't say what kind."

"The police will have to be called in," said Holmes.

"That's why I'm here. I want you to take a look at him. Perhaps you can sort this out without informing them."

Holmes gave the agitated academic a stern gaze.

"We will, as you say, take a look at him, but the police will have to be told eventually. And if we come to the conclusion that someone who was at table with him, or one of the catering staff, was responsible, we will not withhold that information from the constabulary. Is that understood?"

"Yes, yes. I have a cab waiting."

As we were driven through the historic mediaeval streets, Holmes asked, "Did the university doctor decide on a time of death?"

"Some time in between two and three this morning, he said," replied Soames.

"That might well suggest that the poison was administered during the dinner. Who discovered the body?"

"Cullingford's scout. He came into the bedroom to wake him, as usual, at about 8:30. It was obvious from the terrible expression on his face that he was dead, and had died in agony. The scout came to fetch me, and I went to summon Dr. Cartwright."

"Did Cartwright carry out the examination *in situ*?"

"Yes. Nothing has been moved, as I decided to ask you in almost immediately."

Soames hesitated.

"Before we reach Cullingford's rooms, there is something I must tell you. You must have gleaned from some of the remarks made when he sat down that Cullingford had not attended the dinners in some time. I learned from Dr. Cartwright that Cullingford came to him some time ago suffering from stomach cramps. He believed that someone was slowly poisoning him, but the doctor assured him that the cramps were caused by overwork and nervous tension. Cullingford apparently did not take the medication Cartwright prescribed in case it was the doctor who was trying to kill him. This obsession grew until Cullingford ate all his meals in town and refused to socialize with the other dons. But now . . . ."

"You think his suspicions may have been justified."

"Yes."

"Did he have any enemies?"

"Dons have rivalries, not enemies – at least, that is usually the case. I can't think of anyone who disliked him enough to murder him."

We arrived at an ivy-covered court very similar to the one occupied by Soames, which was arranged on virtually the same pattern.

Cullingford's rooms were on the ground floor. A porter admitted us, and Holmes turned to Soames.

"We will come to your office as soon as we have anything to report."

"Thank you."

As the don hurried across the court, I remarked, "You were rather harsh with him."

"I only agreed to this because Soames was obviously distressed. There is little we can do here. The police must know, and soon. A lengthy investigation will probably ensue, and we have no time for that. We are due to return to Baker Street tomorrow."

We entered Cullingford's suite of rooms. The late lecturer in Ancient History lay on his back in bed, and his mouth was contorted into a truly horrific rictus. Dr. Cartwright had not closed the dead man's eyes, and their pupils had rolled upwards to the limit of their orbit. I concurred with the university doctor's diagnosis that poison was the probable cause of death.

"Let us see if the other room can afford us any useful data," said Holmes. That room was dominated by books and papers, the shelves being crowded almost to the point of collapse with teetering towers comprised of further volumes in front of them. There were two piles of essay papers, presumably marked and unmarked. There was also a locked cupboard, but Holmes drew my attention to an escritoire in the corner of the room which was entirely free of clutter, there being only one sheet of paper on it.

"Presumably this paper was of some importance, since Cullingford appears to have made a point of keeping it separate, so that it would be to hand when needed. Let us see what is on it."

He looked at it for about half a minute. Then, handing the paper to me, said, "How's your Latin, Watson?"

"A little rusty."

I read:

> *Nobilissimum autem est Mithridatis, quod cottidie sumendo rex ille dicitur adversus venenorum pericula tutum corpus suum reddidisse. In quo haec sunt: costi P 1.66acroi P.V 20; hyperici, cummi, sagapeni, acaciae suci, iridis Illyricae, cardamomi, singulorum P.8 II; anesi P.12 III; nardi Gallici, gentianae eradj, aridorum rosae foliorum, singulorum P.16 IIII; papaveris lacrimae, petroselini, singulorum P.17 IIII casiae, silis, lolii, piperis longi, singulorum 20. 66 V styracis P.21 V castorei, turis hypocistidis suci, murrae, opopanacis, floris iunci rotundi, resinae terebenthinae, galbani, dauci Cretici seminis, singulorum P.24.66 VI nardi, opobalsami, singulorum P.25 VI thlaspis P.25 VI radicis Ponticae P.28 VII; croci, zingiberis,cinnamomi, singulorum P.29 VII Haec contrita melle excipiuntur, et adversus venenum, quod magnitudinem nucis Graecae impleat, ex vino datur. In ceteris autem adfectibus corporis pro modo eorum vel quod Aegyptiae fabae vel quod ervi magnitudinem impleat, satis est.*

I endeavoured to translate what I could.

"*Rosae foliorum* – rose leaves. *Cardamomi* and *cinnamoni* are almost the same in English. *Anesi* is anise, *terebenthinae* is turpentine, and *zingiberis* is ginger, and *croci is* saffrón. Is this some sort of recipe?"

"In a way, yes. I believe this lists the ingredients of a *mitridate*, named after an ancient king of Pontus, who is mentioned in the first line. Have you heard of it?"

"As a doctor, of course I have. It is a concoction supposed to act as a universal antidote against any form of poison. But surely, it's entirely mythical."

"Well, whoever wrote this clearly didn't believe so, and neither did Cullingford. As a professor of ancient history, he would have heard of Mithridates, who wished to avoid the fate of his father, who was assassinated when Mithradates was twelve. According to one version, he took different kinds of poisons in small doses to build up immunity against them, but others say he developed this universal antidote, and after his death at a ripe old age there were several attempts to recreate it, of which this, I fancy, is one – probably from Celsus' *De Medicina.* Some of the ingredients here would have been very difficult and expensive to get in those days, so its efficacy probably wasn't often put to the test, but there would be little difficulty obtaining them now. Do you begin to see how this explains Cullingford's behaviour?"

"He didn't attend the meals because he thought someone was trying to poison him, but he put the mitridate together and took it before the dinner. Believing himself immune, he ate and drank freely. But the mitridate didn't work, and he succumbed to whatever poison was administered to him."

"Possibly," said Holmes, "but I believe there is a simpler answer, and if I am not mistaken, the answer may be found in this locked cupboard. Fortunately, it is my reprehensible habit to carry my lock picks wherever I go."

He worked at the doors for a few seconds, then threw them open. Inside were three shelves, on which stood a number of large bottles of the type found in chemists' shops.

"The ingredients, I believe. In large amounts, because the effect of each individual dose would not be permanent – assuming one believes it would work at all."

"Did he eat all those things?"

"No. According to the paper they have to be dried and then ground, so there's probably a mortar and pestle here somewhere. Yes, here at the back. So they were dried and ground and mixed with honey, then formed into a pellet which was swallowed."

Holmes unscrewed the lids and examined the contents one by one, until, on opening the seventh, he gave a small "Ah!" of satisfaction.

"You have found the answer?"

"Yes. Let us go and inform friend Soames of the news.

"Come!" yelled Soames in answer to Holmes's knock.

"Good news, Mr. Soames," said Holmes. "You may safely report this matter to the police without an ensuing scandal or investigation. Marcus Cullingford was the author of his own demise, as the police autopsy will confirm."

"Suicide?"

"No, no. An accident, the unfortunate result of a misinterpretation of a Latin text. Mr. Cullingford must have been slightly less proficient at Latin than he imagined, and he certainly had no knowledge of toxicology."

"Please explain."

Holmes gave Soames a brief description of what we had found, and the significance of the paper bearing the Latin text, which he had brought with him.

"The formula contains rhubarb. Cullingford must have interpreted this to mean rhubarb *leaves*, of which he had a large supply, rather than rhubarb *stalks*. Now, while rhubarb stalks are harmless, the leaves contain a high concentration of oxalic acid, which can cause failure of some of the vital organs. Drying and grinding them probably concentrated it further.

"Normally that would produce great pain, so I can only surmise that one or more of the other ingredients in the mithridate acted as an analgesic while it did its work, enabling him to attend the dinner with no signs of the ill effects. No doubt the autopsy will also reveal the truth of that."

"Thank you, thank you, Mr. Holmes. And you, Dr. Watson."

"You're welcome, Mr. Soames. And now, Watson – Baker Street calls."

The Adventure of James Edward Phillimore

It had been raining heavily in London for more than a week. One morning after another, I awoke in semi-darkness with a chill in the air and water streaming down the panes. It was a pleasure, then, to rise from sleep that day in late April to see and feel the sun beaming through the windows of my bedroom in Baker Street. I had no doubt that the cessation of the daily downpours would also be welcome to my fellow-lodger, Mr. Sherlock Holmes. He was largely indifferent to the weather except when it affected his practice as London's first and only consulting detective, and, as he had remarked to me on more than one occasion, clients were less likely to call, and criminals to carry out their misdeeds, when there was heavy rain.

I shaved and dressed with a light heart and descended the stairs, eager to see what Mrs. Hudson had provided for our breakfast. When I entered our sitting room, I found Holmes already half-way through a plate of kedgeree, a dish for which I had acquired quite a taste during my time in India.

"Good morning, Watson," he said with a wide smile. "A pleasant morning, is it not? Perhaps when you have consumed Mrs. Hudson's excellent meal, you might like to come for a walk with me in this spring sunshine."

"By all means," I answered as I spooned a portion onto my plate.

I haven't spoken much in these chronicles of the frequent excursions that Holmes and I made from our lodgings into the wider world of the metropolis. He often claimed that he allowed his brain to retain nothing other than that which was strictly necessary to the pursuit of his profession, but in his more relaxed moments he was prepared to concede that this wasn't strictly true. A thorough knowledge of the layout of the city was, naturally, of great practical use to the detective, but this could not be said of the majority of the out-of-the-way facts he had accumulated over the years. Wherever we went, it seemed, he had an anecdote about the district's past inhabitants or the story of the origin of the name of a particular road or area.

When we had finished our coffee, and Holmes had smoked his first, malodorous pipe of the day, we went down into Baker Street and set off at a leisurely pace in a north-easterly direction.

After a pleasant stroll into lower Islington, during which Holmes informed me that the name of the borough had originally been "Giseldone", meaning "Gisla's Hill", after an early Saxon inhabitant, we returned to Baker Street some two hours later. On our entry, Mrs. Hudson handed Holmes a visiting card and informed us that a lady had called in our absence – young, about twenty-two or -three, and well-to-do.

We climbed the stairs to the sitting room and when I had sat in my accustomed armchair Holmes passed me the card, saying, "Let me hear what you can deduce from this."

On the printed side it said: *James and Viola Phillimore, The Poplars, 17 Oulton Rd, Bromley, Kent.*

I turned it over. On the other side was written, in a neat, feminine hand: *Will call again at half-past eleven. VP.*

"Well," I began, a little hesitantly, "the Phillimores are evidently well-off. The card is particularly thick and stiff, and the information is embossed, rather than merely printed on it."

"A reasonable inference."

"While it is clearly expensive, it is not ostentatious, which indicates modesty and good taste on their part."

"Sound enough. Anything more?"

"Not to my eyes."

"It isn't your eyes that are at fault, since they see no less than mine. You fail to deduce from what you see."

I passed the card back to him, sighed, and reached in my pocket for my pipe and tobacco pouch, saying as I filled the bowl with Ship's, "What do you deduce then?"

"We already know from Mrs. Hudson that Viola Phillimore is a young woman. I would add that she and her husband have probably not been married long, are childless, and have only recently moved into The Poplars, which is in all probability their first marital home. Mrs. Phillimore is a sensible woman, not given to hysteria, so we may take it her visit to us has a serious purpose."

He handed me back the card.

"Observe," he continued. "Despite its stiffness, the card is slightly bent, and there are two small indentations on the lower edge."

"Why, yes. And what does that tell us?"

"That too many cards have been pressed into a card case. Which also tells us that the carrier of the case anticipated handing out many cards on the day the case was filled. When would one hand out more cards than at any other time? When one has just moved into an area and is calling on one's new neighbours."

"Very well, but your other deductions? Their childlessness, and the rest?"

"Both of the couple's names are on it. If the husband is, as we may infer from their address and the quality of the card, a member of the professional class, he doubtless has his own supply of cards with only his name upon them. His wife doesn't have her own cards, which indicates that she does not yet move comfortably in her new social circle unless accompanied by her husband. That is a characteristic of the early days of a marriage, especially among younger women. It is also her youth which persuades me that she has no children. It is among the lower orders, to which she clearly doesn't belong, that we must expect to see early marriage and young parenthood."

"How do you arrive at your conclusions about her personality?"

"Really, Watson! We have a sample of her handwriting, brief though it is! Women tend to write in a smaller hand than men and, allowing for that, her writing is of the middle size, which generally indicates a well-balanced personality. This inference is corroborated by the neatness of her script and the fact that the letters of her words are consistently connected."

"Well," I glanced up at the clock where it sat on the mantelpiece next to Holmes's jack-knife, "we don't have long to wait before we can test the accuracy of your conclusions."

Mrs. Viola Phillimore was a handsome young woman of the middle height, dressed in a modest outfit of dark blue taffeta, and with a small dark hat pinned to her hair, which was a deep chestnut in colour. Distress was visible on her pale, heart-shaped face.

"Good morning, Mrs. Phillimore. I am Sherlock Holmes, and this is my colleague, Dr. John Watson."

"Dr. Watson. I have, of course, heard your name in connection with that of your friend."

"Please take a seat, Mrs. Phillimore," said Holmes, "and tell us how we may be of service."

"Certainly, Mr. Holmes. My husband is James Edward Phillimore, a junior partner at the solicitors' firm of Killroy and Hay in the City, and we have recently moved into The Poplars, in the southern part of Bromley in Kent. Four days ago, on Saturday, we had just left the house at about half-past eight to visit my mother in Norwood, and were about to walk to the station when James realized that he had left his umbrella in the stand in the hall.

"'I'd better go and get it,' he said. 'It'll rain today, if the last few days are anything to go by. I'll just be a moment.'

"He turned his key in the lock once more and went in, closing the door behind him.

"Getting the umbrella should have been the work of a few seconds, so when a couple of minutes had gone by without his return, I took out my own key and opened the door, which had automatically relocked when James re-entered. The umbrella was still in the stand, but James was nowhere to be seen. I thought perhaps that he had forgotten something else, from another part of the house. I called out his name once or twice, but there was no reply. I went back to the door and looked down the street in either direction, but still he was nowhere to be seen. I stood for a while, dazed and baffled, then I went to the local police station to report his disappearance."

"Where, I would imagine, they were less than sympathetic," said Holmes.

"They seemed to think that either he was playing some absurd prank on me, or that he wanted to leave me and had chosen this particularly cruel method of doing so. They told me to wait a few days for his return. I have done so, with no result, so now I have come to you, Mr. Holmes."

The detective leaned forward, resting his elbows on his bony knees and pressing the tips of his fingers together.

"Before I take your case, let me warn you that should I discover the truth, it may not necessarily end your distress."

"I understand that, Mr. Holmes. Nevertheless, I wish to know it."

"Very well. Now, if you would be so good, I have some questions to ask you. Were there any servants in the house on that day?"

"No. We have a cook, and a maid, but neither of them lives in, and as we visit my mother every Saturday, we give them that morning and afternoon off."

"You said that you looked up and down the street without seeing your husband. Did you see anyone else?"

"It was quite early in the morning, and a Saturday. The street was empty except for a deformed man I had never seen before, about thirty yards from the front door. As I looked at him he turned and hobbled away. Since my husband has a straight back and a strong physique, it couldn't have been him, even if for some outrageous reason he had been disguised."

"Have you made inquiries at Killroy and Hay?"

"I have just returned from there. When I didn't find you in, I decided to use the time to call on them."

"And?"

"He hasn't been at their offices since last Friday."

"Now I must ask you some questions of a more delicate nature."

"Please proceed."

"How were the relations between your husband and yourself?"

"No marriage is ever perfect, Mr. Holmes, or utterly without conflict, but I believe that ours was as harmonious as one could reasonably expect. I am certainly happy, and James gives no indication that he is not."

"You have never had any doubts as to his fidelity?"

"Certainly not. James is a quiet man. He seldom goes out without me, and while he sometimes stays late at his chambers, he often brings any extra work home. I cannot see when he would have the time to be unfaithful, even if he had the inclination, which I can assure you he does not."

"Has there been any change in his habits of late?"

" He had been spending rather more time in his study over the last few days before his disappearance, but I gather that he has several important cases on at the moment."

"I see," said Holmes, standing up. "Dr. Watson and I will need to see your house. May we do that this afternoon?"

"Yes, of course."

"Then we bid you goodbye until then, Mrs. Phillimore."

After Mrs. Hudson had shown the lady out, Holmes asked, "So, my friend, what did you make of her story?"

"Well, people don't simply vanish into thin air."

"Don't they, now? What about Bathurst?"

"No doubt I am very slow, Holmes, but I fail to see what Australia has to do with this."

"I was referring to Benjamin Bathurst, not the gold centre of New South Wales. On 25 November, 1809, Bathurst, a British diplomatic envoy, and his German courier, a Herr Krause, travelled by chaise to the town of Perleberg, west of Berlin. After ordering fresh horses at the post house, Bathurst and his companion walked to a nearby inn, The White Swan. They ate an early dinner, and then Bathurst spent several hours writing in a small room set aside for him at the inn. The travellers' departure was delayed and it wasn't until nine p.m. that they were told that the horses were about to be harnessed to their carriage. Bathurst immediately left his room, followed seconds later by Krause. Bathurst entered the chaise, but when Krause went in, he found it empty. He went around the horses to see if, for some reason, Bathurst had stepped out through the other door. But there was no sign of him anywhere."

"So what had happened?"

"No one knows. That's my point. Perhaps I am being a little vain in thinking that had I been in Perleberg at the time, I would have solved the conundrum. In this instance, I'm rather afraid that Mr. Phillimore, as the Bromley constabulary suggested, has left his wife, though at present I am at a loss to explain why he should have done so in such a bizarre manner. However, let us not speculate further until we have more data."

After a light lunch, we made our way to Liverpool Street and caught the two o'clock train to Bromley South. From there it was a short walk to Oulton Road. Mrs. Phillimore greeted us with a countenance suffused with hope. I had expected Holmes to make a thorough search of The Poplars, but instead he asked, "Is there any part of the house to which only your husband has access?"

"Yes, there is his study. He doesn't even allow the maid into it, which I grant is a little eccentric, but as I told you in Baker Street, he sometimes brings work home, and if he needs absolute privacy to concentrate on it, then so be it."

"May we see it?"

"I'm afraid that my husband has the only key, which he keeps on a ring that only he handles. It will have been in his pocket when he . . . when he . . . ."

Mrs. Phillimore's calm demeanour broke down and she burst into passionate sobbing. In that moment, she seemed like a desperate young girl rather than the composed married woman we had first met that morning. Clearly this business was putting her under considerable strain

"Put your faith in Mr. Holmes," I said soothingly. "If this mystery is capable of solution, then he is the man to solve it."

"And if we are to solve it," said Holmes, "then I am afraid that, with your permission of course, I must pick the lock of Mr. Phillimore's study."

"You have it," said Mrs. Phillimore, "but you will forgive me if I don't watch you at your work. I shall be in the parlour."

Once the lady had gone, Holmes took a little soft leather case from the pocket of his jacket and selected two metal tools from it.

"This will take but a moment. The lock isn't a sophisticated one." And within an instant, the door was open, and we stepped into James Edward Phillimore's private sanctum.

It was a square, spacious room with one small window, unremarkable at first glance except for a deal table covered with jars of chemicals and scientific equipment. It seemed that, like Holmes himself, Phillimore was an amateur chemist. The detective looked at the jars one by one, then turned to an examination of the rest of the room. Its walls were covered with a plain, conventional wallpaper, another indication of that modesty and lack of ostentation hinted at by the visiting card. The dark blue, unpatterned carpet, the brown mahogany desk, the white lampshade, the utilitarian furniture, all pointed to an occupant of simple, unaffected tastes.

On the wall behind the desk were two framed photographs, one of the couple together, clearly taken on their wedding day, and the other of Mrs. Phillimore by herself. Between the photographs was a set of shelves bending slightly under the weight of the books upon them.

"What a man chooses to read is among the best indicators of his character," said Holmes, and we began to scan their spines. As might be expected, given Phillimore's profession, there were many books on the law, but they were all crammed onto the top shelf. Those below were of more interest and, to judge from their condition, more frequently read:

The Zincali, *Lavengro*, and *The Romany Rye* by George Borrow, *Travels with a Donkey in the Cevennes* by R. L. Stevenson, *Confessions of an English Opium-Eater* by Thomas de Quincey, *The Gold Mines of Midian* and *The Lands of Cazembe* by Sir Richard Burton, *Tales of the Grotesque and Arabesque* by Edgar Allan Poe, and two volumes *of La Comedie Humaine* by Honore de Balzac.

"Are you beginning to discern a theme?"

"Travel. Escape."

"Certainly, but I think we can infer a little more. Let us consider the authors for a moment, rather than the content of their works. Stevenson rebelled against his Presbyterian background and the path laid out for him by his father. Borrow and Balzac both studied law, but found it stultifying, and rejected it in favour of literature. Poe was always at odds with his foster-father and failed at the military career planned for him. When Burton was at college, he deliberately tried to get rusticated by breaking every possible rule. De Quincey was sent to Manchester Grammar School, so that after three years' stay he might obtain a scholarship to Brasenose College, Oxford, but he ran away after only nineteen months."

"All rebels, " I said. "Defying what was expected of them."

"Indeed, and unless I am very much mistaken, if we look into Phillimore's background we shall probably find indications that he wished for a different life, but hadn't the strength of character to go against his family's expectations."

"Holmes, both de Quincey and Poe were opium eaters. Do you think Phillimore emulated them?"

"One thing is clear: While part of him longed to escape from the prison of respectable conformity, he remained within it because he loves his wife. Here, in his private space, where no one else would ever see them, he has a wedding photograph and a portrait of her."

"What now?"

"A visit to Messrs Killroy and Hay, I think. But first, a word with Mrs. Phillimore."

Holmes locked the door once more with the aid of his metal picks and we made our way to the parlour.

"I require a little more data, Mrs. Phillimore," said Holmes, "Are any of your husband's clothes missing? Any personal effects, such as toiletries?"

"No, everything is just as he left it that morning."

"I see. May we have the address of Mr. Phillimore's law firm?"

"Of course. It is Killroy and Hay, 34 Austin Friars, EC."

"Thank you. And now, Mrs. Phillimore, we must bid you good day. Rest assured that your case has my entire attention.

"Now, Watson," said Holmes as we settled into a carriage on the Victoria-bound train from Bromley, "we can use the half-hour or so of travel we have before us to smoke a pipe or two and review the case of Mr. James Edward Phillimore. Let me have your thoughts."

"Well, your last question of Mrs. Phillimore tells against the idea that the whole thing was planned. Surely he would have taken some clothes with him if his aim was to leave her."

"No, I am afraid her answer doesn't prove that it was unplanned. He is a fairly wealthy man. He could, for example, have already rented himself a room somewhere, bought a fresh set of clothes, and established a new identity."

"Why did you ask the question, in that case?"

"Had she said, yes, there were clothes and toiletries missing, it would certainly have meant that it was planned. I was expecting a negative reply, but I had to ask. My belief is that his actions were a spontaneous response to something that must have happened to him in that brief span of moments. He saw something, or heard something, or possibly even felt something, that caused him to do what he did. But what?"

"Holmes! The deformed man in the street – that's what he saw! He must have known the fellow, and perhaps recognised him as someone who would use violence against him, and even against his wife. So he went back into the house and hid somewhere inside until his wife left for the police station. Then he came out and faced the man."

"Your idea isn't entirely without merit, but there are too many points which contradict it. If Phillimore had genuinely forgotten his umbrella, then seeing the man was a strange coincidence. He suddenly had both a motive for going back into his house and an excuse for doing so. You may recall that Mrs. Phillimore described her husband as being the possessor of a strong physique, bookish and sedentary as he was. A man of the kind she described would be unlikely to attack someone stronger and fitter. And how do you explain the fact that the fellow ran away – or, as Mrs. Phillimore put it, hobbled away – when she looked at him? And yet, there is a possibility that in some way he is a factor. Perhaps it would be better if we waited to see if our visit to Killroy and Hay can shed any light on this. You have your newspaper, I see, and I my Pocket Library edition of Marcus Aurelius' *Meditations*, so let us spend the remainder of the journey reading quietly."

Charles Dickens would have found the premises of Killroy and Hay, Solicitors, familiar. The room filled with copyists and clerks, the smell of ink and wood polish and the rustle of documents, the self-important head clerk keeping a close eye on his young underlings, the short flight of stairs that led to the partners' rooms, the clients coming in and out, their faces beaming, sullen, or downcast, depending on the nature of their dealings with the law and how they had turned out – all were there. Holmes and I were shown into the office of Benedict Hay, a senior partner and a descendant of one of the founders of the firm, which I later learned dated back to the sixteenth century. Hay was a tall, thin man with wiry grey hair and piercing blue eyes. He shook us both firmly by the hand.

"Pray be seated, gentlemen," he said. "It isn't every day that our office is graced by the presence of so famous a visitor as you, Mr. Holmes. Oh, and you too, of course, Dr. Watson. I assume you are here because of the disappearance of our Mr. Phillimore. James is a first-class solicitor and we feel his absence deeply. His wife came here earlier today and said that she was about to consult you, as she had been disappointed in the response of the police."

"You last saw him this past Friday."

"That is correct, sir."

"In the last few days before his disappearance, was there any decline in the quality of his work?"

"None whatsoever."

"Was there any change in his general demeanour? Did he seem worried, for example, or overly excited?"

"No, he was the same as ever."

"Mrs. Phillimore told us that he sometimes worked late at the office. Would he have been here alone on those occasions?"

Hay's eyebrows lifted.

"Worked late? He never did that. None of the partners do, junior or senior. It is a policy of the firm."

Holmes briefly turned his head and met my gaze. I instantly understood the meaning of that swift glance. For the first time, we had caught Phillimore in a lie to his wife. There must surely be something he had been hiding from her. A double life, perhaps.

"Who is handling Mr. Phillimore's cases in his absence?" asked Holmes.

"That would be Mr. Ockendon, another of the junior partners."

"May we speak with him?"

"Certainly."

Hay took us down the corridor to another office. He opened the door without knocking and we found it occupied by a fresh-faced young man in his early thirties, who was in the middle of giving instructions to one of his clerks.

"This is Mr. Sherlock Holmes," said Hay, "and his colleague Dr. Watson."

The young clerk's mouth fell open, and he was clearly disappointed when Ockendon sent him off to carry out the work they had been discussing.

Hay departed for his own office.

"I take it you're here about Jim," said Ockendon.

"I believe there might be a key to his disappearance in the cases he was dealing with at the time," said Holmes.

"It's all fairly workaday stuff. A contested inheritance – that's *Jarrowby v. Markham*. Pursuance of a debt, *Laker v. Collins* – breach of promise. *Arlen v, Coniston* – an inquiry for the relatives of Michael Enderby. The – "

"Did you say – *Michael Enderby*?"

"Yes, sir. Michael Enderby. You'd have thought, being a lawyer himself, that Enderby would at least have left his papers in order when he died, but everything's in a terrible mess. He died intestate, and we're making inquiries to see if he had any relatives. I suspect he may not have been of sound mind at the end."

Holmes stood up and, reaching across the desk, shook Ockendon by the hand.

"Thank you, your assistance has been invaluable," he said.

"But I – "

I followed Holmes through the door, bidding Ockendon a polite farewell.

A minute or two later we were seated in a hansom bound for Baker Street. My friend was silent, a grim expression on his face.

"Don't keep me in suspense," I said. "You have solved the case, have you not? Or at any rate, are in receipt of a vital clue. What is the significance of this Enderby?"

"My friend, I advise you to wait until you are sitting in a comfortable chair in our rooms, with a strong drink in your hand, before you ask that question."

"Just as you wish."

"As a literary man," said Holmes when we were back in Baker Street, "and also as a lover of sensational fiction, you have no doubt read *The Strange Case of Dr. Jekyll and Mr. Hyde*, by Robert Louis Stevenson."

"I would hardly describe the work as sensational. Stevenson may have begun his career as a writer of boys' adventure stories, but he has a good deal of psychological insight. The business with the potion is somewhat far-fetched, but the work overall is a metaphor for the human condition."

"I stand corrected, my dear doctor. Clearly, then, you have read it."

"Yes."

Holmes poured us both a brandy, then reached into the coal scuttle and took a cigar from his box.

"It may surprise you to learn, then," he said, holding a match to the end of his *Hoyo*, "that while the work is fiction, it is based on fact. You recall the death of Dr. Anthony Adamson?"

"Yes, I read about it in an English newspaper, sometime after it happened, as I was in the base hospital in Peshawur at the time. He was a respected and highly-placed member of the profession, and only about fifty when he died. Of a heart attack, I think it was."

"Yes, that is what was given out at the time. In fact, Adamson is still alive, and incarcerated in an asylum. Stevenson based the character of Henry Jekyll upon him."

"You surely aren't suggesting that Dr. Adamson invented a potion that could transform a man both physically and mentally?"

"A complete physical transformation as described in the novel is, of course, impossible. But while, as you said, the potion is pure fantasy, it conceals a truth which can be scientifically verified, though it is far outside the experience of the majority of Englishmen."

"Holmes, you have yet to connect all this to Michael Enderby, let alone James Phillimore."

"This is what I believe has happened: Enderby was Adamson's lawyer, an old friend and the executor of his will, though he had no role in drafting it. Enderby died intestate, and the task of finding his relatives, as we heard this afternoon, was given to Phillimore, who then had access to Enderby's papers. Among them must have been either a summary of Adamson's own papers, or the papers themselves."

"Something in those papers is the key to Adamson's incarceration, and to Phillimore's disappearance."

"Just so. I shall keep you in suspense no longer, and I apologise if I have tried your patience. Over the years, I have made a special study of the effects of various types of hallucinogens. Oh, don't look so worried. My experience has been confined to reading up on them. As a medical man, perhaps you should look into them yourself."

"I hardly think that, as a general practitioner, I am likely to encounter their use."

"As I've said before, education never ends, and you never know when such knowledge may prove valuable. However, let us return to the matter in hand. One of the key aspects of such drugs is that they can cause a feeling of liberation, of transcendence. The Masatec Indians of Oaxaca in Mexico have for centuries chewed a hallucinogenic mushroom called *psilocybe* to achieve those effects. The ancient Greek worshippers of Dionysus appear to have used something similar. The Masatecs and the Maenads used them infrequently, mainly at religious rites, so their systems were able to recover from the effects. Repeated doses at short intervals, particularly if the taker is unused to them, can cause mania, and an absence of conscience which may be accompanied by bursts of great physical strength. Another symptom of frequent use is that the drug's effects may reoccur even if the individual hasn't used it for several days."

I was beginning, in a vague and tentative manner, to see where Holmes's argument was taking us, but I kept silent as he continued his narrative.

"I knew none of this when I was called in to help investigate the murder of Sir Daniel Cremers. I was lodging in Montague Street at the time, and living a more or less hand-to-mouth existence. Lestrade asked for my assistance, which I took as an admission that he had some small faith in me, though he wouldn't have said as much to a third person.

"There had been one witness to the crime, a maid servant, who had seen the murder clearly from her window. The night was cloudless and there was a full moon. She saw a white-haired old gentleman coming down the lane. The old man was accosted by a second man, whose face she couldn't see. He took out a bludgeon and without warning, in a burst of inhuman strength and rage, showered blow after blow on the head and shoulders of Cremers until the aged man fell dead to the cobbles."

"That exactly mirrors the murder of Sir Danvers Carew in the novel."

"Yes, but unlike the detectives in the book, we didn't have so straightforward a clue as the broken half of a cane belonging to the murderer. I had one very slender thread, which by great good fortune turned out to be a key to the mystery. From the maid's evidence that the killer had suddenly appeared, I conjectured that he had been waiting for Cremers in the house next to the maid's, which was derelict and untenanted. On the floor of that house, I found an old newspaper with a distinct bootmark upon it. As well as its size, there was a pattern on the rubber sole which suggested that it came from one particular bootmaker and had possibly been specially made. I might have saved myself much time and effort if I had told Lestrade and let his men do the legwork, but I preferred to do it myself. If I succeeded, I would get the credit, and if I had made a false assumption, only I would know of it. It was weary, uphill work, and had none of those features of interest with which you delight your readers. To cut a long story short, the boot led me to Dr. Anthony Adamson. I informed Lestrade, and Adamson was taken to Bow Street Police Station.

"He claimed to have no memory of the evening in question and could provide no one who could vouch for his whereabouts. In the cells later that day, he experienced one of those reoccurrences of the drugged state I referred to before. This involved some powerful hallucination, as he screamed loudly, claiming that all the other inmates of the holding cells had been transformed into semi-human monsters who were planning his death. An alienist who was brought into Bow Street to examine him concluded that this was a deep-seated mania and recommended that he be transferred immediately to an asylum.

"The alienist reported the situation to the British Medical Association, who then petitioned the Metropolitan Police Commissioner to keep the matter from the public in the interests of the dignity and reputation of the medical profession. Word was given out that Adamson had died of heart failure. He was given a new name in the asylum, and I was likewise sworn to secrecy."

"How did Stevenson find out about it?"

"A good question. One of the policemen or one of the doctors involved must have outlined the bare bones of the case to him, which he then covered with fictional flesh, producing that fable on the duality of man you praised a few minutes ago. Some years later, while I was investigating the effects of these substances, it occurred to me that some of the symptoms described exactly fitted Adamson. I gained permission to visit him in the asylum. He had accepted his responsibility for Cremers' death, but even after so long a period of abstinence from the drug he was still prone to those bouts of temporary mania. He confirmed that he had experimented with a cocktail of hallucinogens in an attempt, as he described it, to expand his consciousness beyond the confines and restraints imposed upon it by the strictures of society."

"But he became psychologically addicted, and continued to take the drugs even when the effect on him was deleterious."

"Indeed."

"I've seen other drugs have a similar effect. Opium, for example."

"So," asked Holmes, "are we now ready to apply our knowledge to the case of Mr. James Edward Phillimore?"

"I think so. Like Adamson, Phillimore longed for something beyond the bourgeois respectability of his life. Adamson's papers came into his hands, and he too saw a means of release in the use of these substances. Perhaps he was a little more cautious than Adamson, as Mr. Hay said that he could see no change in his demeanour or in his work. Phillimore may, as you suggested, have taken a room where he took small doses which had an effect, but didn't prevent him from going home to his wife the same night with his story of working late."

"Excellent, Watson! And what of his disappearance, the starting point of our labours?"

"No doubt you have reached a conclusion."

"Yes. Here is what I believe happened on that Saturday morning. As Phillimore and his wife prepared to leave the house, he began to feel the cumulative force of the effect of the drugs. He had, as you said, probably been taking them in small doses, but he had been doing so regularly. He must have felt that he was on the verge of some outbreak of madness, as he may well have been. He loved his wife and didn't wish her to see whatever it was that was about to happen to him. He deliberately left his umbrella behind so that he would have an excuse to go back into the house. He then made his exit through the back door, clambered over the wall and out into the street. That is when his wife saw him. He was the deformed man in the street."

"But you said there was no physical transformation."

"Not of the kind that Stevenson described, no. But one possible effect of these chemicals is muscular spasms, which can cause the victim to bend his back and lose full control of his limbs. He ran away as best he could to preserve his secret. Had Mrs. Phillimore been trained in my methods of observation, she might have noticed that the figure was clad in the clothes her husband had been wearing the last time she saw him."

"She did say that he was thirty yards away."

"True."

"This is all well and good, Holmes," I said, "but we are still left with the question: Where is James Phillimore? Is there any chance that he too has become a murderer? He must be apprehended, before, like Adamson, he commits some unspeakable outrage."

"Crimes of violence are common in the poorer parts of London, and the culprits seldom caught, so it is entirely possible that in the four days since he vanished, Phillimore has already committed some of those everyday atrocities which regularly go unsolved and unpunished."

James Phillimore was never seen again in this world, alive or dead, and his fate remains a mystery. Holmes was forced to swallow his pride and admit his failure, and his discomfort at being unable to provide any solace for the unfortunate Mrs. Viola Phillimore. Because this case is unsolved, and because of the unsettling nature of the revelations concerning Dr. Anthony Adamson's experiments, I am consigning this account to my old tin dispatch box in the vaults of Cox and Company, Charing Cross, where it will remain unread until seventy-five years after my death.

The Adventure of the Unfortunate Cardinal

It was shortly before my friend Sherlock Holmes's retirement that we received the news that Pope Leo XIII had died. While neither Holmes nor I had any specific religious convictions, and the Pontiff's death hardly came as a surprise, as he was ninety-three years old and had been in poor health for some years, nevertheless, we heard the report of his passing with sadness. We had been of service to him on two separate occasions, the recovery of the Vatican cameos and the murder of Cardinal Tosca. While the first case received more publicity, Holmes was wont to dismiss it as "a little affair" because he had been able to solve it after a few hours' contemplation of the facts, without moving from his armchair. Needless to say, the Holy Father and his Cardinalate did not take the same view. The cameos dated back to the late fourth century and were said to have been created at the behest of St. Siricius, who had formulated many of the rules still adhered to by the priesthood. So, while they were not technically Holy Relics, they represented a link with the past whose absence would have been keenly felt.

As well as rewarding Holmes handsomely, Leo had been loud in his praise of the detective, and it cannot be doubted that this added to Holmes's growing international fame. Nor did it come as a surprise to us when, some years later, we were summoned to Rome to deal with the rather more delicate and potentially scandalous matter of the death of Cardinal Tosca.

The Cardinal had died, apparently from poisoning, not long after an unscheduled audience with the Pontiff. Holmes was uncomfortable if he had to leave his books and his scientific equipment, and the comforts of our life in Baker Street, for longer than a few days, so while the summons might have been expected, I was a little taken aback when he immediately dispatched a telegram agreeing to the trip. It transpired that, however complex or simple the case might prove to be, Holmes was eager to actually meet the Pope. I was happy to accompany him, for who could resist a journey to the Eternal City, even if the circumstances were unfortunate, and there was little likelihood that there would be time to view the full splendours of the ancient capital. Holmes informed Mrs. Hudson of our impending absence, and also sent a telegram to Inspector Lestrade to let him know that he would be unavailable for consultation until further notice. Then we were off, and we had ample opportunity to discuss the matter during the four days we spent on the Continental Express.

"What do you know of Cardinal Tosca?" Holmes asked me on the first evening after we had just finished a splendid meal and were partaking of brandy and cigars.

"Not very much, I'm afraid."

"Then let me enlighten you, as after we received the telegram I spent some time examining his career in my index, where I found him between a German music-hall performer and an American admiral. The name is Italian, but he was French, born in a little village in Provence in 1857."

"Young to be a Cardinal."

"Indeed. His family was poor, but he managed, on the basis of his ability, to get a place at the Sorbonne. He apparently came to the priesthood after a long spiritual struggle, which I understand isn't uncommon among intellectuals who embrace the Church, but once in, his talent guaranteed him a swift rise up the echelons. There were those who thought he would be a worthy successor to Peter's chair, even though he would have been the first non-Italian Pope in four-hundred years – since Adrian VI, that is, who was Dutch. Leo looked favourably upon him at first, doubtless seeing in him a man of potentially equal ability to himself."

"I take it that something caused a rift between them."

"Yes, indeed. In 1891, Leo issued an encyclical called *Rerum Novarum* – in English, *Rights and Duties of Capital and Labour*. It was an open letter, passed to all Catholic patriarchs, primates, archbishops and bishops, and in it Leo rejected both socialism and *laissez-faire* capitalism, and championed the right of workers to form trade unions. Despite coming from a humble background, Tosca was opposed to trade unions. He believed that if employers operated their businesses on Christian principles, as was their duty, then there would be no need for unions, and in any case, they were the thin edge of a wedge that inevitably led to communism and atheism."

"And you think Tosca's death may somehow be connected to this disagreement?"

"Well, it is certainly a possibility, but it would be a capital mistake to assume that it were so until we have had the opportunity to examine all the data."

At the end of our journey, we were met at the elegant Stazione Termini in Rome by Cardinal Salvatore Lombino, a vigorous man with iron-grey hair in his early sixties who spoke near-perfect English, having spent some years in London as a young man as a deacon in St. George's Cathedral, Southwark. He was, duties permitting, to act as our interpreter throughout our stay. I had no Italian at all, and Holmes, characteristically, had little command of the language other than words connected with crime.

As a porter helped us load our luggage onto a smart little horse-drawn carriage, Lombino told us, "Accommodation has been arranged for you at the Hotel Emilio, which is in St. Peter's Square, within walking distance of the Apostolic Palace."

As it turned out, I would be glad of that last fact, for while that ride through the streets of Rome was a parade of magnificent buildings and places of historic interest, the surfaces of the roads were in bad need of refurbishment, which made for a jerky and uncomfortable journey, When we arrived at the Emilio, somewhat shaken up, Lombino gave us an hour or so to rest and refresh ourselves before taking us into the presence of the Pontiff. When we arrived at the Apostolic Palace, it transpired that unexpected business would delay the start of our audience, so Holmes took advantage of this waiting period to question Cardinal Lombino.

"Have you any idea why Tosca wanted to see the Pope?"

"That, of course, is a private matter between Cardinal Tosca and His Holiness, but it was clearly something urgent."

"Why do you think so?"

"Because a list is always prepared in advance of who the Pope will see and the order in which he will receive them. Tosca wasn't on the list. He simply arrived, sent in a note, and was admitted into the audience chamber on the Holy Father's order, before he saw anyone else."

"Do you have any idea why this was?"

"I can only speculate. Perhaps Tosca's faction had secretly grown, and he felt he had the power to urge the Pope to retract *Rerum Novarum*. But it seems equally possible that Tosca had come to assure His Holiness of his continuing loyalty, despite their disagreement and the growing number of his adherents. But – and this is the strange thing that seems to even further complicate the matter – there was another victim. He didn't die, but is seriously ill in hospital."

Holmes's eyes narrowed.

"Another victim? Who is he? Does he have any connection with Tosca, other than being high in the Church?"

"He is Michael Schwerzinger, the Bishop Emeritus of Sion in Switzerland. I think it doubtful that he and Tosca even knew each other, except perhaps by sight."

"Has Schwerzinger ever expressed any opinions about *Rerum Novarum*?"

"Not to my knowledge, no. In fact, Tosca was one of the few non-Italians who had strong feelings about it one way or the other. Nearly all his followers are Italian. Besides, my impression of Schwerzinger, from the little I know of him, is that he wants a quiet life in which he can enjoy the privileges of his position. I doubt that he would be drawn to factionalism of any kind."

"Has he been questioned?"

"No, the doctors have determined that at the present time he is too weak."

"Why was he visiting the Pope?"

"He isn't in Rome very often, so I imagine he was simply paying his respects."

"After we have seen Pope Leo, I would like to speak to the doctor who signed Tosca's death warrant."

"That is easily arranged. His name is Dr. Rizzio. Ah, I believe the Holy Father is ready for us."

To be in the simultaneous presence of Sherlock Holmes and Leo XIII was a remarkable experience. It need hardly be said that both were highly intellectual, but there was an immense contrast in the form that that intellect took in either man. It wasn't merely that the Pontiff was more than forty years older than the detective. Leo's faith had given him a serenity that underlay his sophisticated theological pronouncements. There was about him, above all, an impression that his very being was permeated with a sense of stillness.

In his most elevated moments, Holmes might attain a similar stillness – as when, for example, he was playing his beloved violin, or listening to a favourite piece of music. But his mercurial nature was such that this mood couldn't stay long in the ascendant. He might descend into near-despair when there was nothing of substance upon which he could exercise his formidable talents, or become voluble and excited when those same talents were being exercised to their highest degree, or, perhaps less forgivably, resort to sarcasm and mockery when dealing with the fumbling efforts of less-astute minds.

The Pope extended his hand for Holmes to kiss his ring but, despite the detective's respect for the Pontiff, he declined to do so, and I felt it incumbent upon me to follow suit.

Cardinal Lombino was horrified.

"You cannot insult the Holy Father in this manner!"

"We wish him no insult," said Holmes, "but we aren't of the faith."

When this was translated, the Pope looked severe, but nodded his head in deference to our principles.

"Let us continue," he said.

Having been given much of the information by Lombino, Holmes decided to keep the interview short in consideration of the Pontiff's advanced years.

"Do you still have the note given to you by Cardinal Tosca?"

"Yes."

"May we see it?"

"No, I am afraid not. Even though Tosca is with God now, the note, and our conversation, must remain confidential."

"Even though it might lead us to his murderer?"

"I assure you it would not."

"Then can you tell us what was said when Bishop Schwerzinger saw you?"

"It was simply a greeting, then an exchange about our health. Nothing more."

"One last thing: May we have the list of visitors for that day?"

"I will ask my secretary to make you a copy. The original must remain in the archives."

Lombino did not accompany us to see Dr. Rizzio in his office, as the doctor spoke excellent English, a legacy from a period at Barts in London.

Rizzio was a big man with grey hair and a neatly trimmed goatee. There was an air of professional expertise about him which inspired confidence. A brief conversation elicited the information that before he had been appointed the Pope's personal physician five years previously, he had worked in France and Spain, and, after he and his wife had decided to return to Italy to start a family, had done a fifteen-year stint as an examiner for the state police, followed by eight years in civil practice.

"I was called to the Hotel Emilio near St, Peter's – Do you know it? Visiting dignitaries are often lodged there."

"We are staying there."

"I see. Well, I often get called in if one of the Pontiff's guests falls ill, since they are mainly clerics of advanced years. When I arrived,

Cardinal Tosca was in convulsions. My assessment was that these were caused by *Aqua Tofana*, probably in a highly concentrated form. Do you know of it?"

"A Sicilian poison," said Holmes, "odourless, tasteless, and colorless. First concocted in the seventeenth century and named after Giulia Tofana, who sold it to women who wanted to do away with their husbands."

"Quite so," said Rizzio. "I administered an antidote, but it was too late. The cardinal died twenty minutes after my arrival. He'd hardly passed away when I was summoned to the room of Bishop Schwerzinger, who was suffering the same symptoms, though not as severely. The antidote was successful, though he still needed to be hospitalised. I immediately asked the hotel staff if the two men had had the same breakfast, since if they had, there was the possibility that other guests might fall ill. But no, Tosca had had croissants and *cafe noir*, while Schwerzinger breakfasted on kipper with fried onions and oolong tea. I sent a message to the Holy Father's secretary to inform him of the situation, and was told not to bring the matter to the attention of the state police."

"Thank you, Dr. Rizzio."

We later dressed for dinner, then went down to the ground floor to the Emilioo's restaurant. But before we went in to dine, Holmes approached the reception desk and asked for the room number of Monsignor Noonan, the second name on the list given us by the Pope's secretary.

"He's in room 127," said the receptionist, in heavily-accented but near-perfect English, "but he's at table eighteen in the restaurant if you want to speak to him now."

The monsignor was a short, stocky Irish-American with a head of wispy greying hair. His nose and ears bore signs that he had boxed in his far-off youth. There was an aperitif glass before him, half-drained, so he must have been waiting to be served his meal.

"Monsignor Noonan?"

"That's me. Whom have I the pleasure of addressing?"

His accent could only be from New York.

"I am Sherlock Holmes, and this is my colleague, Dr. Watson."

"The detective? Then I guess you're here to investigate the death of poor Tosca."

"Yes. Did you know him?"

"A little. Can't say I agreed with him on everything. *Rerum Novarum* struck me as exactly the right stance for the Church to be taking. Still, Tosca was an upright sort of man, and I don't think anyone questioned his right to follow the dictates of his own conscience."

"May I ask you," said Holmes, "were you ill on the morning of the fourteenth?"

Noonan made an amused face at the oddness of the question, then said good-naturedly, "Well, since you ask, I was a little nauseous, and a bit dizzy, but I lay down for about half-an-hour, and then I was fine. How did you know?"

A waiter was approaching Noonan's table with a tray bearing a bowl of soup, a plate of vermicelli, and a glass of wine.

"I didn't. I was testing a theory. Thank you for corroborating it. And now we shall leave you to enjoy your meal in peace."

"Have you come to any conclusions?" I asked Holmes as we climbed the hotel stairs after finishing our own meals.

"Well, I think I know how it was done, but as to who, and why? That will take a little more investigation."

We had arrived at the adjacent doors to our rooms. I said, "It seems to me that all we have is that what the three have in common is that they all had an audience with the Pope. And for some reason, however the poison was administered, it was done in decreasing doses."

"What else did all three do in the audience chamber, besides talk to the Pope?"

I thought for a few seconds.

"Presumably they all sat down."

"True, but that wasn't it."

With that enigmatic statement, he entered his room and closed the door.

The following morning we stood once more before the Pope, but this time the role of translator was taken by the Papal Secretary, Lombino being occupied on some other business.

"Thank you for seeing us again," said Holmes. "We have only a few questions. First, does anyone have access to your bedroom at night, other than yourself?"

"Only my head of security, Mateo Bisch, and his deputy."

"Which one was on duty on the night in question?"

"Bisch."

"Would he have access to the following day's audience list?"

"Of course."

"Your Holiness, are you a heavy sleeper?"

"What is the possible relevance of such a question?" the Papal secretary demanded.

"It is relevant, I promise you. Please translate."

The Pope replied with a wry smile.

"Yes, I am. The burdens of office . . . ."

"And lastly, do you remove the Papal ring when you go to bed?"

"Always. When I am awake, I am Leo XIII, Pontifex Maximus, Head of the Roman Church, Christ's Vicar on Earth. In my nightshirt, without the ring, I am once more, for a few brief hours, only Gioacchino Pecci from Lazio."

"And you keep the ring by your bedside?"

"Yes."

"Thank you. And now, Sir Secretary, if you can arrange it, we will need a small room in which we can question Mateo Bisch,with a member of the Swiss Guard posted at the door."

Mateo Bisch was a tall, muscular man in his late thirties with a strong-jawed but sensitive face below close-cropped dark hair.

"Signor Bisch," Holmes began, "it is a tenet of your faith that confession is good for the soul, so I give you this opportunity to tell us freely how and why you brought about the death of Cardinal Tosca."

Bisch put his elbows on the table and said nothing.

"Very well, I shall tell you the how. You went into the Papal bedchamber once you were sure the Pope was asleep and you smeared his ring with concentrated *Aqua Tofana*. You did this because you knew that the first thing that happens in a Papal audience is that the visitor kisses the Pope's ring. Even that little contact would be enough to kill. But you overdid it. You killed the first man, but enough remained on the ring to make the next man gravely ill, and even then there was enough left to make a third person dizzy and nauseous. And then of course there is the fact that you killed the wrong man. Your target wasn't Cardinal Tosca. It was Bishop Michael Schwerzinger. You saw the list of audiences the previous evening and realised that at last your opportunity had come. You couldn't know that Tosca would arrive early the following morning and see the Pope before Schwerzinger. Am I right?"

Bisch's features writhed.

"Oh yes, you are right, you oh-so-clever Englishman, Mr. Sherlock Holmes."

"Why do you hate Schwerzinger enough to want to kill him?" I asked.

Bisch stood up.

"You ask me why? Why? I'll tell you why! Because he is a foul, disgusting creature! Because he killed my brother, as surely as if he had put a bullet through his head. I had to make my own justice. Where was justice for Alesio, if I didn't make it? I swear, I would go into that hospital and squeeze the life out of him now with my bare hands if I could."

Bisch fell back in his chair, put his head into his hands, and burst into passionate sobbing.

Holmes and I fell silent. At length, Bisch wiped the tears from his face with the back of one large hand.

"All my life, I have been a devout son of the Church. All I ever wanted was to serve it in some capacity. I wasn't academic enough, or unworldly enough, to join the priesthood, but I was tall and strong and vigorous, so I applied to join the Swiss Guard, and was accepted. When I was deemed too old for the Guard, I sought a job in the Vatican security service, and again was accepted, and rose to be the chief.

"I was born in Basle of a good family, the oldest of eight children. We have all served our church or our country with honour – all save one. Alesio, the youngest. He started out well. Better than I, certainly. He was a good scholar and sang in the church choir, but then, around thirteen or fourteen, he started committing petty crimes. He went to drink and cocaine, and joined a gang of ruffians. His crimes became more serious, and eventually he was sent to prison. I believe the shame of it hastened my parents' deaths. I was now the head of the family, and as such, it was my duty to visit him in that terrible place.

"I could scarcely believe that the piece of human wreckage I saw before me was my own flesh and blood.

"I was bitterly angry with him. 'How did you come to this'? I yelled at him. 'How could you sully the family name? You were a better scholar than me! You were a choirboy . . . ."

"Tears rolled down his cheeks. 'Yes, a choirboy,' he said. 'That's where it began.' I asked him what he meant, and he told me a horrible story. If I hadn't been there – if I had not seen the sorrow in his eyes, and heard the pain in his voice, perhaps I would not have believed him. He had loved his choirmaster like a second father, and when the man singled him out, he believed that he loved him like a son. But then the choirmaster began . . . *interfering* with him. He forced him to commit obscene acts. Alesio felt that this was wrong, but the choirmaster was an adult, and a respected priest of the Church. Who could he tell? Who would believe him? Was it his fault? Had he invited it without knowing? What would his life be? These thoughts rolled around and around his head until all he wanted was escape from the pain they caused. Alcohol and cocaine numbed him. They also led him to crime. I thought that telling me of his pain might exorcise it. Instead, it brought it closer to the surface. He suffered. A week later he took his own life.

"The choirmaster left Basle. He had friends high up in the Church who helped him rise. You know his name, and what he became. Now do you see?"

"I see that if your brother told the truth, Schwerzinger was guilty of a heinous crime. Why did you not report it?" asked Holmes.

"I could not prove it! Who would believe me? Who would even consider it possible? Now I have caused the death of an innocent man, a good man, even if he had his disagreements with the Holy Father. For that I must die."

* * * * *

"Well," said Cardinal Lombino, "the killer wasn't a priest. That's a relief. No scandal on that score. Now he has confessed, it will not be necessary to inform His Holiness of what Bisch claims was his motivation."

"Perhaps not," said Holmes, "but you might do well to investigate any other claims against Schwerzinger."

"Well, that is something for the Swiss Police. Now, the Pope is very appreciative. He would like you to stay another week, as the Church's guests. I'm sure you would like to see the Sistine Chapel, the Castel Sant Angelo, and the rest of the marvels of the Eternal City."

Holmes and I exchanged glances.

"Convey our greatest respects to the Pontiff, but I think we have had enough of Rome for the time being," said Holmes. "Perhaps you would arrange for a carriage to take us from the Emilio to the Stazione Termini."

Shortly after our return to Baker Street, Holmes received a telegram from Cardinal Lombino informing him that due to a severe reaction to one of the curative drugs that had been prescribed to him, Bishop Michael Schwerzinger had died in hospital of a massive heart attack.

I hadn't even considered the idea of turning our experiences in Italy into one of my accounts of my doings with Holmes, but the death of Leo XIII brought it back to my mind. It was a sordid tale, and yet, Holmes's intellect and deductive powers were well on display. I record it here, and will place this narrative in my old tin dispatch box, with instructions that it be published something past seventy-five years after my death.

The Disappearance of the Cutter *Alicia*

One morning in June 1926, I was pleased to find, among my meagre correspondence, a letter postmarked from Sussex. I knew of only one person living in that particular county, and instantly recognized Holmes's handwriting, which, though he was a mere two years my junior, was as firm and clear as it had ever been in those far-off days when we had shared rooms together. I confess that I felt a thrill of the old excitement as I eagerly slit the envelope open.

My dear Doctor,

I trust that you are in good health. You may wonder at my writing to you after so long a silence, but the enclosed papers, which are in the nature of a death-bed confession, finally provide the solution to a long-standing mystery. You went so far, in the introduction to one of your little fables, as to describe our participation in the case as "a complete failure". But now I find that my speculations, wild as they may have seemed at the time, had some basis in truth, though of course they went unsubstantiated. I refer to the affair of the cutter Alicia, *which sailed into a patch of mist and disappeared, and whose crew were never heard of again.*

The sting of Holmes's few defeats had remained in my memory just as clearly as the elation of his many successes, and I laid the letter on the table and fell into a reverie.

That year saw Holmes at perhaps the peak of his powers and the greatest height of his international fame. The social status of any potential client was entirely irrelevant to him, and while he was far from indifferent to the state of his bank balance, he refused to examine many cases which would have brought him a princely fee in favour of those which offered him an intellectual challenge or appealed to his sense of justice.

It was, I recall, a fine morning in late spring. Holmes was looking through a pile of the letters and telegrams which were now arriving at our lodgings every morning. I confined myself to a close examination of the morning papers, for I knew that if he found nothing in the post to pique his interest, his next move would be to ask me if there was anything worth scrutinizing in the news.

"Well, well, " he said suddenly, "it seems that wonders will never cease."

He waved the thin paper of a telegram in my general direction.

"We are about to have a visitation from my brother, Mycroft. Now, as you will recall, he rarely leaves the fixed circle of his existence to visit these humble rooms unless it is to warn us away from a sensitive subject, or to engage our assistance with something he perceives as being of national importance."

"Well," I said, lowering the newspaper, "you must admit that he has been generally right about the latter. So which is it?"

I smiled as Holmes read out the telegram in a fair facsimile of his brother's somewhat deeper and more portentous tones.

"'*Sherlock – Drop whatever case in which you may be involved and expect me to call on you at eleven o'clock this morning on a matter of national security. Be sure to be in your rooms at that hour. Mycroft.*'"

Holmes tossed the telegram onto his desk and rubbed his bony hands together.

"To do him justice, every case he has brought to my attention has been of interest. Luckily, he calls when I have nothing on hand. You will recall that I sent a message to Gregson at Scotland Yard last night."

"Yes."

"It was the final piece of evidence that will secure the prosecution of Thomas Lansdown. And as for the Treharne matter, I am confident that there will be no new developments in the next few days. Was there anything in the papers that might be connected to Mycroft?"

"Not that I saw."

"Then perhaps the matter is still secret."

"We'll soon find out," I said, pulling my watch from my waistcoat pocket. "It's almost eleven now, and your brother has never been less than punctual."

Holmes rose, went over to the window, and gazed down into the street.

"His carriage is just arriving now, and he isn't on his own."

"Lestrade? Bradstreet?"

"No, I've never seen the man before."

There was a knock at the downstairs door, and shortly after we heard the heavy clump of Mycroft Holmes's ascent, accompanied by the sound of the footfalls of a somewhat lighter man.

The older Holmes brother entered, accompanied by a shorter man whom I took to be in his early fifties. His wavy brown hair and beard were sprinkled with grey, and his face was somewhat swarthy and creased with lines. He was wearing a black pea-jacket, dark canvas trousers, and a pair of heavy brown boots.

"This is my brother Sherlock, and this, his friend and colleague Dr. John Watson," Mycroft Holmes began, "and this, gentlemen, is Arthur Coppard, the – "

"Indulge me, Mycroft. Let me exercise such small powers as I possess."

"Oh, if you must."

Holmes took Coppard's hand and shook it vigorously.

"I am pleased to meet you, Mr. Coppard. You are a sea captain, though you have come up through the ranks from a private seaman, and haven't been in your present position for very long."

"That is true, sir, but how did you know it?" Coppard said, in an accent which smacked of the West Country.

"Mycroft, would you care to explain?"

"No doubt my brother observed you leaving my carriage and coming with me to the door. Though a short distance, it was enough for him to see that you have that distinctive gait which is the mark of one who has been long at sea. When you entered the room, he noted your air of authority, which indicated your position of command, but when he shook your hand he felt its hardness, and the callouses which come from the work with ropes and tackle which is the lot of the common seaman. Hence, you haven't long left the fo'c's'le for the captain's cabin."

"Well," said Coppard, "I hadn't thought there was one such a man in the world, let alone two!"

"Let us be seated, gentlemen," said Holmes, " and you can tell us the reason for your visit."

Mycroft gestured to Coppard that he should speak.

"I am Arthur Coppard, captain of the *Christabel*, a ship in the employment of the Liverpool Cotton Association. We transport raw cotton from the Americas. A week ago, we were making our way back to the port with a full cargo when I saw a cutter some five-hundred yards to the west of us. Apart from the fact that she was a little far out to sea for such a small vessel, she appeared to be in distress, for she was moving erratically, with the changes of wind and current. There seemed to be no one at the tiller. We shifted our course to go to her aid and, as we did so, she entered a patch of mist. We followed, but when the mist dissipated a few minutes later, the cutter had vanished. Into thin air, not a sign of her."

"Had the mist entirely dissipated when you noticed the cutter's disappearance?" asked Holmes.

"No, there was some left a few feet above the water, but it was clear that the ship had somehow vanished, so we turned our course to Liverpool, and I told the authorities what I had seen at the earliest opportunity."

"Thank you, Captain Coppard," said the elder Holmes. "I must ask you now to return to the carriage and await me there, for what I must now discuss with my brother is a case of national importance."

"As you wish, sir. Good day, gentlemen."

"Do you wish me to leave too?" I stood up as the sailor made his way downstairs.

"Stay where you are, Watson, " said Holmes. "My brother knows that it is both or neither where you and I are concerned."

Mycroft raised one broad, flat hand in a gesture of acquiescence.

"So, Sherlock," he said, "what do you know about smuggling?"

"I assume from Captain Coppard's story that you are referring to smuggling by sea, rather than across land borders. When I embarked on my examination of the various forms of criminality in this world, I studied the subject with some assiduity, but I confess that since fewer cases involving smuggling have come my way, my knowledge of it has somewhat atrophied. I'm aware that it still exists on the western coast of the United States, in China, and some parts of Africa. It used to be widely practised in the West Country, but surely that ceased at the beginning of this century."

"Well," said Mycroft, "not entirely. It still occurs from time to time in that part of the country, and all the coasts of the British Isles are still regularly patrolled to prevent it. That brings us to the relevance of Captain Coppard's experience. The majority of the boats performing that service are cutters. The only such vessel that hasn't returned to its designated berth is the *Alicia*, currently captained by one Albert Hutchinson. My suspicion is that the craft Coppard saw was the *Alicia*, and the reason that she was moving erratically, why there seemed to be no one at the tiller, was that the crew had been abducted. Now, if that is the case, our national safety is at risk."

"How so?" I asked.

Mycroft answered, slightly impatiently. "Of necessity, all the captains of the cutters employed by the government in this capacity are kept informed of all the movements of all the craft plying the coast, and this includes those patrolling the sea against the possible incursion of foreign vessels whose intent is, shall we say, not peaceful. If Captain Hutchinson has fallen into enemy hands, they may force him to reveal what he knows, enabling them to evade the security patrols and attack the mainland. Now, thus far we have had no such events, but the situation must be resolved. Captain Coppard and his crew have been ordered on pain of prosecution to keep silent about the matter. Now, Sherlock, I am leaving this in your hands because I have more immediate business to deal with. A revolution in San Bartolo is imminent, which threatens our mineral interests in that country, and there is the possibility that the Korean *won* will be subject to inflation. Good day, gentlemen. Should you wish to contact me, you know where I am."

"A pretty mystery, is it not, Watson? And in his understandable eagerness to ensure the country's safety, Mycroft ignored the chief feature of the story: How did the *Alicia* vanish after sailing into that patch of mist, whether its crew was on board or not? It is a mystery which by its nature might seem to most who hear the story to be explicable only in supernatural terms. Was the *Alicia* the victim of some giant, undiscovered creature from the sea bottom which rose from the depths and dragged the cutter and its unfortunate crew down to destruction in a matter of moments? Or perhaps Captain Hutchinson was a sinner equal to the legendary Vanderdecken, and the Devil rendered the ship invisible and sentenced him and his crew to sail the seas until Judgement Day. Or if, like the mathematician Charles Howard Hinton, we wish to dress our speculations in a cloak of pseudo-science, then the ship may, in some inexplicable manner, have entered another dimension. There is, of course, a more simple and fully rational explanation."

"Which is?"

"You studied Latin and Roman history at your school, I imagine?"

"Yes, of course."

"Then you will no doubt remember that the notoriously debauched Emperor Nero was also a matricide."

"Yes, and when the assassins came for his mother, she pointed at her womb and said, "Strike me here," because it had been guilty of bearing such an unfilial son."

"Correct. But before that he tried another method."

"How is any of this connected to the fate of the *Alicia*?"

"Patience, my dear Doctor, patience."

He stood, went over to his bookshelves, and took down three volumes, opening each one after another and skimming through the pages until he found the passages for which he was searching.

"Here is Suetonius, from his *Twelve Caesars*," he said," passing me one of them. I read:

> *Nero's next stratagem was to construct a ship which could be easily shivered, in hopes of destroying her either by drowning, or by the deck above her cabin crushing her in its fall.*

"And Tacitus, from *The Annals*."

> *The vessel had not gone far, Agrippina having with her two of her intimate attendants, one of whom, Crepereius Gallus, stood near the helm, while Acerronia, reclining at Agrippina's feet as she reposed herself, spoke joyfully of her son's repentance and of the recovery of the mother's influence, when at a given signal the ceiling of the place, which was loaded with a quantity of lead, fell in, and Crepereius was crushed and instantly killed.*

"And lastly, Cassius Dio's *Roman History*."

> *Sabina, on hearing about this, began to persuade Nero to get rid of his mother in order to forestall her alleged plots against him. One day they saw in the theatre a ship that*

automatically separated in two, let out some beasts, and came together again so as to be once more seaworthy, and they at once had another one built like it.

"Now, Watson, I am sure you will concede that if there were shipbuilders in the First Century who were capable of constructing such a vessel, it would present no problems to a modern builder who would have access to our century's superior techniques."

"The accounts don't exactly agree."

"True, although they all concur that Agrippina survived by swimming to shore. Suetonius is often accused of purveying malicious gossip, and while Tacitus has a somewhat better reputation, he is not without his critics. Dio was writing a little later, but still, most of our contemporary historians think the story essentially true. I think we can take the use of such a stratagem as a working hypothesis in the case of the *Alicia*. You may have noted that I asked the good captain if the mist had entirely dispersed. If he hadn't turned the *Christabel* and left before it was completely gone, I fancy he would have seen wreckage floating on the water. The presence of both the *Christabel* and the mist cannot have been planned, so the perpetrators presumably intended flotsam bearing the *Alicia*'s name to be found."

"But why was it done? And by whom?"

"Clearly, what our friend the captain saw wasn't the *Alicia* herself, but a collapsible replica, as I don't think it would be possible to alter an existing vessel to fall apart in that manner. This implies that the real *Alicia* is still in existence somewhere, and that there are those who gain an advantage from her being believed lost."

A thought suddenly occurred to me.

"Holmes! Supposing the *Alicia* has been captured by smugglers. In her, they might approach other Navy boats, which, perceiving her as friendly, would allow her to draw alongside. The smugglers could then swarm aboard and kill or capture the revenue men."

"That isn't impossible, but such a theory has an insurmountable flaw: If it had happened, would Mycroft not have informed us? He can be secretive, true, but he would gain nothing by concealing the fact."

"Who, then?"

"The only others who could carry it out would seem to be the crew themselves. They would be able to take her into a harbour where it could be duplicated. It must have been a long-term plan, since the construction of the false *Alicia* would take some time. I have no experience of such matters, so I don't know how long, but it must surely be measured in weeks."

"But why should they do such a thing? What advantage could they gain from it?"

"It would be believed that they were dead, drowned in the sinking of the vessel. To me that hints at some crime in which they were all complicit. Dead men are notoriously difficult to prosecute. Now, unless it can be proved that all combined to carry out some crime on land, which I consider unlikely, we must consider those crimes which are connected with the sea."

"Mutiny?"

"As I said before, the construction of the false *Alicia* must have taken some time, and mutiny is usually carried out spontaneously, or at least planned not long before the act. I am inclined to think that, as with so many misdeeds in this fallen world, monetary gain is at the heart of it. Who could they steal from with absolute impunity? The smugglers themselves. Let us say that they captured a smuggling vessel which had accumulated a large amount of loot. Tempted by greed, they take the money and dispose of the smuggling vessel's crew. But how are they to spend the money without arousing suspicion? Presumably there is enough, cutters' crews being small in number, for them to start new lives elsewhere, so they secrete the money in a safe place, using some of it to pay an unscrupulous shipbuilder to construct the false *Alicia*. They then sail away in the real one, after setting the replica adrift at sea. Will it serve?

"I'm sure you have hit on it. But there are problems."

"Indeed. How do we prove it, and even if we can, how do we bring the perpetrators to justice?"

I will not try the reader's patience with a lengthy description of the fruitless efforts we made over the ensuing weeks. The wives and families of the missing men were interviewed by Mycroft's agents, but they clearly knew nothing of the matter, and were given financial help on the basis that their menfolk appeared to have died while in the service of the government. The only shipbuilder with criminal antecedents who could be identified had left the country, which supported but didn't corroborate Holmes's hypothesis. In the end, he was forced to concede defeat. Mycroft Holmes was far from satisfied with this outcome, but his annoyance with his younger brother subsided when none of the dire predictions he had made that morning came true.

And there it had stood for many years. I turned my attention once more to Holmes's letter.

I received this communication from a gentleman in Australia who signs himself P.J. Webb, *although from the internal evidence, assuming the tale is true and not some peculiar hoax, he would seem to be in truth Arthur Swinscomb, the youngest of the six crewmen of the* Alicia. *In any event, I am sure it will be of interest to you, as it was to me.*

Yours sincerely,
Sherlock Holmes

The enclosure read:

Dear Mr. Holmes,

My doctor informs me that I have little time left in this world, and before I depart it altogether I would like to make my confession. I have never been a religious man, and have no conception of what, if anything, awaits me when I have quit this life. Word reached me that you were charged with the investigation into the disappearance of the cutter Alicia.

[Next to this was a marginal note in Holmes's handwriting: *This suggests that despite Mycroft's precautions, Captain Coppard revealed that he had visited us, though how that information then reached Swinscomb is likely to remain a mystery.*]

I would gain no solace from conversation with a priest, but as I know you came to no firm conclusion concerning its fate, [No doubt he had read that piece of sensational fiction you entitled "The Problem of Thor Bridge"!] *it would please me to finally enlighten you after the passage of so many years. I believe I am the last survivor of our little band of brothers, and so there is none other who can perform this service, and I now have no family to be adversely affected by my revelation. I was the youngest of us, but I was, nevertheless, a grown man, in full control of my destiny, so I cannot use my relative youth as mitigation for my misdeeds.*

I was born in Whimple, in Devon, to honest God-fearing parents, and I swear it is no reflection on them that I turned out the way I did. I was as proud as a man might be when, at the age of twenty-three, I was assigned to the cutter Alicia, *with the responsibility of keeping a section of the west coast of our islands free from smugglers. In truth, we rarely encountered any, but we proudly put that down to our presence, and felt sure that had we not been there, the sea would have been rife with them. There were six of us, including the captain, Albert Hutchinson. He was a tall, imposing man with a great red beard. He was hard as nails and brooked no nonsense, but he was generous and fair, and we all respected him.*

His mate, Thomas Groome, had served with him for several years, and when he was assigned to the Alicia, *it was only natural that Groome should join him. Groome was almost as tall as Hutchinson, but was slim and wiry, and could scramble up the rigging with the speed and surety of a monkey. Next came John Tremayne, at forty-seven the oldest of us all, fair-haired and golden-bearded, still fit and muscular though probably not fated to stay in the service for much longer. Then there was Simon Gascoyne, who had come from what was known as "a good family", but had joined the Navy after that family had been bankrupted by bad investments. A few years my senior, he too was taller than average, with a face that remained pale no matter how hard it was battered by the weather, slim with curling dark hair.*

Bob Roberson, my closest friend on the Alicia*, was, like me, of middling height, though we didn't resemble each other in any other respect. He was married and I was single. He was fair and I was dark. He was loud in his laughter while I was quiet and shy. He loved to gamble, drink and sing, while I kept a close hold on my money. But of all my comrades, he was perhaps the easiest to like.*

We all worked together as a smooth unit under Captain Hutchinson's steady eye and there were no complaints of our conduct by those in charge. What, then, caused our downfall? What led to one of us lying dead on the deck of the Alicia *and the others dispersed to the corners of the world?*

In a word, greed. The oldest trap in the world. The love of dead pieces of paper and metal that somehow becomes more powerful than the sense of duty and responsibility towards one's fellow-man. And in truth, though the money we took has assured me a comfortable life, it has also been a lonely one, with the shadow of my guilt hanging ever over me.

Enough. To my tale. If you were a man of the sea, and especially if you were also a native of the West Country, you would have heard of the legend of Black Bart's Treasure. Of all the smugglers of the eighteenth century, he had been the most successful, and the story was that he had secreted a vast hoard somewhere, in some cave on the Devon coast. His plan was to make one final smuggling voyage and then escape with his accumulated wealth to the New World, but on that last voyage he had quarrelled with his first mate and in the course of a bloody duel with cutlasses, each killed the other. A storm then hit the ship, and it went down to Davy Jones' Locker. One sailor escaped, clinging to a piece of wreckage, and after he was found on the shore he survived long enough to tell the story to his rescuers. So the legend grew up, and in time it was said that there was a curse on Black Bart's loot. Perhaps there was.

Like Black Bart's ship, the Alicia *was caught in a fearful storm. The night was falling fast, and there was no sign of a lighthouse. But unlike Black Bart, in the teeth of a storm we managed to make our way to safety in the form of a sheltered cove. We dropped anchor and prepared to spend the night, but there was no fresh water on board. Bob Roberson and I volunteered to go ashore and look for some. What we found, instead, was a cave. With typical bravado, Bob suggested that we go inside and look around, for who knew, maybe Black Bart's treasure was in there.*

And yes, against all reason, and in keeping with a hoary, improbable tale, that was what we found. Some of it was in the form of paper money unusable in this day, but the majority of it was gold and silver coins, innumerable great piles of them. Like the two honest fellows we felt ourselves to be, we went back and told the others of our find. Soon all six of us were there, staring at more money than we could have hoped to see in a dozen lives. It was then that the great sickness of greed began to overtake us. I certainly knew in my heart that this wasn't ours, that we should notify the authorities to come and retrieve it, that such an injection of money would greatly benefit the county and even perhaps the country. Were we not bound to be given some reward, some honour, for the selfless act of handing it over? No doubt this went through all of our minds, but not one of us said anything to that effect.

We began instead to discuss how we might escape with it, how it could alter our lives so much for the better. Those of us who were married, Groome, Tremayne, and Roberson talked of how they couldn't bring any of it home to their wives and families without arousing suspicion. It was Groome who said that if we could make it seem that we had perished at sea, then our families would get compensation and we could take the hoard aboard the Alicia, *drop anchor on a foreign coast and divide it. Then we could scuttle the ship and go our separate ways. From there the plan grew with the relentlessness of an avalanche. Gascoyne knew of a boat builder who could make a replica of the* Alicia. *When, just before our next scheduled voyage, we consulted him, he assured us that if nails made of beeswax were substituted for certain crucial iron nails, it would be possible for the ship to drift on the ocean until the heat of the sun and the action of the seawater melted them, at which point the false* Alicia *would collapse into wreckage. With luck, that wreckage would eventually be found and our loss confirmed.*

The weeks during which we awaited the replica's completion were tense. None of us were able to speak of it, but then one day John Tremayne found his voice.

All six of us were on deck when he said, "I can't keep my peace any longer. What we are doing is wrong. You know what I'm saying. Abandoning our families, all for gold and silver. Betraying the trust that's been placed in us. Dammit, in your hearts you all know it isn't right!"

"So what would you have us do, Johnny?" asked the captain. "Go back to our lives of toil and danger when there's a way out, a way to safety and a comfortable life? Is that what you want?"

"All right. If I can't move you, at least I can go."

"Then go," said Gascoyne, "and more for the five of us."

"How do we know you'll not betray us? asked Groome.

"We don't," said Gascoyne.

Suddenly there was a flash of smoke and the report of a gun, and to my horror I realised that Bob Roberson had shot Tremayne, who fell to the deck with a scream of pain. Moments later he was dead.

"That solves the problem," said Bob, and I stood aghast at the transformation of my best friend into a cold-blooded killer. In that moment, I knew that I was complicit, that as a participant in the whole scheme I shared in the guilt of Tremayne's death.

"Don't look so pale, boy," the captain said to me. "Help me throw his body overboard."

The rest you can no doubt deduce. Everything went according to plan. Where the others went, I cannot say. I used my share to carry myself to the other side of the world, as far as I could from England.

Signed this day, the 18th May, 1926, by

P.J. Webb

The Adventure of the Remarkable Worm

It was a beautiful, balmy evening, and I had thrown wide the windows of our sitting room at No. 221b Baker Street to let in the cooling breeze. I was content to do nothing more than sit back quietly and relax, but my fellow lodger was of a rather different humour. He'd had no cases for a full five days, and this idleness rendered him a difficult companion. The previous fortnight had been filled – indeed, crammed – with activity, which made his present lack of work the more frustrating. There had been the singular experience of M. Aristide Dubois, a merchant banker who had gone to bed in Paris and woken up two days later on the floor of the British Museum, and the case of the Thornton Heath Horror – to say nothing of the affair of Carew, the blind cracksman, which had so nearly cost us both our lives.

To do him justice, my friend had tried to fill the time constructively. He had spent a day on some malodorous chemical experiments, and then, perhaps sensing that the noxious fumes were making me uncomfortable, put his test tubes and Bunsen burner to one side and turned to the production of a first draft of a monograph he had long intended to write upon the specialised argots of various professions. For a few hours he made preliminary notes and consulted his scrapbooks, but then he stood up with a gesture of frustration and paced back and forth across the room, threw himself into his armchair, sat there for a short while, stood up again, and went over to the window.

He gazed down upon the street below for a minute or so, then turned and gave me a searching look, as if hoping to deduce something from my appearance and facial expression. As I hadn't left our rooms for some time, and felt relaxed and contented, I fear there was little for his genius to work upon.

He then went to the corner where he kept his violin, pulled the instrument from its case, and ran his bow across it, producing a gentle melody which I didn't recognise and presumed to be one of his own compositions. He continued in this vein for one or two minutes, and then concluded with a discordant cadenza. He threw the violin and bow down on a chair with an exclamation of disgust.

"A whisky?" I said, reaching across to the tantalus.

"No, thank you."

"A case will come, my friend. Depend upon it."

"I wish I shared your optimism, Watson. If I don't have work soon, then I shall be forced to seek stimulation elsewhere."

I confess I went a little cold at these words, for I had been struggling to help him rid himself of his addiction to cocaine, and knew that the little morocco case containing his hypodermic needle lay within easy reach in the drawer of his desk. My relief, then, when I heard the ringing of our doorbell may be readily imagined. Mrs. Hudson opened the door to our rooms to admit a little ferret-faced fellow in a grey lightweight cotton suit.

"Good evening, Mr. Holmes. Doctor."

It was Inspector Lestrade, the tenacious Scotland Yarder whom the consulting detective had assisted on many occasions.

Holmes smiled broadly.

"Lestrade, my dear fellow! Please, take a seat. Watson, perhaps the inspector would like a glass of whisky."

"Thank you very much," said the wiry little professional. "Don't mind if I do."

"And one for me, if you'd be so good. Now then, my friend," said Holmes when we were all seated with a drink in hand, "what brings you to our humble abode on this fine evening?"

"Well, Mr. Holmes, it's like this: Have you heard of Isidore Persano?"

"The journalist? I've read one or two of his articles. I can't say they were especially to my taste. What has he done?"

"Well, we've had our eye on him for some time at Scotland Yard. He lived in Paris for a while, and got himself quite a reputation there as a duelist."

"Ah, yes," said Holmes. "There was some contretemps in Pere Lachaise, I seem to recall."

"Yes. I don't know if that's why he left Paris, but since he's been in London, he's had a couple of very public altercations with men who later appeared to have sustained bullet wounds: Thomas Marlowe, another journalist, and Arnold Campbell, a hotelier. We couldn't pin anything on him on either occasion, but it seems highly probable that he had shot them in duels. Since dueling is illegal, neither man could press charges without incriminating himself."

"But what was the nature of these disagreements? They must have been serious to provoke such a reaction."

"Well, by all accounts, he's a bit of a strange chap. Spanish, I take it, by his name, with a proud and passionate nature. Claims to be thirty, but looks a good deal younger. Short, slim, a bit swarthy."

"Essential as these details are, you haven't answered my question: Why should he challenge these men to duels?"

Lestrade cleared his throat and looked somewhat uncomfortable.

"Persano has a very close relationship with the noted chemist, Dr. Thomas Poulteney, of 17 Margrave Villas, Stoke Newington. Dr. Poulteney is a bachelor of forty-five, and . . . well . . . ."

"And these two men suggested that the relationship between them is . . . *unnatural*?"

"You've hit on it, Mr. Holmes. Persano is also unmarried and lives by himself."

"Was there any indication of blackmail? You are aware, I'm sure, that homosexuality is at the root of the majority of such cases?" The whole subject was clearly a source of embarrassment to the Scotland Yarder.

"Thankfully I've had little to do with that sort of thing. There was no evidence of blackmail."

"So, Lestrade, what is there for me to do? Have there been fresh clues to these mysteries? Perplexing threads that you would wish me to untangle?"

"No, sir. It is the strange disappearance of Mr. Isidore Persano that we need your help to solve."

"Disappearance? Pray continue."

I offered Lestrade another whisky, and he accepted it gladly, taking a short sip of it before resuming his account.

"Persano was residing at 24 Monckton Street, just off the Strand. He came home two evenings ago at about six and asked the maid to bring him a cup of coffee before dinner. When she came into his study a few minutes later, she found him in a state of raving madness, hysterical and incoherent, and pointing at a matchbox that lay in front of him."

"A matchbox? Was there anything in it?

"I have it here, Mr. Holmes. See for yourself."

Holmes took the proffered Vestas box and pulled out the little cardboard drawer. I leaned over eagerly to see what it might contain. Inside lay a dead worm, but such a worm as I had never before seen in my life. It had a distinct head of a slate-blue colour, while its fat body was a darker blue mottled with red-and-yellow dots. "No one at the Yard had ever seen anything like it. I sent a man to Westminster Library and he looked it up, but it wasn't there. The Inspector brought in the curator of the Kensington Museum, and he didn't recognise it either. It seems to be completely unknown to science."

"Fascinating. But the disappearance?"

"The girl went to the door and called a boy to fetch the nearest doctor. The man was just a general practitioner and didn't feel confident diagnosing a mental illness, so he just gave Persano a sedative and despatched a message to Colney Hatch to come and get him. They sent a carriage with an attendant. When they arrived at the asylum he was still asleep, so they locked him in a room and waited till he woke up so they could make a proper diagnosis. When they opened the door some time later, there was no one there. The room was completely empty. They contacted the Yard, so I took a couple of constables with me to search the building and grounds while I questioned the staff. My men did a very thorough job and found nothing."

"How often did the nurses check on him?"

"Once every quarter-of-an-hour."

"Any signs that the lock or hinges had been tampered with?"

"None at all. The windows were barred and the room was on the fourth floor."

Holmes pressed the tips of his long bony fingers together. "Did Persano's maid accompany him to the asylum?"

"No, Mr. Holmes. It was all she could do to get a lad to the nearest doctor. I spoke to her the next day and she was still shaken up, poor girl. She was relieved when I took that thing out of the house."

"How long has she been in Persano's employ?"

"Ever since he's been in London, apparently."

"Has he any other servants?"

"Not that I saw. She appears to be the only one that lives in, at any rate."

"What measures have you taken?"

"Well, the whole area's being combed for him, naturally, but I thought – "

"I am much obliged to you, Lestrade," said Holmes, standing up. "If you care to leave this with me, I will give it my fullest attention. Oh, by the way," he added as the inspector turned to the door, "would you mind if I take possession of that singular worm?"

"Certainly not," said Lestrade, handing over the matchbox. "As I said, we can make nothing of it down at the Yard. Well, good night, Mr. Holmes. Dr. Watson." When the street door had closed behind Lestrade, Holmes reached for his clay pipe and filled it with tobacco from the toe of his Persian slipper. "Well, Doctor, what do you make of it?" he asked through preliminary puffs of smoke.

I took a moment to think. "It seems to me that what we have here are two mysteries, and both are equally perplexing. What can be the connection between the two, other than that the same person is involved in both instances?"

"That is for us to discover. We must make a thorough investigation of both ends of the case, and as we progress they will doubtless throw light on each other. But give me your first impressions."

"The worm certainly seems to be of an exceptional character, but that is surely not enough to drive one insane at the mere sight of it. Fear of snakes is common enough. It even has a scientific name, *ophidiophobia*. But fear of worms – "

"*Vermiphobia*?" asked Holmes with a smile.

"Perhaps. It may exist, but it would be the first I have ever heard of it. That particular species of worm must have some special significance for Persano. But if it is unknown to science, how could he have seen one before?"

"How indeed? And what of his disappearance?"

"Supposing Lestrade's men didn't search as fully as they thought? From what I recall of Colney Hatch, it has a high wall and very secure gates. What if Persano is hiding somewhere in the building. Or the grounds?"

"If that's the case, then he'll be discovered very soon. I think, however, that you are being a little unfair to Lestrade and his men. They may be lacking in imagination, but we shouldn't cast aspersions on their diligence."

"Perhaps not. But then we have another mystery: The gates aren't only locked – they are guarded. How could he get through them? As for the locked door, I believe I have a solution to that." Holmes smiled again and sent a plume of smoke upwards.

"Pray tell."

"The windows were barred. Lestrade described Persano as small and slim, but even if he had been slender enough to get through the bars, the room was on the fourth floor. The walls are sheer."

"Ergo?"

"The door must have been unlocked, Persano freed, and the door locked again."

"Bravo, my dear Doctor! In this instance, the simplest and most obvious solution is the only one that will serve. But by whom was the door unlocked? Persano was asleep, so there was no opportunity for him to get a key. You will recall that I asked Lestrade if the maid had accompanied him. She hadn't, so who was there at the mental hospital who had any motive for being his rescuer? I shall think a little more on this matter and then have an early night – as should you, for I expect we shall have a busy day tomorrow."

The sun rose early the following morning, and after a light breakfast we set out by cab for Monckton Street. The traffic was fairly heavy, but our destination was no great distance from our lodgings, and we were there within twenty minutes. 24 Monckton Street was a narrow, elegant, terraced house with three floors. Holmes rang the bell, and a few moments later, it was answered by a pale-faced, petite young woman in a neatly pressed maid's uniform.

"Good morning. I am Sherlock Holmes, and this is my friend and colleague, Dr. John Watson. We have been engaged by the police to aid them in their investigation into the disappearance of your employer. I should like to come in and ask you some questions."

"Please do, sir," the maid said eagerly. "I shall do anything if it helps Mr. Persano." She showed us into a spacious drawing room. We seated ourselves in two of the four chairs.

"Please sit down, Miss – ?"

"Maisie Tiverton, sir."

"You are from Devon, I think, Maisie."

"Yes, sir, but how on earth did you know that?"

"Despite your years in London, you still retain slight traces of your original accent, and Tiverton is a very common name in the west of England."

I have mentioned before in these memoirs that while my friend had no great respect for the female sex in general, he was capable, when the occasion demanded, of treating individual women with care and consideration. I sat silently listening while he gently coaxed information from this girl, who was clearly still upset by the event which had overtaken her employer.

"Is Mr. Persano a kind master?"

"Oh yes, sir, one couldn't hope for a kinder. Very considerate, he is, sir. Very understanding and very generous."

"On the day of Mr. Persano's . . . *illness*, did anything come through the post for him? A package, perhaps, or a letter?"

"Oh no, sir. I was in all day and there was nothing."

"Were there any callers?"

"No, sir, not one."

"Thank you, Maisie. And now, could you show us to Mr. Persano's study?"

The maid's already pale face blanched still further. "Oh, please don't make me go in there again, sir!"

Holmes reached out and patted her little hand.

"You needn't come in with us. Just show us where it is."

She took us up two flights of stairs to a small door, and then reached into the capacious pocket at the front of her starched white apron and produced a small key, which she pressed into Holmes's hand. Then she turned and hurried back down to the ground floor. Holmes turned the key in the lock and we entered Persano's private room. It was small and square, with one window looking down on a backyard, and sparsely furnished. There was a leather-topped desk with a plain chair in front of it, where Persano presumably produced his journalistic efforts, and on the opposite side of the room was a comfortable armchair with a little round table next to it. This was doubtless where he took occasional refreshment and rest from his labours.

The walls were painted a uniform cream and had no pictures on them. The floor was covered only by bare wooden boards, save for a thick round rug which lay under the leg space of the desk. I stood in the doorway and watched as Holmes carried out a very thorough examination. He pulled out his glass and ran it along the sill, the edges, and catches of the window. After covering the floor, he went to the desk and pulled out its three drawers. The second and third contained some sheaves of paper, which he gave only a cursory glance, but a small revolver lay in the first. Holmes opened it up and looked at the chambers, then sniffed the barrel and put it back.

"Well, Watson, I think the study has provided us with all the information it can. Let us return downstairs." On the ground floor once more, Holmes asked Maisie to let us see the backyard. It was a small square space covered in concrete with three walls, about six-and-a-half-feet in height, which separated it from the yards of the houses on either side and of that of the corresponding house in the next street. The back wall of Persano's house was plain, save for a drainpipe about a foot-and-a-half from the window of the study.

"Thank you for your help, Maisie," Holmes said to the maid as she showed us to the door. Once we were back in the street, he turned to me, and, before I could ask what he had learned from the house, said, "You may as well return to Baker Street. I have several more visits to make, and some laborious tasks to perform. But have no fear. I assure you that as my friend and chronicler you will be present at the denouement of this little drama."

He waved his long thin hand in farewell and was gone. It being a warm, sunny morning, I decided to walk back to our lodgings and arrived there to see that the morning papers had been delivered. I sat down to read them, but found the problem of Isidore Persano preying on my mind, so that I had to lay *The Daily Telegraph* aside and give my thought over to it entirely – but I could come up with no solution to the mystery that didn't either rely on some untenable coincidence, or failed to address all the aspects of the case. In the end, I gave up the enterprise and concentrated on the splendid lunch Mrs. Hudson served me at two o'clock. Two hours later, Holmes returned in an excellent mood.

"Well, Watson, I have managed to carry out all my researches successfully."

"And?"

"I will apprise you of the results on our journey to Stoke Newington."

"Where have you been?" I asked.

"Oh, to the shipping office, the Registrar of Births, Marriages and Deaths, the files of *The Daily Star*, Colney Hatch, and West Kensington. But come, I have a hansom waiting for us."

Once in the cab, I was eager to hear what progress Holmes had made in the case.

"Were you able to find out anything about the worm?" I asked as the hansom moved off.

"While the flora and fauna of Africa have yet to be fully categorised, those of South America are even less so. I considered that the balance of probability was that any hitherto unknown species was likely to originate there, and my supposition turned out to be correct. I took the liberty of having the worm examined by Professor George Edward Challenger, who has recently returned to London from one of his expeditions to the Matto Grosso. He recognised it instantly. The creature is indigenous to a very confined region on the banks of the Amazon River. It is the totem animal of the Sigoro Indians. The Professor himself had intended to bring a sample of it to the Royal Society, but it was lost, along with several other interesting specimens, when a pack mule missed its footing and plunged to its death while the expedition was negotiating a narrow cliffside pass."

"Interesting, but how one did come to be in a matchbox on Isidore Persano's desk?"

"Clearly it was placed there by someone who wished Persano no good, since they must have known what kind of reaction it would produce. You will recall that Maisie assured us that no packages had been delivered that day. So either Persano had brought it in himself, which was unlikely, or another person broke in and left it there. When I examined the window, I found signs that it had, indeed, been forced. Persano's study looks out onto the yard and the study is on the third floor. But a young, fit man might have climbed over the walls and up the drainpipe, and done the deed without being observed."

"But why his extreme reaction?"

"I have formulated three possible answers to that question, but I have as yet insufficient data to form a definite conclusion."

"You said you went to the shipping office."

"Yes, to ascertain the most recent arrival times of ships from Rio de Janeiro. Brazil figures largely in this case, and I shall be surprised if we don't discover that Isidore Persano's native language isn't Spanish but Portuguese. It has to be said that the English aren't a race noted for our ability with foreign languages, and the two are easily confused."

"So someone has come from Brazil with the intent of harming Persano."

"So I read it."

My features, which Holmes has often told me are a true mirror of my thoughts, must at that moment have displayed the bafflement I was feeling.

"Why didn't they simply kill him? If they were able to get into his study, why didn't they just wait until he arrived home and went in there, do the deed, and then escape by the way they came?"

"Clearly his immediate death wasn't part of their plan. My apologies, my dear Watson. Again, I have suppositions, but I will not share them with you until they have some substance. Anyway, from the shipping office I went to the Registrar of Births, Marriages, and Deaths, where I made an interesting discovery concerning Dr. Thomas Poulteney: Far from being a bachelor, he has been married for the last seventeen years to one Alice Poulteney, *née* Dawson, of Selsey in the county of West Sussex."

To my mind, Holmes's endeavours seemed to have produced more questions than answers.

"Then why does he represent himself as single, particularly when people are interpreting his friendship with Persano as meaning, well . . . that he is of the 'other persuasion'? And if he really is that way, wouldn't marriage be a way of silencing that sort of gossip?"

"I have no experience of the married state, Watson, as you well know, but I imagine that sort of arrangement wouldn't make for a happy union, whether the spouse knew the truth or not. It would explain his estrangement from his wife, but I'm reasonably sure that Thomas Poulteney isn't, as you so quaintly put it, 'of the other persuasion'. From the Registrar, I went to the offices of *The Daily Star*, where I spent rather longer sifting through the back issues in search of details of his career. It turned out that while he is now most famous as a chemist, he began as an alienist. While researching the composition of certain drugs used in the repression and control of undesirable mental states, he discovered that chemistry was more congenial to him, took a second degree in that subject, and has flourished ever since."

"Are you saying that Persano has always been mad? That his friendship with Poulteney is rather a relationship between a doctor and his patient?"

"No, Watson, that is not what I am saying, though Poulteney's former career certainly has a bearing on the case. But if you have any more questions about Dr. Poulteney, you may ask the man himself, for unless I am mistaken, we have arrived at 17 Margrave Villas, Stoke Newington." The hansom had indeed drawn to a stop even as he spoke.

The house was old and large without being ostentatious, and was surrounded by a small border of greenery with a sturdy iron fence. While I paid the cabbie, Holmes jumped out, opened the gate, bounded along the concrete path, and pulled at the bell. I managed to draw alongside just as the door was opened by a tall and imposing butler with muttonchop whiskers and an air of command.

"Yes?" he said, raising his bushy eyebrows. Holmes produced one of his cards and handed it to the man. "Sherlock Holmes and Dr. John Watson to see Dr. Poulteney."

The butler took the card into his master and returned after a few seconds. "The doctor will see you, gentlemen," he said, and ushered us into Poulteney's receiving room. The man sitting behind the desk was in his mid-forties, his thick wavy black hair and beard streaked with grey, but still remarkably trim and handsome. As he rose to greet us, it could be seen that he was a little under the average height, but this slight lack of stature did nothing to diminish the aura of power and intelligence that hung around him like a cloak.

"That will be all, Hanson. You may go."

"Hanson," said Holmes as the servant turned to the door, "you were a sergeant-major."

"Yes, sir."

"In the infantry."

"Yes sir, 13th Regiment."

"Hanson?"

"Begging your pardon, sir. Good day, gentlemen."

"Clearly a non-commissioned officer, but too heavy to be a sapper or a lancer," said Holmes after the butler had closed the door behind him.

"Mr. Holmes," Poulteney began, "I have heard a little of your reputation. I take it you haven't come to my house merely to demonstrate your ability at parlour tricks."

Holmes gave a little smile. "I do apologise, Dr. Poulteney. The exercise of the faculty of logical deduction can become a little addictive. No, we are here to ask you some questions about the disappearance of your friend, Mr. Isidore Persano."

"I gave all the information I have to the police yesterday, but I have no objection to giving it again if you think it will be of value."

"I think that it will, Dr. Poulteney, but let me first say that, unlike the detectives of the official force, I am a free agent, and therefore not restrained by professional delicacy. I trust you understand me."

"Completely. Ask me whatever you like. I have nothing to hide."

"Very well," said Holmes, leaning back slightly in his chair and crossing his ankles. "Firstly, can you tell us exactly where and when you first met Mr. Persano?"

"It was something like three years ago. I was invited to a literary dinner by a mutual friend and Mr. Persano was also present."

"And did you hit it off straight away? How did you become friends?"

"Well, he certainly struck me as a charming and erudite individual, but as to when I began to truly consider him a friend, who can say? How does someone cease to be merely an acquaintance and become a friend?"

"Would you say that Mr. Persano is your best friend?"

"Yes, yes I would."

"Then I must say I am rather surprised at the lack of concern you appear to be showing at his disappearance."

"I am not the kind of person who puts his emotions on display, but I assure you, I am deeply disturbed by this event, or I wouldn't have agreed to answer your questions. Though I must say, I doubt the relevance of what you have asked me so far. And now, if you don't mind, I generally have a cup of tea at this time. Will you join me?"

"Why not?" said Holmes. Poulteney tugged at the bell pull, and a minute later the door behind us opened and a maid brought in a tray. I caught no more than a glimpse of her slim back and a loose black braid of hair surmounted by a little white cap, and then she was gone. "And now," resumed Holmes after a sip of tea, "I must ask you a question which will seem the height of impertinence to you, but which must be asked if I am to penetrate to the heart of this case."

"Then ask, sir," said Poulteney calmly.

"Were the relations between you and *Señor* Isidore Persano . . . *abnormal* in any way?"

"I can promise you," Poulteney said with a steady voice, "that our 'relations', as you call them, were in no manner what could be termed unnatural. Nor has there been any impropriety, of any kind, between us."

"Such was my belief," said Holmes, "but I was bound to ask. Do you know anything of Mr. Persano's life before he came to London?"

"I was aware that he had lived in Paris, but I know nothing of his life before that."

"And do you have any inkling of his present whereabouts?"

"None whatever. If I had, I would of course have informed the police."

"Dear me, Dr. Poulteney," said Holmes, shaking his head in mock sorrow, "for the most part, you have, with some difficulty, stayed broadly within the bounds of truth, but your last two statements were outright lies."

Dr. Poulteney rose to his feet, his face white with anger. "How dare you, sir! I must ask you and your colleague to leave my house this instant!"

"Sit down, Doctor," said Holmes imperturbably. "Allow me to assure you that my sympathies in this matter are entirely on your side, and that the best possible outcome will be achieved by your complete cooperation." The chemist resumed his seat, but his expression was tense and wary. "I shall reconstruct the situation as I understand it, and you may correct me whenever my deductions diverge from the strict truth," continued Holmes.

Dr. Poulteney nodded. "Very well."

"On the evening in question, you received an urgent message from *Señor* Persano's maidservant, informing you that her master had been taken to the asylum at Colney Hatch. You immediately put a set of women's clothing and a long wig in a valise and hurried by carriage to the asylum. There you had no difficulty obtaining entry, for this was the place where you had been a resident immediately before your change in profession, and your face was still well known. You had either retained a set of keys, or knew where in the building a set could be easily obtained. You also knew the location of the holding cells where a new patient was likely to be brought. You waited until an orderly had checked on *Señor* Persano and, being aware of the asylum's routine, you knew how long it would be before he or she returned.

"You opened the cell door, stripped Persano of his male attire, and dressed him in the woman's outfit. Doubtless you put his clothing in the valise, since it wasn't found in the room when his disappearance was discovered. I don't know if Persano was conscious or not by this time, but in any event, it would have been easy to take him to another cell until he awoke. Then you waited until a new security shift came on, and you and Persano were allowed through the gates. The new guards recognised you but didn't know that you had entered the asylum on your own. They had no reason to assume that the woman accompanying you was an inmate. And so you and Persano made your escape."

"I had kept my keys from the time of my residency," said Poulteney. "I found Isidore asleep, and yes, I carried him to another cell. But after he awoke, I allowed him to change his clothes himself while I kept my back turned. Otherwise, your deductions are correct. However, for all your cleverness, sir, there is one crucial aspect you haven't uncovered."

"Oh, I have uncovered it, Dr. Poulteney, I merely haven't mentioned it yet. Watson here can tell you that I have a lamentable predilection for the dramatic." So saying, he leaned forward and gave the bell pull a sharp jerk. Moments later the maid reappeared, her head modestly bowed, and moved to take the tray. As she bent to do so, Holmes seized her cap and hair and pulled them off, revealing a closely cropped head. "Watson, allow me to introduce Isidore – I beg her pardon – I should say, *Miss Isadora* Persano." For while her face might have passed for that of a handsome young man, her form, though slim, was unmistakably female.

Dr. Thomas Poulteney instantly stood and enfolded her in a protective embrace. "It began as friendship," he said in a gentle tone, "but it blossomed into something deeper. Then one day Isadora revealed her secret to me, and I realised we were in love. But there was a reason why I couldn't ask her to be my wife."

"You were already married – to Alice Dawson."

"Yes, and I rue the day that ever I stood beside her at the altar. She had deceived me into completely misreading her character, and no sooner was the ring on her finger than she embarked on a series of adulterous affairs. She drank, and experimented with stimulants of various kinds. It became obvious to me that while there had as yet been no public scandal, it was only a matter of time. Finally, I reached an agreement with her that she should move out of my house. I provided her with a monthly allowance on the condition that she lived under another name and made no further demands on me. My existing friends knew of this arrangement and kept my secret, so that when I made new acquaintances, I was thus able to represent myself as a bachelor. Although in the course of my social life I met many women, I had hardened my heart against the emotion of love. And then I met Isadora." As he said this, he took the young woman's hand in his own. Both smiled, and they gazed into each other's eyes with such clear affection that I felt a wave of warmth and sympathy towards them.

"And now, Miss Persano," said Holmes, "I believe the time has come for you to give us an explanation of those points which we haven't already resolved."

"Very well, Mr. Holmes," she began in a low, melodious voice. She lowered her eyes, and when she raised them a few seconds later they were full of frankness and resolution.

"I was born on the banks of the Imara, a river which runs into the Amazon some five hundred miles from its source. My father was a Portuguese missionary named Dr. Jorge Persano, and my mother was a member of the Sigoro Indian tribe which inhabits that region. My father converted many of the tribesmen and women to Christianity – including of course my mother – but the majority of them continued to adhere to the cult of Tumaq, a god whom they worshipped in the form of the worm that appeared in my study. For some years this was of no matter. My father also ran a school, and all were encouraged to make use of it, whatever their religious persuasion. But the time came when the followers of Christ began to outnumber those of Tumaq, and the priests began to mutter that my father should be expelled, and those he had converted forcibly returned to their original creed.

"Sensing the danger, my father formulated plans to send me to Manaus to ensure my safety, but before this could be done, there was an uprising. My parents were killed, and the worship of Tumaq restored. I was then nine years old. It was decided that when I attained womanhood, I was to be a 'Bride of Tumaq', which meant that I would be sacrificed to the god at the summer solstice following my first menstruation. Until that day arrived I would be a prisoner, although I would be clothed in the finest fabrics and given the choicest foods. I lived in dread of the day when I would first experience my monthly courses, but before that evil hour arrived, I was spirited away by a small group who still secretly adhered to Christ, and taken to Manaus as my father had originally planned. There I sought out the Archbishop, who was an old friend of my father and grieved much to hear of his fate. He raised me in his house and saw that I was educated.

"I turned sixteen, and thought that my previous unhappy experiences were well behind me, but I discovered, to my sorrow, that I was wrong. I mentioned that my father had run a school in the Sigoro village. He had unwittingly nurtured a group of young men who could speak Spanish, Portuguese, and English, but remained fanatical devotees of the Worm God. When they heard of my escape, they swore that, if it meant going to the ends of the earth, they would capture me and take me back to become a Bride of Tumaq, for if one who had been promised to him didn't meet her fate at the designated time, the whole tribe would suffer for it until the situation was rectified. An attempt was made to kidnap me in Manaus, but it was thwarted, and one of the offenders captured by the police, and it was he who warned me that, go where I would, the followers of Tumaq would track me down.

"I determined that I would go to Europe, and the good Archbishop readily gave me the wherewithal. I arrived in Paris, where I first cut off my long hair and assumed men's clothing. As further protection, I carried a gun and learned how to use it well. My education enabled me to obtain work as a journalist, but I was young, and unwise enough to write an article criticising an eminent businessman and accusing him of corrupt practices. He challenged me to a duel in the cemetery at Pere Lachaise, and I killed him. Both his sons then challenged me, and met the same fate as their father. I thus acquired a reputation as a duellist, though I had challenged no one. I was unhappy with this, so I quit Paris and came to London. It was here, as you have heard, that I first met Thomas, and when an intimate friendship began to turn into love, I revealed my true sex to him.

"Because of the English divorce laws, we couldn't marry, but we spent as much time together as possible. A fellow journalist named Marlowe made sly accusations. I lost my temper and challenged him to a duel. Later, we took adjoining rooms at a hotel run by Arnold Campbell when we holidayed in Brighton together. He also accused my darling of having a perverted passion. For myself I didn't care, but these men were impugning the honour of the best man who ever drew breath. I couldn't let such insults pass. I challenged Campbell too, and in both cases I was careful to merely wound them. Honour was satisfied. As to the Sigoro totem, I confess that when I came home that evening and found that despicable worm on my desk. I succumbed to hysteria.

"Do you wonder at that, Mr. Holmes? Dr. Watson? Since the age of nine this thing had been a symbol of horror in my life, and now at the age of thirty, when I believed that I was more or less safe, and felt secure in the love of the best of men, this abomination was back to haunt me. I understood only too clearly the message its presence sent: That the followers of Tumaq had managed to pursue me to London, that they would capture me and take me back to the banks of the Imara to die at the next summer solstice. I suppose that by taunting me thus, they hoped to frighten me so badly that I would be rendered incapable of clear thought or action. The rest I think you know."

At Holmes's instructions, the police made a thorough and painstaking list of all those who had come into London from Brazil in the last two months, and by a process of elimination and identification, assisted by Miss Persano, they were able to arrest the handful of men from the Sigoro tribe who had threatened her life. All suffered permanent deportation. For the first time in her life, Isadora felt completely free.

We were back in Baker Street a few days later, enjoying a pipe after our evening meal, when I turned to Holmes and said, "There's one thing I don't understand. I almost got the feeling that Poulteney wanted us to find out the truth. Why else did he ring for Isadora to bring the tea?"

"Well, Dr. Poulteney isn't a criminal, but in this respect he shares one of their characteristics: That when an imposture has been carried off successfully, the perpetrator has an unspoken desire for it to be discovered, so that everyone may see and admire his cleverness."

"That is surely rather fanciful."

"Is it? Well, if that doesn't serve your turn, consider this: Here we have two people who for almost three years have been forced to conceal their true relationship and unable to openly express the deep love they feel for each other. Imagine how great a relief it must be to finally be able to openly acknowledge those feelings, even if there is still an element of danger in the revelation."

"That, I suspect, is closer to the truth."

"And is, no doubt, the version you will give your readers."

"No, Holmes. I may make a record of this case, but I hardly think it can be published in our lifetimes. It contains certain themes, certain references . . . ."

"Ah, to what Lord Alfred Douglas called 'the love that dare not speak its name'. But there was no true instance of such a love here. It was all in the minds of a few individuals."

"Even so, I suspect that the public wouldn't wish to hear of it. Perhaps one day . . . ."

"Yes, let us hope so."

Little more remains to be said. Thomas Poulteney and Isadora continued to remain in their celibate state for another year or so, when they received news that Poulteney's estranged wife, Alice, had been killed in a boating accident, freeing them to marry. Thomas received a knighthood for his services to science in 1905. He and Lady Poulteney became well-known members of high society, to say nothing of producing three beautiful, olive-skinned children. "Isidore Persano" was never heard of again.

A Yuletide Mystery

Elsewhere in these memoirs, I have stated that of all the cases in which I acted as the companion and amanuensis of my distinguished friend, Mr. Sherlock Holmes, there were only two which I brought to his notice: That of Colonel Warburton's madness, and that of Victor Hatherley and his missing thumb. Since the publication of that story, however, I have had occasion to draw his attention to one other, which the newspapers at the time dubbed "The Yuletide Mystery", as it took place towards the end of a dark and snowbound December.

The King's Road, Chelsea, was crowded with shoppers on that winter afternoon, as I made my way determinedly through the thick snow towards a particular little shop that sold old, second-hand, and obscure books. I was warmly dressed in a thick coat over a tweed suit, a woolen muffler, stout boots, and leather gloves, with a cloth cap covering my head, but a chill, cutting wind was swirling the heavy snowflakes along the busy street, and I would be happy to be back in front of the fire in our rooms in Baker Street.

The bell rang as I stepped inside old Mr. Penfold's shop and pulled off my gloves. The interior felt pleasantly warm, and smelt reassuringly of leather-bound volumes and old ink. Mr. Penfold stepped out of his back room and gazed at me over his half-moon spectacles.

"Dr. Watson! Hello! I haven't seen you or Mr. Holmes in here for some time."

I smiled. With the fluffy little ring of whitening hair about the back of his head, his old-fashioned fingerless gloves, and his embroidered waistcoat, there was something distinctly Dickensian about the old bookseller. He might have stepped from the pages of *The Pickwick Papers* or *Martin Chuzzlewit*.

"I'm here to buy Mr. Holmes a Christmas present," I said. "Do you have any suggestions?"

"Well," said Mr. Penfold, "I've just had a delivery of a complete library. You know, relatives selling off the property of the deceased. I haven't had time to take them out and look at them. Perhaps you'd like to go through it with me, see if anything takes your fancy."

"I'd like that very much."

"Splendid! The crates are just inside the back door. The delivery man was in a hurry, so we just made sure they were out of the cold. Let me get the first one into the office."

"Let me do it, Mr. Penfold. They must be heavy."

"All right, let's do it together."

We pulled the crate next to the desk in the bookseller's office, where a coal fire was glowing in the hearth. Mr. Penfold sat in his wooden chair, leaving me to occupy the rather more comfortable armchair opposite. I took off my hat and coat and sat down.

"Right," he said. "I suggest I take them out first and hand them to you. If it isn't clear what a volume is, I have a better chance of identifying it than you. Oh, while I think of it, would you like a cup of tea? Sorting through books can be dry work."

"I'll do it. That will give you a chance to start going through them."

"Very well. The kitchen is just through there. You can see where everything is."

I was pouring boiling water into a big brown ceramic teapot when Mr. Penfold cried, "Ah, I think I've found something Mr. Holmes would like."

"Oh, what's that?"

"*The Course of Positive Philosophy*, by Auguste Comte."

I put the pot, two cups, the milk jug and the sugar bowl on a tin tray and carried them into the little office.

"I'm afraid he already has it," I said as I laid the tray on the table. I had made a thorough survey of Holmes's bookshelf before coming out.

"Harrison Ainsworth – *The Tower of London* and *Rookwood* and *The Lancashire Witches*. Sir Walter Scott's *Kenilworth*, *Peveril of the Peak*, *Rob Roy*, and *Redgauntlet*. Old Mr. Greville seems to have had quite a taste for historicals. Ah, what about this? *The Mystery of a Hansom Cab*, by Fergus Hume. "

I couldn't help smiling.

"Mr. Holmes has very little patience with the detectives of fiction. None of them seem to come up to his intellectual standards."

"Well, it was quite a big seller a few years ago, I seem to recall."

"That would cut no ice with him. 'What does the general public know?' he'd say. 'They cannot even tell a shoemaker by the state of his trousers or a journalist by the condition of his second finger, so how can they be trusted when it comes to evaluating the plausibility of an invented crime investigation?'"

Just then the bell rang. As Mr. Penfold rose to go into the shop, he said. "Carry on looking. I shouldn't be too long."

There was nothing Holmes would have cared to read in the rest of that crate, so I went to the back door, made a pile of about twelve books from the second crate and carried them into the office. I put the pile on the floor next to the armchair and picked up the first volume. It was a copy of Kipling's first collection of short stories, *Plain Tales from the Hills*. Now, the reader might imagine that given my experiences in our Eastern possessions, the wounds I had sustained during the Afghan campaign, and my subsequent bout with enteric fever, I would have no desire to revisit those dark days, even via the medium of fiction. It is a curious fact, but with the passage of time, what remained with me was the memory, not of my pains, but of the stout fellows I had met and befriended, and of the courage and self-sacrifice they had shown. I set the Kipling volume to one side for myself.

The next two books in the pile were distinctly promising – a collection of the poems of Francois Villon in French – Holmes disdained translations if he had a grasp of the original language – and a book on fingerprints by Sir Francis Galton.

I could hear Mr. Penfold finishing up with his latest customer.

"Right, sir. So, the complete Galland *Thousand and One Nights*, Sir Richard Burton's *The Gold Mines of Midian*, and *The Episodes of Vathek* by William Beckford. Not many of that last one about. Nice edition, too. That'll be twenty-five pounds, thank you sir. And a good Christmas to you too, sir."

I placed my empty cup in its saucer, put on my cap and coat, and went out into the shop, handed Mr. Penfold the little pile and reached into my pocket for my wallet.

"I've found three things I'd like. How much is that?"

"Six pounds, please."

I pulled out the exact amount and Mr. Penfold wrote me a receipt.

"Would you like these delivered?"

"No, I'll take them now."

"Oh, in that case I'll wrap them up and put them in a bag for you. Don't want the snow getting at them, do we? Now, where did I put that brown paper?"

He turned to a shelf behind him.

The bell rang, and there was a brief gust of cold air as the door was opened and closed. Mr. Penfold turned around. The shop was empty.

Sherlock Holmes took a sip from his hot toddy and leaned forward eagerly in his armchair.

"Ah, at last, Watson, you come to the nub of the matter! Why did you leave old Mr. Penfold's shop in so precipitous a manner? You had seen something, I take it, but what?"

"I saw a murder, Holmes. What made me glance through the window of the bookshop at precisely that moment I cannot say. It was already dark and snowy, but there was a streetlamp nearby. The victim was leaning up against the lamppost, and the other man – the killer – was very close, right in front of him. I saw something glitter in his hand, and then he thrust upward, up through the ribcage into the heart. The victim must have died instantaneously. Then the murderer pulled the knife out, put it in his pocket and left his victim propped against the post."

"And no else saw the killing take place?"

"Apparently not. As I said, it was dark, and snowing heavily. After a second's hesitation I decided that I had to pursue the killer, as there was nothing I could do for the victim. At that moment, a tram pulled up at a nearby stop, and the culprit jumped on board. As it pulled away, I was forced to run after it, fearing all the time that I would lose my footing and tumble forward onto the icy road. But I managed to reach it and pull myself up onto the platform."

"Well done. That was no small feat for a middle-aged man with a damaged *tendo Achillis*."

"I was in time to see him climbing the stairs to the upper deck, so I took a seat on the lower deck and waited for him to come down. When the conductor asked me for my fare, I had to buy a ticket for the terminus at Highbury, as I had no idea where my quarry would be getting off. Eventually he descended at The Angel, Islington. His face, as before, was half-obscured by a woolen scarf, but I had no doubt as to his identity. I had also seen that the collar of his overcoat had a distinctive red trimming."

"Excellent, old friend! Your powers of observation certainly seem to be improving. What happened then?"

"He crossed the road and I followed him, at a distance, through a maze of very similar streets, until he entered a house. Number 43. I went to the end of the road and made a note of its name, Allingham Street. As you know, I do not have your encyclopedic knowledge of the metropolis, so I found myself wandering those near-identical streets, trying to find a way back to the Pentonville Road."

"Where you knew there was a police station, from one of our previous exploits in that area."

"Quite so. I was lucky enough to encounter a beat officer who escorted me to the station, where I made a full statement of what I had seen and how I had followed the fellow to his house. I don't doubt that I will be called upon to testify when the case comes to trial."

"A fine afternoon's work, dear doctor. And now, I am sure you are more than ready for one of Mrs. Hudson's splendid suppers."

The following morning, the papers were full of the King's Road murder. The condition of the victim, whose identity remained as yet unknown, was not discovered until a passerby bumped into him, and his corpse was knocked to the snowy ground, where it left conspicuous red stains. As of the next day, the Metropolitan Police stated they were confident that an early arrest would be made, as they had already received vital evidence from an eye witness, whose name they declined to reveal in the interests of that individual's personal security.

I imagined that the matter was settled, and that there was no more to be done until I was summoned to appear before the court. When the early edition of *The Evening Standard* arrived, however, it told a different story. The Christmas murder, as they were calling it, the 25th being only a few days away, was still unsolved. The suspect, when questioned by the police, pointed out by the still-unnamed eye-witness had an unshakeable alibi, having been with his sister and brother at the time in question.

"Hardly what I'd call unshakeable," said Holmes after I had drawn the article to his attention. "I'm sure the Scotland Yard files are bursting with cases where a spouse or a sibling, or a parent, has lied to support a murderer. Does it mention anywhere who is in charge of the investigation? I can't imagine Bradstreet, or Gregson, or even Lestrade making such a cardinal mistake."

I glanced further down the article until I reached the name.

"Inspector Drayton."

"No, I don't know him. He must be a recent addition, or elevation, to the ranks of the detective division."

"Holmes, it's always possible that I followed the wrong man. That is the conclusion most people would come to. It was dark, and the snow was heavy."

"If I had to cite every instance of 'the conclusion most people would come to' being utterly and demonstrably wrong, we'd be here 'til tomorrow morning."

My old friend reached forward and patted me reassuringly on the arm.

"As so often, your characteristic modesty leads you to underestimate your own abilities. I have no doubt that the man you pursued was the culprit, as I am sure our investigations will confirm."

"Our investigations? You intend to look into the matter?"

"I can hardly see how I could do otherwise, so let us begin. You said the killer put the murder weapon straight in his pocket?"

"Yes."

"So, Inspector Drayton should have had the pockets examined for bloodstains. On the basis of what we know so far, that gentleman doesn't seem fated to rise any higher in the force."

"Perhaps not, but what should we do?"

"We find out the name of the man, and as much as we can about him. It would help if we can discover the identity of the victim, too. It's unusual for someone to have no form of identification on him at all, not even a wallet."

"Should we call on Inspector Drayton and ask him about the suspect?"

"As far as Scotland Yard is concerned the fellow's been cleared, so he will not be permitted to give us that information. But we have the man's address, so it will only require a visit to the Town Clerk for Islington and an examination of the electoral roll to provide us with his name. No, stay where you are, Watson, and remain by the fire. This task only requires one of us."

He stood, took his heavy coat from its hanger, and went to the door.

The Islington electoral register revealed that the inhabitants of 43 Allingham Street (or at least, those eligible to vote) were two men, Jonathan and Christopher Morton.

"Our next move," said Holmes, "must be to ascertain what employment the man has, if any. We will keep the house under surveillance, and when he comes out, I will follow him, while you continue to watch the house. That will mean getting there early in the morning, before most people are up, so I suggest that you get a good night's sleep."

"Holmes, the fellow is a murderer. Should we not both follow him? What if he should turn on you?"

"Your concern is touching, Watson, but a little misplaced. However bulky and formidable the man may be, I have my knowledge of the Eastern martial arts, and I am confident that I can hold my own in any confrontation."

"Nevertheless, he may be armed. I will take my revolver, and I urge you to do the same."

"Very well, if it will ease your mind."

Perhaps my awareness of the importance and potential danger of our task was colouring my perceptions, but my memory of the following morning is that it was the darkest and coldest of the year. Even as we made our way through the pre-dawn streets in a hansom cab which Holmes had ordered the previous evening, the snow was descending in great sheets which were then scattered and dispersed by the icy swirling winds. Looking through the cab window, it was almost as if we were inside one of those glass snow globes, and in my imagination a giant hand might at any moment shake the globe and plunge us into a hazy white chaos where up was down and back was front.

At last we arrived at No. 43 Allingham Street. Holmes paid the cab fare, and I wished the driver a Merry Christmas. Then we alighted and began to look around for a suitable location from which we might observe the door of the murderer's dwelling. By great good fortune, a house which was almost opposite No. 43 was derelict and unoccupied. Holmes glanced briefly around to make sure that we were unobserved, then plied his lock-pick, and within moments we were inside. Through the windows of the front parlour, we had a clear view of the killer's door.

We didn't have long to wait. At about half-past-six, the man himself came out of the house.

"That's him," I whispered.

"You're sure?"

"Same height, same coat, same hat."

Holmes waited a few seconds, then made for the front door. I followed, and gripped his arm for a second.

"Be careful."

Holmes said nothing, but smiled at me, and then he was gone.

He returned to the empty house at about half-past-two in the afternoon. We walked to Pentonville Road, where we found a cab to take us home. On the journey back to Baker Street, we said little. I was waiting to return to the warmth and comfort of our rooms before sharing my experience, while Holmes appeared to be contemplating what he had seen and sifting through it for what was relevant and what might be discarded. A fire was blazing in the sitting room grate when we arrived at No. 221b, and as we took our seats, our landlady brought in a plate piled high with sandwiches and laid it on the table between us.

"You went out early without any breakfast," she said, "so I thought you might be hungry. I didn't make anything hot, because I didn't know what time you'd be back."

"And you lit the fire too," I said, reaching for a cheese-and-tomato sandwich. "Mrs. Hudson, you are an absolute angel."

"Well, I don't know about that. Would you like some coffee?"

"An excellent idea," said Holmes. "Just the antidote to a short night's sleep and several long hours spent out in the cold."

When most of the sandwiches had been consumed and the coffee cups were empty, I looked across at Holmes.

"I have little doubt that your morning was more interesting than mine,"I said, "so I'm eager to hear about it."

Holmes reached into the coal scuttle for his cigars and we each took one from the box. When they were both lit and drawing well, he began.

"Our friend caught a tram from the Angel, and I just managed to get on it. He alighted at Bank Station and walked to what I imagine must be his place of work, a law firm called Stringer and Cunliffe in Mercer's Lane. Judging from where he lives, he cannot be a solicitor, so he must be something like a clerk. If he was a messenger, he would have gone out, and I would have seen him, as I was seated on a little bench opposite the building. Anyway, he left at about quarter-past-twelve, and I followed him to a cafe where I assume he was having his lunch, and I came back to you. When exactly did you see him outside the shop?"

"At about half-past four."

"He started work at seven-thirty, so I wouldn't have thought he'd be out until four at the earliest. Bank to King's Road, Chelsea. That's an eleven tram. With the traffic at that time, in this sort of weather, it's unlikely he'd be there by half-past four."

"He might have had the afternoon off. Some companies do that at Christmas so their employees can go shopping for presents. Or perhaps he doesn't start at the same time every day."

"Possibly, though neither of those things usually apply to law firms. What did you see?"

"The only person who called, at a quarter-to-ten, was a tradesman of some sort, and I caught a glimpse of a wife, or sister or whatever she might be, when she answered the door to him. I didn't see anyone else."

Holmes stood up.

"I have to go out again."

"Whatever for?"

"I have to buy an overcoat."

"I can't see that there's anything wrong with the one you have."

"Nor is there. I should be back in time for dinner."

When he returned at about half-past-six, he was carrying a parcel wrapped in brown paper which I assumed contained his new overcoat. As we ate our evening meal, he made it clear that he didn't wish to discuss the case. After our long association, I was used to this reticence on his part, nor did it come as any surprise to me when, the following morning, he steered our conversation over breakfast onto trivial and commonplace lines. I knew that when he saw fit, he would give me a full account of his doings, whatever they might be. He left at about half-past-eleven, wearing his new purchase, and returned at about two. After taking a light lunch, he lit a cigarette and embarked on an explanation.

"Human beings, as you know, are creatures of habit, so my purchase of an overcoat similar to that of Mr. Morton was predicated on the belief that he would lunch at the same cafe as he had the previous day. When a man finds an establishment to his liking within a few minutes' walk of his place of work, he is likely to return to it. And so it proved. The cafe, which was in South Place, E.C., was fairly crowded, but fortunately there were one or two empty places. I watched through the front window as he hung up his coat. He then went over to the counter to order his lunch and sat down opposite another diner to wait for the arrival of his food. I went in, took off my coat and hung it on the hook next to his. I ordered and paid for a cup of tea and found a sear near the window. When my tea arrived, I drank it at a leisurely pace, after which I left, making sure to lift Morton's overcoat from its hook instead of my own."

"You wished to examine it, and using this subterfuge, you could claim that you had taken it by mistake if he challenged you on it."

"Exactly. A swift glance in his direction as I went through the door told me that he was only halfway through his meal. I went a few yards down the street and turned a corner. Then I took off the coat and looked at the pockets, where I found his wallet, which identified him as *Jonathan*, rather than *Christopher* Morton. Fortunately that style of overcoat has pockets you can pull out and examine. In the other there was a distinct bloodstain, which by its colour seemed to be fairly recent. When I returned to the cafe Morton was just finishing his first course and was about to start on a bowl of apple pie and cream. I put his coat back on the hook, donned my own, and made my exit. Then I went to Scotland Yard to tell them what I'd found. There was a little bit of a stink – Drayton was in charge of the case, but Gregson was there too, and as the senior man, he had some harsh words for Drayton for not having had Morton's clothing examined the first time they brought him in. Anyway, speaking of coats, get yours."

"Why?"

"They're bringing Morton in, and Gregson convinced Drayton that we should be there."

By the time we arrived at the station, there had been fresh developments. The corpse had been identified as Michael Byrne of 22 Arlington Road, Peckham.

"You took the afternoon off from Stringer and Cunliffe because you said there was a family emergency and you needed to get back to Islington," Drayton, a big young man with a head of frizzy red hair, was saying to Morton as we came into the interrogation room with Inspector Gregson. "What was the nature of this 'family emergency'?"

"None of your damn business."

"Since your presence at 43 Allingham Road constitutes your alibi, I'd say it's very much 'our business'. You weren't at Allingham Road, were you? You were in King's Road, Chelsea, at approximately four-thirty, stabbing Michael Byrne to death. Then you went back to Islington and convinced your brother and sister to tell us you'd been there since you got back from work. Isn't that what really happened?"

There was a knock at the door. It was opened to reveal the station sergeant, accompanied by a young man, who, to judge from the similarity of their features and their blond hair, could only be Morton's brother.

"This is Mr. Christopher Morton," said the sergeant, "and he says he has information vital to this case."

The other brother half rose from his seat and cried, "No, Chris, no!" before he was pushed back into his chair by Drayton.

"I'm sorry, Jon, but the truth must be told. This business has gone far enough."

"What about what we swore to mother? What about the lambs?"

"Curse the bloody lambs! You've given up the best years of your life, and for what? So that this could happen?"

"Why are you here, Chris? And what have you done with her?"

"I gave her a pill and locked her in her room. She'll be out for hours."

"I think it would help," said Gregson. "If you could tell us what this is all about . . . ."

"On the morning of the murder, Jonathan thought the weather was going to be a little warmer, so he left his heavier topcoat at home and put on a lighter one – "

"Chris, don't do this!"

"Our sister Alice is Jon's twin. They're the same height, and Alice is quite broad-shouldered for a woman. Alice has had mental problems for quite a long time – "

"Oh God!" said Jonathan, and covered his face with his hands.

"But when mother was dying, Jon promised that he'd always look after her – that we'd both always look after her. And as long as one of us was there, she was usually all right. Jon is better with her than I am, but we needed money, and as he is also a better earner than I am, he worked and I stayed home with Alice. But lately, she's been getting more difficult to handle, and we started giving her drugs. I suppose whatever they did to her, she blamed it on me. I was about to give her that morning's medication. I turned my back on her for one moment, and the next thing I knew, she hit me on the back of my head with something, and I came around at about two. She'd taken Jonathan's overcoat, one of my hats, and a sharp knife we use for cutting vegetables. I got one of the boys on our street to take a message to Jon to summon him home. When he arrived, there was nothing we could do but wait. Alice came in and we feared the worst. We knew she could be violent because – because – "

"No, Chris, no. Please."

"We knew she could be violent because my mother died because Alice stabbed her. Our doctor was an old family friend. He falsified the death certificate to say she died of heart failure."

"You should have put her in an institution," said Drayton. "They would have known how to deal with her there."

Jonathan turned to the inspector, his eyes blazing with anger.

"Have you ever seen the inside of one of those places? Well, have you? If you had, you'd never, ever think of putting someone you loved in there."

"I'm afraid the price paid for your reluctance to do so was the life of an innocent man," said Holmes, "killed at random by the sound of it."

Christopher resumed his narrative.

"She came home at about six, in a state of exhaustion, not knowing where she'd been, or what she'd been doing. We put her to bed, and I found the bloody knife in one pocket and this in the other."

He tossed a brown leather wallet on the table. The letters "*MB*" were embossed on one corner.

"That doesn't tell in her favour," said Gregson. "It makes it look as if a robbery was a motive. But from what you have told us, she may well be found irresponsible due to insanity. As for you gentlemen, I'm afraid the penalties for being accessories after the fact can be severe, whatever the judge decides about your sister's culpability. We must arrest you. Take them to the cells, Sergeant, and then arrange for their sister to be brought here."

"We weren't like the lambs after all, were we?" said Jonathan.

"No, we weren't," his brother replied.

After the Morton brothers had been taken to the cells. Drayton said, "So what the Hell was all that business about '*lambs*'? What have bloody sheep got to do with any of it?"

"It wasn't '*lambs*' with a small '*l*'," said Holmes. "It was '*Lambs*' – the name – with a capital '*L*'. Charles and Mary Lamb. They were part of a literary circle that included William Hazlitt and Samuel Taylor Coleridge, and wrote a book for children together called *Tales from Shakespeare*."

"I'm no wiser," said Drayton.

"Well, they were brother and sister. In 1796, Mary suffered a mental breakdown and stabbed her mother to death. She was put in an asylum, but in 1799, Charles took sole charge of her and they began living together in London. As long as she was with Charles, she was balanced and sane. Charles devoted the rest of his life to her and they both died unmarried. Do you understand it now?"

"Pardon me," said Drayton. "I didn't have the benefit of a university education."

"I doubt that the Mortons did either," I said. "Some families read, some don't."

"A sad story all round," I remarked to Holmes the following evening. "Poor Michael Byrne killed, Alice Morton likely to spend the rest of her life in an institution, separated from her brothers, and the pair of them doomed to serve whatever term in prison the judge deems fit."

"We cannot always hope for a happy ending, Watson, as you well know, and I'm sure you will agree that it is better for all concerned that there should be no chance of Miss Morton roaming the streets with murderous intent, even if she cannot be held responsible. As for her brothers, they may come before a sympathetic judge."

"Or they may not."

"Come, old friend, tomorrow is Christmas, one of your favourite times of the year, and I happen to know that Mrs. Hudson has made a special effort this Yuletide. I don't believe I've ever seen so large and plump a goose."

Christmas! In all the flurry and activity of the previous few days, I had completely forgotten the books I had purchased at Mr. Penfold's shop.

There was a ring at the door. Mrs. Hudson answered and a few moments later a dapper elderly man appeared on our threshold bearing a brown paper parcel. I failed to recognise him at first, but then I knew him.

"Mr. Penfold!"

"I'll only stay a moment. I'm just bringing these around."

He handed over the parcel.

"I'm sorry I didn't bring them earlier, but you know, I close quite late, and I live in the opposite direction. Tonight I'm on my way to spend Christmas with my daughter Susan and her family in Camden Town, so you're on my route,"

"We were just about to have some mulled wine," said Holmes. "Stay and have one with us. Something to warm you up before you go back out into the cold."

"Oh, don't mind if I do. Just the one, though."

"Thank you again, Mr. Penfold," I said, "and Happy Christmas to you."

"And to you, gentlemen. And to you."

The Adventure of the Silver Snail

Mr. Sherlock Holmes and I were seated at the dining table in our sitting room at 221b Baker Street, smoking an after-breakfast pipe and perusing the morning newspapers, when Holmes gave vent to a short, barking laugh. I looked across at him questioningly. He folded his paper and proffered it to me, tapping the relevant section with the mouthpiece of his pipe.

"As a literary practitioner, dear Doctor, what do you make of that?"

I put down *The Telegraph*, took *The Courier* from him, and looked at the article. It read:

At the Supper Table
A weekly column by
The Daily Courier*'s restaurant critic*
Raymond Arnoux

Those of you who are gracious enough to peruse my little essays each week will know that I am not a man to mince my words. I state my conclusions in no uncertain terms. Indeed, how could it be otherwise, when it is my duty to act as a culinary advance guard, braving restaurants where the foot of cultured man has never before trod, and to bring back accurate reports of the wonders, or horrors, that I find there. If, therefore, my conclusions as set out in the following paragraphs seem harsh and acerbic, you may nevertheless rest assured that the establishment in question deserves every iota of the opprobrium I heap upon it.

Like many, I was full of anticipation when I learned that a new French restaurant, L'Auberge de Jehan Cottard, was due to open at 17 Moulton St, Fitzrovia, W. In accordance with my usual policy, I allowed the new enterprise a grace period of two weeks before visiting its premises for the purposes of assessing its value as a venue for the consumption of comestibles worthy of the sophisticated palate. It cannot be gainsaid that the proprietors have made a conspicuous effort to ensure that the decor and ambience are redolent of Magny's or Le Grand Vefour. The waiters are modest, efficient, and inconspicuous, the linen spotless, the cutlery and glassware impeccable."

"It seems somewhat verbose and pretentious," I said.

"Two characteristics which are at least conspicuously absent from the modest products of your own pen."

"Thank you. I think. Does he ever get around to mentioning the bill of fare?"

"Read on."

The food, on the other hand, can only be described as execrable. My devoted readers will no doubt recall that it is my custom to always order la specialite d'hote *and the most expensive item on the wine list. The latter, a Chateau Leoville Bordeaux 1864, was excellent, and, indeed, was the only element of the entire experience which prevented me from running screaming into the night.*

"I think the point is made. He doesn't recommend the place. Does anybody pay attention to this pompous windbag?

"Oh, you'd be surprised," said Holmes. "Apparently, there are quite a few people in polite society who regard his convoluted verbiage as 'good writing' and hang on his every word."

He sighed.

"Well, it provided me with a minute or two of harmless amusement. Anything of interest in *The Telegraph*?"

"Nothing that would concern you, or I would have brought it to your attention."

I glanced across at the clock on the mantelpiece.

"It's only a quarter-to-nine, Holmes. Who knows what the day may bring?"

No sooner were the words out of my mouth than there was a ring at the doorbell, and within minutes we were plunged into a case of paramount importance which, after the passage of a suitable amount of time, may be the subject of one of these narratives. It was, in any event, of sufficient urgency and complexity to drive any remaining thought of Raymond Arnoux completely out of our minds, and it wasn't until several months later that he was thrust once more into our attention, and we found ourselves investigating the murder of the restaurant critic of *The Daily Courier.*

Regular readers of these humble sketches may have noticed that my distinguished friend had a certain affinity with France, and the French. His maternal grandmother had been the sister of the famous French artist, Horace Vernet. His knowledge of French literature far exceeded his acquaintance with that of England, and he could quote freely from

Flaubert, Zola, and Georges Sand. And it should be noted that while he refused a knighthood from the English Crown on more than one occasion, he was happy to accept the Order of the *Legion d'Honneur* from the French President, in recognition of his vital part in the arrest of Huret, the infamous boulevard assassin.

One of the ways in which this Gallic connection manifested itself was in a liking for French food. We did not dine out exclusively in French restaurants, but we could usually be found in such establishments two or three times a month. One particular favourite of Holmes was *L'Escargot D'Argent* – in English, *The Silver Snail*. It was small, tucked away in a cul-de-sac in Covent Garden called Little Burbage Street. As well as the attractions of its excellent food, it was a convenient place to dine because of its proximity to the Opera House.

Holmes had had no clients for a week, and I had suggested to him that as a means of occupying himself, he should finish a monograph he had left half-completed on the specialized argots of various professions. He acceded, and spent the next two days researching the subject, riffling through his records of past cases, his own and others', and making copious notes. At last he put pen to paper, and late in the afternoon he stood up from his desk and stretched his long arms.

"You've finished it?" I asked.

"Well, I shall read it through once more tomorrow morning before I send it to the publisher, but I am certainly done for today. How does the idea of an evening out appeal to you?"

"Very much."

Holmes rang the bell, and when Mrs. Hudson appeared, he informed her that we wouldn't be in for dinner, a courtesy which, it has to be said, he didn't always extend to her.

We made our leisurely way on foot to Little Burbage Street, the evening being fresh and clear.

L'Escargot d'Argent was founded, owned, and managed by one Theophile Dumont, who had come to London in 1872. Born in Le Havre, he had fought in the Franco-Prussian War. He survived several of the great battles of that conflict with a few wounds, none of them with any permanent effects other than scars, and after the Battle of Sedan he decided that rather than remain in a country suffering the ill-effects of defeat, he would go to London. He was charmed by the ambience of Covent Garden and its environs and decided to open a restaurant there, which he did with some financial assistance from his parents. Two old friends from his student days, Maurice Leclerc and Alphonse Duvivier, came from Paris to join him as chef and head waiter. Within two years, all had married Englishwomen, assuring their permanent residence in the capital and the continued existence of L'Escargot d'Argent. The place was not, as yet, well known, but had numerous regular patrons, which maintained its success.

It was relatively small for a restaurant, being of enough size to accommodate some twenty diners at one time. The walls were faced with pine and decorated simply with framed photographs of Parisian locales, theatrical posters, and the occasional painting donated by the artist, for, like his fellow-restaurateurs across the Channel, Dumont would often accept a work of art in lieu of payment for a meal. The furniture was of a basic design, and the tablecloths were cotton checkerboards of red and white.

Alphonse Duvivier was a short, slim individual with black hair smoothed to the back of his head and an impressive waxed moustache that ended in two diminutive curls. When Holmes and I entered the restaurant, he came up and greeted us effusively.

"Ah, Monsieur Holmes! And Doctor Watson! Once more you

honour us with your presence! It is very pleasant to see you again! Marcel!" he said, clicking his fingers to summon one of the white-uniformed waiters who were gliding efficiently between the tables with their trays of food and wine.

"You remember the famous detective and his colleague?"

"*Bien sur*. Good evening, gentlemen."

Marcel was also somewhat below average height and, like his superior, sported a moustache. His accent was not that of a Parisian, but I couldn't place it.

"Show Mr. Holmes and Doctor Watson to the window table, and take their order."

After we were comfortably seated, and the little waiter had hurried off to fetch a bottle of wine to accompany our meals, Holmes smiled and said, "Marseilles."

"I beg your pardon?"

"Marcel is from Marseilles, in the *departement* of Bouches-du-Rhone As I have said many times, your face is an extremely accurate barometer of your thoughts. Marcel has seen us here before, but has never served us, so you hadn't heard him speak. You know that Alphonse is Parisian, and I could see that you were a little puzzled by the difference in accents."

He then gave a brief discourse, to which I listened avidly, on the regions of the French nation and the variations in stress, intonation, and modulation to be found in the accents of each of them.

The waiter returned with our wine and two plates of *vichyssoise*, which we consumed in silence. Then, during the main course, Holmes drew my attention to a new poster on one of the walls, and we embarked on a conversation which began with the career of Jean-Eugène Robert-Houdin and wandered from there to the conquests of the Roman Emperor

Aurelian and the likely effects of devaluation on any given currency. I was about to express my own thoughts on the latter subject when the character of the evening was radically changed.

Two men had entered L'Escargot D'Argent while Holmes and I were eating our *vichyssoise*, and I had glanced idly over at them as one of the waiters seated them at a table near the back of the restaurant.

The first was a slim, dapper man of the middle height. The uniform colour and sheen of his thick black hair led one to suspect that they were the result of dye. His features were regular, but his facial expression was one of barely suppressed disdain. His companion appeared to be about ten years older and was about the same height, but rather rotund. His clothes were neither as well-fitting nor of as good quality as that of his companions, and he was carrying a little leather briefcase. His hair was greying, with a distinct bald patch at the back, and I had the impression that for some reason he wasn't comfortable with his surroundings.

After a few minutes, the hum of conversation in the restaurant came to an abrupt end as both men uttered piercing cries. The first slid to the floor and lay prostrate, while the other fell forward onto the table a moment later, his arms outstretched. Heads were turned in curiosity and stayed fixed in horror.

"It seems there is work for us," said Holmes, rising to his feet. "Come, Watson."

Together we hurried to the table where the two men lay inert. I knelt beside the man on the floor and felt his neck for a pulse. There was none. I stood and performed the same action on the other.

"This man is still alive. We must call an ambulance."

"And the police," said Holmes. "Did they have soup?" he asked the white-faced young waiter who had served the pair.

"They both started with *vichyssoise*, and then they had *tournedos*

Rossini. And they shared a bottle of Pinot Noir."

Holmes nodded. The bottle of wine stood half-finished on the table, and the two men had clearly just started eating the tournedos.

"The soup plates will have been washed, I suppose."

"Not necessarily, Monsieur Holmes, but there will be a pile of them, and it will be impossible to say which came from this table."

One of the other diners rose and questioned Holmes. "Is it poison?"

"That would seem to be the most likely cause of death," he admitted.

"Food poisoning? Are we all in danger?"

"They had exactly the same meal, but whatever it was is unlikely to have been in the main course, because they had hardly eaten any," said Holmes. He then turned and addressed everyone present "Did anyone else have the *tournedos Rossini*?"

Several diners had, but had eaten them and gone on to their desserts with no ill-effects.

"That leaves the *vichyssoise* and the wine."

"Surely it must have been the wine," I said. "We both had the *vichyssoise*, and we're unharmed, to say nothing of all the others here who must have had it."

"If he has been poisoned," said one of the waiters, gesturing to the unconscious man at the table, "shouldn't we give him something to make him bring it up?"

"No, no," I interjected quickly, "that would be the worst thing to do. We don't know yet what type of poison it was, if it was. When it comes back up it could get into his lungs, or damage his oesophagus. They'll know what to do at the hospital."

A horse-drawn vehicle from the St. John Ambulance Brigade arrived to take the survivor to University College Hospital, followed shortly by the police in the person of one Inspector Lanner, an alert, eager young Scotland Yard Inspector who had called on Holmes for assistance more than once in the recent past. He was accompanied by his sergeant, Ross, a burly ex-military man, and two uniformed constables.

The next to arrive was Theophile Dumont, a tall, imposing man with the traditional ample girth of the successful restaurateur. He hadn't been present at the restaurant but entered now, in an advanced state of agitation, having been summoned by Alphonse. He went from table to table, assuring the customers that under the circumstances they wouldn't be charged for their meal. On reaching the table where we sat, he seized Holmes's hand and cried, "Ah, praise be to *le bon Dieu* that you are here! I confess, I don't trust your English police. But you, Monsieur Holmes, surely you can solve this crime and save my restaurant from shame and ruin?"

Holmes gently disengaged his hand from Dumont's.

"I'm afraid that we must leave the matter to the official force for the time being. If they cannot find the culprit, I promise that I will take up the case. At the moment, however, Monsieur Dumont, I am afraid that Dr. Watson and I are merely witnesses."

Holmes stayed in communication with Lanner for the next week. That was how we learned that the murdered man was restaurant critic Raymond Arnoux. The other man, Charles Morgan, had the same occupation, writing for another newspaper, *The Daily Clarion*. The remaining wine, and the two glasses, had been examined and yielded no trace of poison, although the police autopsy had confirmed that this was the cause of death. The lethal substance was *botulin*, which has the twin advantages, so far as the malefactor is concerned, of being both odourless and tasteless, and easily manufactured, so that unlike arsenic, for example, it need not be purchased at a chemist's, where a record would be made of its sale.

At the end of the week, Lanner called on us, looking rather haggard and woebegone.

"I have my theories, Mr. Holmes," he said, as he took a seat in our living-room, "but no solid evidence to back them up."

Holmes reached for one of his pipes and filled the bowl with tobacco.

"Pray tell me what they are, then," he said, striking a match.

"Well," the inspector began, "French-speaking waiters are a close-knit group. There cannot be more than a hundred of them in the whole of London. Arnoux is at least indirectly responsible for the failure of quite a few restaurants over the last few years. A brother, or a close friend, or the murderer himself, loses a job when one fails, and the killer fixates on the person he holds responsible. The waiter comes to work at L'Escargot d'Argent, and when Arnoux books a table, the murderer sees his time has come."

"Is that feasible?" I asked.

"Oh, yes," said Holmes. "And in terms of motive, waiters who have been employed by the same restaurant for a long time can feel a great sense of loyalty toward the place, and their employers. Ask Alphonse Duvivier. Presumably you have questioned the waiter who served Morgan and Arnoux?"

"Thoroughly, and he would seem to be in the clear. He has only worked there for two weeks, and in fact has only been in London for three. I sent his name and description to the *Sûreté*, and they confirmed his identity. The other person I concentrated on was the chef, Maurice Leclerc, and he most definitely had a motive, of the kind I mentioned earlier. His younger brother had had followed him to London and was employed as the chef at the Auberge de Jehan Cottard, which closed down not long after Arnoux gave it a particularly scathing review, and after that no other restaurateur would employ him."

It was at that point that I recalled the conversation Holmes and had had some months before, and it struck me that to one of a passionate Gallic temperament, that might indeed be motive enough for murder.

"I questioned him long and hard," continued Lanner, "but he didn't break."

"The problem is method, not motive, at least for the moment," said Holmes. "How did the botulin get into the soup, for that is surely where the poison was? If it was done by the chef, or by the waiter, it is difficult to see how it could be carried out without the complicity of the other. The waiter knows to whom he is serving the soup, but how does he get the lethal dose into it without being sure that he will not be seen? True, he is in the middle of the busy kitchen, or the equally busy restaurant, but he is either holding one plate in each hand, or bearing both on a tray. The poison is presumably in a vial or some other small receptacle which he must take from a pocket and pour into the *vichyssoise*. How can he do that without setting down the plates?

"Now let us consider the chef. You will recall that *vichyssoise* is served with a garnish of chopped chives, which is added just before serving the soup. Under cover of this action, it would be easy for him to add the poison. The problem then would be that, unless the waiter were an accomplice, the chef couldn't possibly be sure that the poisoned soup would go to the correct table."

"But why poison both of them," I objected, "if Arnoux was his target?"

"Possibly the killer didn't know him by sight," said Lanner. "He'd have to kill both of them to be sure of Arnoux's death."

"A reasonable assumption," said Holmes.

"Kill an innocent man to ensure the death of a guilty one?" I expostulated.

"It would hardly be without precedent," replied Holmes, "and recent history provides us with several examples. In Adelaide in 1879, Thomas Hawkins killed a pair of twin brothers. He discovered that one of them had seduced his sister, to whom he had an unhealthy attachment. She sought to protect her lover by pretending she didn't know which twin it was, so he murdered both of them. Then there's the case of Sven Jorgenson in Stockholm in '83. He poisoned a dinner party of twelve people by putting strychnine in the dessert. It was revealed at the trial that he only had a motive for killing one of them. And only last year, the case of Wing Fat in San Francisco was along similar lines. But let us not forget, Charles Morgan is still alive, is he not, Lanner?"

"He's still in University College Hospital. They'll be letting him out in a few days, apparently."

The next morning Holmes stood up immediately after breakfast and put on his light summer jacket.

"You are going out?" I inquired.

"Yes, to Scotland Yard, and then to L'Escargot D'Argent."

"You have, then, some clue to the solution of this mystery?"

"Like our friend Lanner, I have a theory which must be put to the test. If it rings true, then I will ask you to accompany me to University College Hospital this afternoon. That is, of course, unless you have more pressing business of your own to conduct."

"Holmes, you know full well that I am currently without a practice," I said with not a little irritation.

"So, I can rely on your presence. Until this afternoon, then."

Having lived with Holmes for this long, I was, I presume, more sensitive to his changing moods than any other man alive, but I confess that when he returned to Baker Street at about two o'clock, I found it difficult to discern his frame of mind. As we rattled in a hansom through the crowded streets of London en route to the hospital, it seemed to me that behind his stoic mask there were signs of both triumph and frustration. No doubt, I told myself, there would be answers at our destination. And so it proved.

There was a middle-aged nurse on duty at the hospital reception desk. Holmes gave her his most winning smile and said, "May we see Charles Morgan? We are friends of his, and we have his briefcase."

I had of course noticed what he had been carrying, but as I had seen it only briefly at the restaurant, I hadn't made the connection. Now he held it up so that the nurse could see the little letters "*C.M.*." where they were embossed into the leather surface just below the closed flap.

"He left it at the restaurant that night. Understandably. How is he?"

"He's still a bit weak, but well enough to have visitors. He's in a private room on the second floor. 24-A."

We climbed the stairs and found the room. Morgan lay on his back in bed, dressed in a blue-and-white hospital gown and in a state of half-sleep. He looker older and fatter, and more out of shape than he had in his suit in the restaurant

"Morgan!" Holmes said in a loud, clear voice. The journalist sat up and rubbed his bleary eyes.

"What is it?" he said. "Who are you?"

"You may have heard of us. I am Sherlock Holmes, and this is my friend and colleague Dr. John Watson. You left your briefcase behind at L'Escargot D'Argent. I had to go to Scotland Yard to pick it up. They thought it might be evidence."

"Oh, thank you. But evidence of what?"

"There were a couple of things in it. The police couldn't understand, but to me those two things suggest, although it cannot be proven, that you killed Raymond Arnoux."

Morgan's face twisted into a mask of contempt.

"What on earth are you talking about? Killed him? I nearly died myself."

"Yes, and it seemed odd to me that a man both older and demonstrably less healthy should survive when a younger, fitter man succumbed. You put your own life at risk in order to take his. That indicates a powerful hatred. What was it, Morgan? Professional jealousy of a richer, more successful restaurant critic? A woman, perhaps, whom you wanted and he had? You may as well tell me. I have already told you I can't prove anything."

"I'm telling you nothing." Morgan paused. "There's nothing to tell. And even if there were, I'm not stupid enough to say it in front of two people. That would be tantamount to a confession."

"Very well." Holmes opened the briefcase and reached into it. "Exhibits *A* and *B*."

Morgan gave a false laugh.

"A pair of soup spoons? Are you insane? What does that prove?"

"Let us use the word 'suggest' rather than 'prove'. As you say, two soup spoons, from L'Escargot D'Argent. And, like all the cutlery in that establishment – " Holmes turned them so that Morgan could see the backs of the handles. " – stamped with the letters '*E*' and '*A*'. Now, I went back to the restaurant this morning and, with the kind permission of the manager, examined all the spoons. I found two that had plain backs." Morgan arched one eyebrow sardonically.

"And what does that 'suggest' to you?"

"It suggests that when you arrived at the restaurant, you had the two plain-handled spoons in your briefcase. You had coated them both with botulin. You had them in separate compartments so that you knew which had the fatal, and which the non-fatal dose. At some point you replaced the restaurant spoons with the poisoned ones, not realising that they weren't identical. Perhaps Arnoux unwittingly made it easier for you by going to the men's room. He ordered first, and you had the same. You knew that by the time the botulin took effect, the spoons would either have been washed or be lying in a pile with many others waiting to be washed, and indistinguishable from them at a casual glance."

"Bravo," said Morgan. "An excellent piece of fiction."

"You are neither as clever nor as original as you may imagine. You are hardly the first murderer by poison who has taken a dose himself to throw the law off the scent. There was Coleraine in Bristol in 1854, and Steiner in Metz in 1873, to cite just two examples. You have escaped punishment on this occasion, but – " Holmes moved a little closer to the bed and lifted an admonitory finger. " – be warned. My eyes are upon you. If you perpetrate any other such crime, I will not hesitate to take the law into my own hands and punish you accordingly."

"Both those eventualities seem unlikely," said Morgan with an unpleasant smile. "And now, I'd like to sleep. Please leave."

I accompanied Holmes out into the cold, antiseptic corridor. I was chilled by the implication of his last words to Morgan, but said nothing. I knew he had spoken the strict truth, for justice was his concern, not the letter of the law.

Holmes informed Lanner of his conclusions, and the inspector agreed that under the circumstances, nothing could be done. Nevertheless, the tale has a sequel. After Arnoux's death, Morgan became the restaurant critic of *The Daily Courier*. Had he known that he would be the likely successor to the dead man's position? Had he feigned friendship and invited Arnoux to L'Escargot D'Argent with that result in mind? Two weeks after starting with his new paper, a fire broke out at a restaurant he had been sent to review. The crowded dining room of Il Piatto d'Oro had suddenly filled with billowing smoke, and although some of the diners had gone to hospital suffering from smoke inhalation, none of them had died. None, that is, except for Charles Morgan.

As for Theophile Dumont, the unsolved murder didn't destroy his restaurant business, as he had expected. In fact, so many people were interested to dine at the establishment where it had taken place that he was obliged to expand L'Escargot D'Argent and bring in more tables. Even after twenty years, Dumont exclaimed, he still didn't understand the English character.

The Adventure of the Surrey Revenant

The year of 1894, which had seen the return of Mr. Sherlock Holmes to 221b Baker Street, and his resumption of his role of consulting detective and last court of appeal, was drawing to a close. The seven months since he had brought Professor Moriarty's deputy, the formidable Colonel Sebastian Moran, to justice, had been amongst the busiest of his professional career, and I had been privileged to accompany and assist him on many of his most important cases, even as I had in those days before his seeming death amid the swirling waters of the Reichenbach Falls.

I had left our lodgings on a brief shopping expedition in search of a new razor, my old one, which I had bought shortly before my attachment to the Fifth Northumberland Fusiliers, having given up the ghost after many years' service. As I climbed the steps to our rooms on my return I heard Holmes's clear, high voice coming through the door. I had passed Mrs. Hudson in the hallway, so he was presumably conversing with a client.

"I'm very sorry, Mr. Bridges, but I don't think I can take your case. While you have my complete sympathy, I think you should consult an exorcist, or at any rate a priest of some kind. Your situation really doesn't come within my purview. Ah, good morning, Watson."

I had entered our sitting room and saw what appeared to be a sane and competent middle-aged member of the rentier class, respectably dressed and well groomed, his straight brown hair neatly combed to the back of his head and his upper lip adorned with a meticulously trimmed moustache.

"Am I interrupting?" I asked.

"No, Doctor, I believe Mr. Bridges is about to leave."

Bridges rose to his feet, his regular features writhing in frustration.

"I came to you because I was told you help people – those who cannot go to the police. People who need things kept out of the papers. People who have nowhere else to go. Obviously I was misinformed. Good day, sir."

"I, at least, would like to hear your story, Mr. Bridges," I interrupted. "Surely there is no harm in that, Holmes."

The detective leaned forward in his chair.

"Please sit down, Mr. Bridges. Perhaps I was a little hasty. I have rather more human weaknesses than one might imagine from reading about me in my friend's accounts of our cases. But you would admit that most people, hearing your story, would find it incredible, and might well come to the conclusion that you were, at the very least, suffering from some kind of delusion. Surely the simplest and most logical solution to the situation is that it was a case of mistaken identity."

"I've known the man for twenty years, I tell you. It was him, not just somebody who looked like him. And as I said, I've seen him more than once."

"Excuse me, gentlemen," I interjected, "but I have yet to hear the story."

"My apologies, Watson. Please repeat what you have told me, Mr. Bridges, and I assure you I shall make no more observations until you have finished."

He reached for his pipe and Persian slipper, and Michael Bridges began his tale.

"Fifteen years ago, I started a business with my friend, Arthur Atwell. We specialised in the production of agricultural machinery. I don't suppose you've heard of us, but amongst farming folk, Atwell and Bridges have a pretty solid reputation. Do you know anything about Haiti, Dr. Watson?"

"Beyond the fact that it is part of the island of Hispaniola, I know virtually nothing of it. Why do you ask?"

"Well, most people don't even know that much. After a rough time of political and social chaos, Michel Domingue introduced a fairer and more democratic constitution in 1874, resulting in a stability which has lasted to this day. In such circumstances, one can usually expect to see an improvement in agriculture, with greater efficiency and higher yields. But Haiti has virtually no industry, and is consequently unable to produce the machinery which would facilitate this. Now, Arthur and I always kept an eye out for potential new markets, and we came up with a plan for Haiti which we believed would be beneficial to both parties. We would sell them our products at greatly reduced prices in exchange for a guaranteed percentage of the profits from their exported goods."

"That sounds like an eminently sensible scheme," I remarked.

"Well, we thought so too. Most of the small-holding farmers there are dirt poor, but we were sure that there were enough big landowners who were rich enough to be interested in what we had to offer, and would have some influence in government circles. The only way to meet those landowners and convince them was for one of us to go to Haiti in person. Arthur was always better at that sort of thing, so he went. It was a long journey – Portsmouth to New York by sea, New York to Miami by train, and then Miami to Port-au-Prince by boat. I received a letter from him, posted a few days after he arrived, telling me that not only had we made a big mistake, but he was in personal danger and was returning home as soon as he could and catching the first available boat to Miami. The mistake we had made was that the landowners had hundreds of people working the land for them, using primitive methods and in conditions of virtual slavery, and the owners liked it that way. So Arthur had to get out, and he did get out, but not alive. It was his dead body that took that long journey back."

"Was there a death certificate?"

"Yes, Arthur's son and daughter made the journey to Port-au-Prince as soon as the news reached them from the British representative there, and it was given directly into their hands. The cause of death was diagnosed as a heart attack. I couldn't believe that at first. Arthur was fifty-five, a few years older than me, but he was pretty fit for a man of his age. But then I thought, he had that long journey, all that time in a hot country, the failure of our enterprise, the threat of death, and even eating food he wasn't used to – all that must have combined to put a strain on his heart. I must confess, I felt – and feel – rather guilty. I should have gone. I'm not married, you see, and I've no one to grieve over me.

"That's the background, but it's time I came to the point. The part you won't believe – that Mr. Holmes here already doesn't believe. It was dark, and I had just been to see Edgar and Amelia, Arthur's children, in Sutton in Surrey, about ten days ago. I suppose it was about eleven at night. I'd gone over there with some documents connected with the business that they needed to sign. The door of their house is at the end of a narrow cul-de-sac, so I had parked the carriage on the main road near the other end of it and now I was walking back down the street. I heard footsteps behind me. I turned, and someone came out of the darkness into the light of a streetlamp, and I thought my own heart was going to stop when I saw Arthur's face. His face, I swear it, but deathly pale and bearing an expression of unutterable horror. His eyes seemed to be staring into the very pits of Hell. I scuttled backwards away from him, then I turned back and ran off as far and as fast as I could."

He took a couple of deep breaths then continued. "I found a cab and got home. The next day, I told my coachman to go and fetch the carriage. I couldn't stand to go back there."

"Why didn't he drive you the night before?" I asked.

"It was his night off, that's all. Wednesday night. I didn't tell anyone what had happened. As you said, if I told most people, they'd think I was insane."

Holmes broke his silence.

"I didn't say that, exactly."

"Well, my own first thought was that I was going mad. I tried to tell myself I'd been tired, or overwrought because of Arthur's death, or that I'd drunk too much while dining with Edgar and Amelia, but none of that was true. If I wasn't insane, the only alternative was that it was really him. I'd had a supernatural experience. Do you know what a zombie is?"

"I've heard the word, that's all," I said, "but perhaps you can enlighten me."

"Certainly. I have done some research into the matter in the past few days. If Arthur had died in Haiti, then the root of the situation was to be found there. As you may know, the religion of Haiti is voodooism. There is no central authority, no Pope or Archbishop, which I imagine stems from the fact that the Negroes who were transported there as slaves came from many different tribal cultures. Their priests are called *houngans*, and some of them are good and virtuous, while others, known as *bokors*, follow what some call 'The Left Hand Path'."

"That of evil."

"Precisely. The *houngans* disinter dead bodies and reanimate them by the use of magical rituals. In this state of half-life, they can perform simple duties for long hours, needing no food or sleep. Being turned into a zombie is a form of punishment. Instead of being borne to the realm of the *loa*, the gods, the perpetrator of a crime – rape, say, or murder – is resurrected from the grave to a living death and condemned to carry out the most menial or irksome tasks until the *houngan* who has created the zombie, or his successor, deems that the zombie has expiated his or her crime."

His use of language suggested that he was quoting verbatim from a book, or books, on the subject.

"My opinion is that the large landowners on Haiti form a small group of *bokors*, or have some working on their behalf, who turn the innocent dead into zombies to use as workers in their fields. You can't get cheaper labour than that – they don't need food, they don't get sick or ask for improved pay and conditions. That would also explain why the landowners rejected our offer."

"You mentioned earlier that you had seen your friend more than once since his death," said Holmes,

"Yes. The second occasion was in the garden of my house in St. John's Wood, the night before last. I was awakened by the garden gate banging at about one in the morning and went down to close it. Arthur stepped out of the shadow of the trees into the moonlight. I wasn't quite as scared this time, because, as I said, now I had an explanation of sorts."

"Did you try to speak to him?"

"I called him by name, and his expression lightened a little, but zombies only fully respond to the one who has been given power over them."

"And you alone heard the garden gate making a noise?"

"My bedroom is on that side of the house. The servants" rooms are all on the other side."

"Did you try to restrain him?"

"Certainly not! Zombies are possessed of preternatural strength. He would have torn me to pieces. No, I let him go, by the garden gate."

"You didn't attempt to follow him?"

"Follow a zombie and their master becomes aware of you? You don't want that to happen."

"Even though they are on the other side of the Atlantic Ocean?" I asked. I confess that I was beginning to find Mr. Bridges' apparent gullibility somewhat irksome.

"It seemed quite possible to me that it might be the work of someone in this country, who had made a deeper study of voodoo. Or, of course, a native *bokor* could have come here by ship."

"Just a few more questions, Mr. Bridges," continued Holmes. "First, do you know where Mr. Atwell is – or rather *was* – buried?"

"In the churchyard of St. Botolph's, near the house in Surrey."

"Which now belongs to his son and daughter?"

"Yes."

"When?"

"The first available day after his body arrived. I was at the funeral. A Saturday, it must have been."

"The Saturday before the Wednesday you first saw him?"

"Yes."

"Did you see Atwell's body before it was interred?"

"No, the coffin was closed. Apparently the facial distortion caused by the pain of the sudden heart attack was beyond the ability of the undertakers to alter, because *rigor mortis* had set in during the transportation of the corpse."

"And his grave is now empty, if your suspicions are correct."

"An exhumation order would prove that one way or another," I said, "but I doubt the authorities would credit the reasons for requesting one. Why do you suppose he has appeared to you, and not his children?"

"We were great friends, don't forget."

"But what do you think he, or whoever may be controlling him, wants of you?" asked Holmes.

"I couldn't say."

"Did you and Mr. Atwood have any enemies?"

"Business rivals, certainly, but none of them knew about Arthur's trip to Haiti. Even if they had, I can't imagine any of them being behind this."

"No others?"

"None that I am aware of."

"Have you visited Mr. Atwood's children since that Wednesday?

"Yes. They invited me again the following Wednesday. All the papers transferring their father's interest in the business to them have been signed and dealt with, but since Arthur's death I think I may have become something of a substitute father for them."

"Did you drive the carriage again?"

"No, this time I asked my coachman to drive me there. He was a little put out, as Wednesday is also his lady friend's night off, but he agreed when I promised him the whole weekend free. He drove me to dinner, and I left at eleven again."

"Now, lastly," said Holmes, "what do you require of us? That we wait with you for a further visitation and witness that your tale is true? Or that we track down whoever is behind this?"

"Oh, no, Mr. Holmes. I want you to help me kill him – or rather, destroy him, since he's already dead. Put him out of his misery. As an old friend, it's the least I can do."

"I see. We shall give you whatever assistance you need, but first I shall give you some instructions you must follow to the letter. Do you have any other residence besides your house in St. John's Wood?"

"Yes, I have a cottage just outside Studley in Warwickshire."

"Excellent. I take it you can leave your business to run itself for a few days?"

"I have a very reliable man who is often left in charge."

"Then here is what you must do: Go home and pack a suitcase, then go to your office and inform them that you will be at your cottage from the eighth onwards – "

"But today is the fourth."

" – and then return here and give me the keys to the property in St. John's Wood, not forgetting to provide us with the address. Then take the first available train to Studley. Tell no one else of your departure. Stay there until we arrive on the seventh."

"But what is your plan, sir?"

"Mr. Bridges, if I am to bring this matter to a satisfactory conclusion, then you must trust me and allow me to keep my own counsel. Mrs. Hudson will show you out."

Reaching across to the bell-pull, he rang to summon that estimable lady.

"Thank you, Watson, If not for your timely arrival, I might have missed out on what looks to be a most interesting case. Mr. Bridges clearly found you a more sympathetic listener, as he told his story at greater length and in more detail than when I was his sole audience. By the way, I trust your quest for a new razor was successful."

"Yes, I went to Hayworth's in the Bayswater Road. But how – ?"

My hand flew up to my face.

"Relax, my friend. Your shave is but an hour or two overdue, and only the trained eye of one who knows of your habits would notice the very slight stubble on your cheeks and chin. Your reputation for scrupulous neatness remains intact. Now, what do you make of Bridges' story?"

"I find it very surprising that an apparently sane man could credit such nonsense for a single moment."

"Well, Watson, a rich vein of supernaturalism runs beneath the surface of our scientific, mechanized society, and as belief in the established religion wanes, folk become susceptible to more *outré* modes of thought. You and I are agreed that these visitations cannot be due to necromancy. How then, may we explain them?"

I thought for a few seconds.

"There is a certain amount of evidence that persons of a hypersensitive nature may be prone to hallucinations, particularly where the individual is suffering from a strong negative emotion, such as guilt."

"There were certainly a few indications that there is more to Mr. Bridges than his stolid exterior would suggest. Anything else?"

"Both these events took place at night. Perhaps whoever is behind this found someone who resembled Atwell enough to pass for him in a bad light. Or even," I continued, warming to the theme, "someone took a cast of his face after death and used it to construct a mask of rubber that would serve a similar purpose. Bridges did say that Atwell's face had an unnatural pallor."

Holmes looked down with a fixed, introspective look in his grey eyes.

"No," he said after a few seconds, "no. There is something else at work here, something deeper."

He looked up at me once more.

"Are you aware, Watson, that some have explained the Greek legend of the Centaurs by saying that they were simply men on horseback, as seen through the eyes of those who had never encountered such riders before?"

"I'm sorry, Holmes, I don't see your point."

"If zombies exist – "

"Oh, come now, Holmes!"

" – then there must be a rational, scientific explanation for their existence."

"If there is one, I have no doubt that you of all men can find it out. But what is our first move? I take it you were not serious when you agreed to help him destroy whoever or whatever it was he saw."

"I would if there were an absolute necessity for such action, but I think it highly unlikely that there will be. You realize, of course, that I sent him off to his cottage in Warwickshire principally to get him out of the way?"

"I imagined that was the reason."

"The presence of one who is convinced of the supernatural nature of these visits, to say nothing of his murderous intent, would hamper our investigation. Here is what we shall do: After Bridges has returned with the key and departed for the station, we will go to his house and take up temporary residence there until the seventh. If we see no zombies, we shall take the train to Studley and stay with our client until we see one there, though I have greater hopes of St. John's Wood."

"And during the days?"

"I will spend the first at the Reading Room at the British Museum, consulting Eckermann and whatever else I can find of relevance. And have no fear. When the hour of action does arrive, your presence will be crucial, or I should not have asked you to come."

Michael Bridges returned a couple of hours later with the key to 83 Perceval Gardens, St. John's Wood.

"I will give you a note to take to my servants," said Bridges when Holmes informed him of our plans regarding his house.

"Servants, indeed," I remarked as I gazed out of one of the windows at our client climbing into his carriage on the street below us.

"You heard him say so earlier. It is hardly remarkable that a rich man would have them."

"True. Has he any inkling of the reason we are sending him out of London, do you think?"

"As long as he obeys my instructions, it is immaterial to me whether he has or not. Now, Watson, have you packed enough for our short stay?"

"Of course."

"And I have already informed Mrs. Hudson of our impending absence, so we can be off without delay, and you can christen your new razor in the bathroom of 83 Perceval Gardens."

Bridge's house was a fully-detached villa-style building of the late eighteenth century with a large L-shaped garden that ran along its left side and back. Between the wall separating the garden from the next-door neighbour and the front of the house ran a set of iron railings with a wrought-iron gate at the centre. Rather than using the key Bridges had given him, Holmes rapped on the door with its brass knocker.

The door was opened by a tall, dark-haired young woman in a maid's outfit.

"Good afternoon," said Holmes.

"Good afternoon, sirs. I am afraid Mr. Bridges is not in."

"He gave us this," said Holmes, proffering the note.

It read:

This is to inform you that Mr. Sherlock Holmes and his colleague, Dr. Watson, will be staying at the house for the next few days in my absence. You will obey their orders as you would mine and serve them in the same manner.

M.A. Bridges
4th November, 1894

"Sherlock Holmes!" said the young woman in a tone of awe.

"You have heard of me, then. Perhaps you would bring the rest of the staff here so that we can meet them all."

The household consisted of a butler, a cook, two more maids, and a boot-boy.

The butler, Wheatcroft, had a slight whiff of brown ale about him and his collar was slightly askew, as if it had been buttoned in haste. While the cats away, the mice will play, as the old adage has it. The cook, a dumpy, maternal woman with a Scots accent, was called Mrs. Guthrie. The maid who had opened the door to us was Mortimer, while the other two, both shorter and pale-skinned, answered to Mullins and Ratcliff. Jackson, the boot-boy, was a scrawny, somewhat-underdeveloped youth of sixteen, who looked two or three years younger. There was also the carriage driver, but Bridges has given him the week off.

"Before you go back to your duties," said Holmes, "I have a request to make of you: From tomorrow onward, if anyone calls at the house during the day, whether you know them or not, you are to tell them that your master is from home, but will be back in the evening. Is that clear? Good. You can go now."

"Dinner will be at half-past-seven, sir,"

"Thank you, Mrs. Guthrie."

I came down to dinner after a short rest, freshly shaven, to find Holmes waiting for me. As we ate the excellent three-course meal served us by Mullins and Ratcliff, Holmes informed me of the part I was to play. I had been given the role of Bridges because my moustache made it possible for me to be briefly mistaken for him, and also because my medical experience made me slightly more qualified for the task I must perform.

When we had finished, we repaired to the smoking room and chatted leisurely about other matters unconnected to the business in hand, smoking panatelas and drinking from a decanter of brandy brought to us by Wheatcroft.

Both of the guest bedrooms were on the same side of the house as Bridges' room, so if our visitor announced his presence by banging the gate, at least one of us would be sure to hear it. He did not call on that first night, nor on the second. Both of us were prepared for our separate tasks, but he didn't arrive until one in the morning on the seventh.

When Holmes returned from his researches at about three o'clock on the afternoon of our first full day, I scarcely gave him time to remove his topcoat before I began quizzing him on the subject. I had had a pleasant enough day leafing through the books in Bridges' library, to say nothing of consuming a splendid lunch, but I was most eager to know what he had learned.

Holmes gave me an indulgent smile.

"Background and colour for your coming account of the case, eh?"

"Well, I've given it a little thought, yes."

"Let us at least discuss it in comfort."

I followed him into the spacious living room, where we each sat down in one of the large, mahogany-brown padded-leather armchairs.

"Well, to begin with, voodoo is not just the religion of the common people, but permeates the professional classes there to such a degree that virtually every lawyer, doctor, and landowner is a *houngan*. One might even say that, despite those democratic reforms Bridges mentioned, they are the country's true rulers.

"As to zombies, they are never seen outside their work area, or at night. Unfortunately, discussion of the whole subject is prone to sensationalism, and it is entirely possible that Bridges consulted some unreliable texts. Even those writers I read who seem to believe that zombies are indeed resurrected corpses said nothing about their masters being able to divine where they are when out of sight, nor do they simply appear and disappear like ghosts."

For my part, the event which took place in the morning of the seventh of November, though brief, is indelibly imprinted on my memory. I had stood beside Holmes on more than one occasion when we appeared to be in the presence of the supernatural, and although he had always proved that there was a rational explanation for the phenomenon, nevertheless, each time I had experienced a chilling moment of atavistic fear, during which, for all my scientific and medical training, it seemed to me that such things might somehow, after all, exist.

We heard the banging of the garden gate – in fact, it was opened and closed with a clatter more than once, doubtless to ensure that Bridges would be awakened by noise. In accordance with our plan, Holmes and I sprang into action. We both hurried down the stairs, and I went into the garden by the back door while Holmes went into the street by the main door. The air was filled with the chill of the late autumn as I took up my position.

A figure moved toward me, its pale, hollowed face ghastly in the circle of light cast by a nearby street lamp, its eyes full of a desperate and terrible sadness. I took a hypodermic syringe from my pocket, but as I raised it to plunge the needle in, the figure caught my arm and held it with an unanticipated burst of strength, such strength as a madman might possess. I flung the whole weight of my body against him, bringing us both to the damp earth. For a moment my hand was free, and I stuck the needle in his neck and depressed the plunger, flooding his system with 300-milligrams of chloral hydrate. For a second or two I feared it had had no effect, but then Atwell fell back in a stupour, his eyes closed and his face somewhat relaxed.

As I pulled myself to my feet, I heard cries and the sounds of a struggle coming from the street.

A minute or so later Holmes appeared, his revolver was in his hand. It was trained upon a tubby, bespectacled young man with his hands cuffed in front of him. He had a hard, spoiled face, and his eyes were filled with malice and frustration, and perhaps fear at what must now lie ahead of him.

"Watson, allow me to introduce Mr. Edgar Atwell, the perpetrator of this little plan."

He reached into the pockets of the man's coat and produced a vial of a colourless liquid.

"Ah, my surmise was correct. You carry an extra supply, in case the last dose proved insufficient. Watson, let us get this fellow inside and restrain him more fully. Then we can bear his unfortunate father inside and lay him on one of the beds."

His arm in Holmes's iron grip, the young man didn't struggle. Once inside, we tied him to a kitchen chair with a length of washing line, and he spoke for the first time, in an unpleasant rasping tone.

"I hope you realize that this is illegal restraint."

"Preventing a criminal's escape isn't illegal. Whereas your treatment of your father is a form of assault, and I don't doubt that a charge of attempted embezzlement can also be laid at your door, at the very least."

We brought the older Atwell inside and laid him on the bed of the room I had been occupying. We then woke Wheatcroft, telling him to summon an ambulance and the police.

While we waited, I said, "What was that liquid you took from young Atwell's pocket?"

"Oh, that? Nothing less than the key to this whole business, and a lot more besides. I'm not yet sure of its chemical composition, but you have seen for yourself what its effects are. Once Atwell Senior has been taken to hospital and his son to the police cells, we must return to Baker Street and analyse it." He took a small bottle from his own pocket and poured half the contents of the vial into it. Seeing my questioning glance, he said, "We must give the police a chance to come to their own conclusions."

We returned to Baker Street the following morning, and while our stay in St. John's Wood had undeniably had its pleasant aspects, I was happy to be back in our humble lodgings, and I was sure that Holmes, who was never completely content when away from his files and reference books, felt the same.

"You played your role to perfection, Watson, said Holmes as we took our accustomed armchairs in our sitting room," and it is only fair that I give you a complete explanation of the case as I understand it."

"May I take notes?"

"Of course."

I went to my desk and pulled a notebook and pencil from a drawer. When I was seated once more, Holmes began.

"Now, as you know, when one is in search of a motive for a crime, a good starting point is the question, "'*Cui bono?*', and it seemed to me that the only possible beneficiaries of this situation were Edgar and Amelia Atwell. By getting rid of both their father and Michael Bridges, full ownership of the firm would come into their hands. Their plan had the advantage that all the possible outcomes would serve their ends. If Bridges shared his belief, he might be considered insane – indeed, with sufficient persecution, he might actually *become* insane. In those circumstances, all that remained was to dispose of the father, who was already thought dead. If Bridges killed his partner in the belief that he was saving his soul, again, it wouldn't matter that the victim was already supposed to be dead, there would be a *corpus delicti*, and Edgar on hand as a witness. In fact, they might even claim that the entire hoax had been engineered by Bridges, rather than by them."

"Diabolical!"

"Indeed. My suspicions were supported by several facts. The first visitation took place near the house in Surrey, and Bridges was alone in the quiet street when he saw Atwell. In all probability, he had told the pair in passing that he had driven himself that night, but the following Wednesday, he was with his coachman, and he didn't see the older Atwell. Either he had told the son and daughter of the coachman's presence, or they had made a point of asking him about it. In St. John's

Wood, much closer to the centre of the metropolis, Edgar waited until one in the morning for the street to be clear before bringing his father into the garden.

"Then there was the burial. As Atwell Senior hadn't died, of a heart attack or anything else, I think it likely that he was secreted somewhere in the house, and the coffin was full of stones, or perhaps even a genuine corpse they had somehow obtained. Let us not forget that even before this plan went into action, they received a considerable allowance from their father, enough to indulge in some selective bribery."

"And still that wasn't enough for them. They wanted it all."

"Quite. Now, as I told you before, the professional classes in Haiti are almost exclusively comprised of *houngans*. The Atwells might have obtained a falsified death certificate, and a supply of that liquid you saw me take from Edgar's pocket, from a corrupt medical man. I believe that they crossed the Atlantic before they claimed to have, once they learned their father was *en route*. That is, something that can be confirmed or disproved by the shipping lines" records of passengers to New York. Whether they formulated their plan in London, or during the crossing, or created it with the aid of a *houngan*, or perhaps more correctly a *bokor*, remains to be seen."

"You have yet to tell me exactly what that liquid was."

"Have you heard of the puffer fish?"

"It is poisonous, is it not?"

"Well, parts of it are edible. Those are known to the Japanese as *fugu*, and can only be prepared by specially trained chefs who know exactly which parts of the fish to cook. The rest contain a deadly neurotoxin called *tetrodotoxin*. If you eat the liver, for example, or the skin, you will die very quickly, and in great pain. Well, the *genus* the pufferfish belong to, the *tetraodontidae*, are found all over the world, including the Caribbean, and many of them have the same toxic properties as the pufferfish. What about *datura*? Do you know what that is?"

"No, I am afraid you have me there."

"It's also known as Devil's Trumpet – Jimson Weed, Hell's Bells, Thorn Apple, and a few other colourful names. Whatever name you give it, it's a plant which also contains deadly toxins. In smaller doses, it can cause hallucinations and temporary paralysis. The liquid in that vial contained both tetrodotoxin and tropane alkaloids, the active ingredient of *datura*, in significant amounts. It is my belief, though I will need to consult a neurologist to be completely sure, that in the right combination they would produce the classic zombie state, which Atwell manifested. Suspension of the higher brain functions with the autonomic system unaffected. To maintain this state, one would need to dose the subject on a regular basis, and if this dosage is stopped, he or she should eventually revert to normal."

"So Arthur Atwell will recover?"

"That is to be hoped for, but I don't envy him on the day he finds out what his own children did to him and Bridges. '*How sharper than a serpent's tooth it is, to have a thankless child!*' as Shakespeare says in *King Lear*. Now, before I forget, we must send a telegram to Studley and summon Mr. Bridges back to London.

Contrary to Holmes's hopes, Arthur Atwell never fully recovered. His mental faculties permanently impaired, he was placed in a private nursing home. Michael Bridges was ready to pay for his care, but the costs were instead met by an anonymous donor, with the condition that Bridges never visit his old friend.

Neither of the Atwell siblings was ever brought to trial. When the police arrived at the house in Surrey to question Amelia, she was nowhere to be found. Her brother's failure to return must have warned her that the game was up, and she fled to save her own skin. As to Edgar, we heard no more of him once we had handed him over into police custody.

These codas to our investigations would have struck both Holmes and I as odd, had it not been for an event which took place a few days after the case was concluded, and from which much might be inferred.

We had just finished our lunch when we heard a heavy footfall on the stair, and the door opened to reveal the bulky figure of the saturnine Mycroft Holmes on the threshold.

"Mycroft! How pleasant to see you! Please take a seat. Would you care for a whisky?"

The older Holmes brother remained where he was.

"This isn't a social call, Sherlock, and while the matter affects you, it is chiefly to Dr. Watson that I wish to speak."

"Me?"

"Yes, sir, you. I am aware that you and my brother have recently concluded what you would no doubt term an 'adventure' concerning a certain substance that has a particular effect upon the human nervous system. No doubt you plan to publish an account of the business."

"Well, I was – "

"No such account must ever be written. Or, if written, it must never be published. Should you ever do so, I promise you that there will be consequences of a most serious nature."

The younger Holmes got to his feet.

"I will endure much from you, Mycroft, but when it comes to threatening Watson, that is something I will not tolerate."

Mycroft's expression softened a little.

"Your loyalty to your friend does you credit, Sherlock. But I must ask you both to seriously consider the results of making the existence of this drug known. As long as these 'walking dead', as one might call them, are considered fables, and confined to a small and inconsequential island, they represent no danger. Imagine, however, what might happen if the story is credited in the palaces and chancellories of the great foreign powers. Surely you can see that they would do everything they can to manufacture or obtain supplies of the mixture. I trust you wouldn't wish to see it fall into the hands of the Kaiser, or of the Sultan of Turkey."

"Very well," I said. "I accept your reasoning, and I will not send the story to be published."

"You have made a wise decision, sir."

"Goodbye, Brother. It was, as ever, a pleasure to see you."

"Sarcasm ill becomes you, Sherlock. Good day, gentlemen."

The Three Archers

Those who have followed my chronicles of the exploits of Mr. Sherlock Holmes from their earliest publication will be aware that the first of them, *A Study in Scarlet*, is described, in part, as being "*A Reprint from The Reminiscences of John H. Watson, M.D., Late of the Army Medical Department*". This has led some of my readers to inquire if it is possible to also obtain a copy of that book. The answer, alas, is no.

Any aspiring author can tell the tale of his or her early frustrations: The return of one's manuscript by publisher after publisher, the loss of a book in transit, (making it necessary to choose between rewriting the entire story and abandoning the enterprise altogether), or acceptance of one's manuscript accompanied by a demand for drastic cutting or revision.

My *Reminiscences* fall into the last category. My publishers determined that the public would not be interested in the story of my upbringing, my schooldays, and my early visits to the United States and Australia, and that the narrative really begins with my meeting Holmes, the main interest being our pursuit and capture of Jefferson Hope. The second section, "The Country of the Saints", while it is based on the experiences of Hope and the Ferriers, contains a strong element of fiction, as I was required to concoct a narrative using the meagre information on the subject I had to hand.

So while *A Study in Scarlet* drew on my manuscript, it cannot truly be described as a "reprint", since the original was never printed, and so does not exist as a separate entity. No doubt the publishers thought that it made the narrative appear more authoritative. I must admit that in all probability, they made the right decision, although I did not believe that to be the case at the time.

Another point which correspondents frequently raise in connection with that first book is: Why does Holmes's practice seem to consist, in those early days, entirely of cases which he can solve without leaving the confines of 221b Baker Street? Was the Lauriston Gardens mystery the first time he solved a case by visiting the location of the crime and questioning witnesses?

Certainly, it was the first occasion on which he asked *me* to accompany him, but from conversations with him over many years. It is clear that both the police and clients had summoned him to various locations during his time in Montague Street. It must also be remembered that during those first weeks during which we shared rooms, I was still in the last stages of a long convalescence, and thus unable in any event to accompany him on cases which demanded that he leave our lodgings.

As time went on, and Holmes's reputation grew, he could both command higher fees and be more selective about which cases in which he would become involved. The number which he could solve without leaving his armchair dwindled, but didn't disappear altogether. I have already related he stories of Mary Sutherland and her duplicitous stepfather, and that of John Openshaw and the five orange pips. The following narrative takes place some years later, but falls into a similar category.

By the year 1896, the popularity of archery had gone a little into decline. It had been surpassed as a fashionable pastime for the middle classes by sports such as croquet and tennis. Nevertheless, some fifty archery clubs still remained in Britain. In 1894, the first Olympics committee, headed by Baron Pierre de Coubertin, announced that the 1900 Games would take place in Paris, and that archery would be among the events. This provoked a fierce atmosphere of competition among that group of practitioners who made up the members of the remaining clubs. The fact that six years must elapse before the British team was chosen seemed to have intensified that atmosphere rather than dissipated it.

The Fernfield Archery Club near High Barnet in north London was one of the oldest in the country, having been founded in 1863, only two years after the formation of the Grand National Archery Society. The GNAS organized the Annual National Championship competitions, and would also have a considerable say in who was chosen to represent the country in the first British Olympic archery team. Fernfield's reputation was good. Only two of its members had ever won the championship, but they were always well represented in the semi- and quarter-finals.

In the year 1896, the club had three outstanding archers: W.H. Cullen, D.N. Edginton, and R.H. McNeil. In June, the month before that year's championship, it appeared certain that one of them would win the competition, though it was difficult to say which, since they seemed equally adept. Under those circumstances, it was understandable that there was a great rivalry amongst them, but that rivalry took different forms in each of the three men, who had starkly contrasting personalities. Robert Hugh McNeil was the most popular of the three among the hundred or so members of the club. A sandy-haired Scot from Edinburgh, he was a lawyer who had moved his practice to London when he married a woman from Hampstead. Fond of a drink, but not to excess, he was easy-going, and while he trained hard, he wasn't obsessive. Archery came naturally to him – he was good at it – but he didn't allow it to interfere with the attention he paid to his wife and child. If Edginton or Cullen beat him, he would be disappointed, but no more.

Dennis Noel Edginton counted McNeil among his friends, and it was as if he saw in the affable Scot the image of what he would like to be, but felt he never could. He was moody and insecure and spent virtually all his free time on his sport. McNeil alone was able to coax him out of his bouts of sullenness with some amicable teasing and a few drinks in the club bar. If Robbie McNeil was the most amiable of the three, Walter Henry Cullen was the most disliked. He was a braggart, and continually sought to undermine his rivals with insults and sneering assertions as to their lack of skill. McNeil had no problem laughing this off, but Edginton's sensitive soul was mauled by it. On one occasion, after some drinks in the bar, Cullen went over to his table and whispered something in Edginton's ear which was so offensive – no one ever discovered what it was – that Edginton stood and was about to take a swing at Cullen. McNeil restrained his friend, and surprised everyone by threatening to hit Cullen himself if he didn't leave.

Cullen's indisputable ability was the only thing that prevented the club committee from expelling him. Not long after he provoked Edginton, he tried to force his attentions on one of the club waitresses, and this, along with his general habit of treating them as grossly inferior, encouraged the entire catering staff to refuse to serve him unless he gave an apology. This was duly given, but thereafter Cullen stopped dining or drinking at the bar and restaurant. Any time he spent at the club was mostly occupied with archery.

A description of the club buildings is necessary at this point, based on photographs taken by the police. At the front of the clubhouse were two doors. The larger one, on the right, led into a hall leading to the reception room, while a smaller door on the left was to a room where equipment could be stored in personal lockers. This also contained small changing rooms for men and women members. Another door at the far end of the room opened onto the club restaurant, which could also be accessed by a side door.

Next to the restaurant was the bar, the only place where smoking was allowed. It was accessed by another door. Connecting to the bar, the restaurant, and the reception area was a large room which also contained the kitchen and a separate seating area for the staff. A door led into reception and, as part of the same wall, there was a space with a reception desk with a curtain behind it so that visitors couldn't see into the room.

The reception area had two windows, both of which looked out onto the large, square flat lawn to the right of the building where the practice of archery was actually carried out. The rest of the clubhouse consisted of two offices and a committee room which shared walls with the kitchen and the bar, but were only accessible by a door at the back of the building.

It was seven o'clock on the evening of June 16th, and because of the heat, many of the doors and windows, including those of the reception room, were fully open. Cullen, Edginton, and McNeil were the only members still out on the butts, and the other members who had been present that day, twenty in all, being either in the bar or at dinner. Cullen was the first to stop. He walked back to the clubhouse and went and sat in the reception area.

A few minutes later one of the staff went into reception and found Cullen dead, lying down with an arrow sticking in the nape of his neck. He kept his head and left the corpse, and the scene, untouched, and then went into the restaurant via the kitchen and informed the Club Treasurer, Mr. Lionel Harris, what he had found. Harris instantly went 'round into his office and telephoned the local constabulary, who, as was common in murder cases, notified Scotland Yard. He then had the main door to the club locked and allowed the rest of the members to finish their meals and drinks (the club closed at nine), and leave. He was later criticised for this action, but defended himself on the grounds that he had been in the restaurant and had seen no one leave.

The door to the bar had been closed, but he knew there were only three people in there and none had passed by the open restaurant windows. His immediate concern had been to neither upset nor panic the members, particularly the female ones. As McNeil had only just come into the restaurant, Harris told him to remain. He asked him if there was anyone else on the butts. McNeil replied that Cullen had just come off but Edginton was either still out there or in the locker room. Edginton had in fact gone into the reception area, and was there when the door was locked as per Harris's instructions.

When the police arrived, Edginton was seated in a chair, gazing down at his rival's corpse with an unfathomable expression. He was still dressed as he had been at the butts and had his bow and arrows. Inspector Stanley Hopkins of Scotland Yard arrived at about half-past-nine, accompanied by the medical examiner, a sergeant, and a police photographer. Hopkins apologised for his late arrival. The examiner, Dr. James Cardew, had been delayed by another murder in Camden Town and none of his colleagues had been available.

The site of the murder was photographed from several angles. Cardew then confirmed that Cullen's death was caused by the arrow in the back of his neck, and that death would have occurred instantaneously, or within two or three seconds at most, and had taken place in the last two to two-and-a-half hours. Hopkins then questioned McNeil, Edginton, and Huggins, the man who had discovered the body, in the Treasurer's office. Notes were taken in shorthand by Sergeant Griffiths.

These were the facts, as they were presented to us by Inspector Hopkins one evening as we sat with the Scotland Yarder in our rooms in Baker Street

"And what did those three gentlemen have to say for themselves?" asked Sherlock Holmes, leaning forward, the expression on his sharp features akin to that of the hound who catches the far-off scent of the fox.

The case had reached an impasse, so the inspector had swallowed his pride and come to ask for assistance from the one man in London who could help him with his investigation.

"McNeil says the three of them – that is, himself, Cullen, and Edginton – were out at the butts for about two hours. Cullen left first. McNeil was going to keep Edginton company, but decided to go to the restaurant and get something to eat."

"Did McNeil see Cullen in the reception area?" asked Holmes.

"He said that the door was open and Cullen was sitting in a chair about halfway between the door and the reception desk."

"Why did he go into the reception area rather than the restaurant?"

"He hadn't been in the bar or restaurant for a while, but he was prepared to pay a bit extra for someone to bring him a drink there. Apparently he would have one or two on his own there, and then get changed and leave."

"So, what did McNeil do after he saw Cullen?"

"He says he went and changed his clothes, put his bow and arrows away, then went into the restaurant. He ordered a meal, but before it arrived Mr. Harris asked him to stay after the club closed. He didn't find out why until we arrived. He took his time over his meal and then went into the bar, where he had a couple of drinks and read the newspapers."

"Did you ask him if he saw Edginton at any point after leaving the butts?"

"He said he hadn't. When I asked him if he had got on with the dead man, he admitted that Cullen was a first-class archer, but he was too arrogant about it, and that if he were honest, he wouldn't miss him.

"I let McNeil go and spoke to Edginton. He said the last time he had seen Cullen alive was when McNeil was leaving the butts to get something to eat. Edginton turned to tell McNeil he'd join him in a little while, and saw Cullen sitting in an armchair near the reception desk. Both windows were open, and he saw him through the right-hand one. That was about thirty yards from where he was standing."

"And Edginton was sure it was him?"

"So he said. Edginton then stayed and took a few more shots, gathered his arrows, and started for the clubhouse. When he got to the main door, he looked in and saw someone lying on the floor with an arrow in his neck. He went along the hall and saw it was Cullen.

"I asked him why he had stayed there, and he said he needed to sit down because he was in shock. There was no one else in the room. I was told later that Huggins had already discovered the body, and informed Mr. Harris before Edginton claims to have seen it. Then one of the staff locked the main door, not realizing that Edginton was in there, as the whole of the reception area isn't visible from the door. It was unlocked when we arrived. McNeil took Edginton to the bar and went behind it and got him a drink. Edginton admitted that plenty of the members had a motive for killing Cullen, but that he was high on the list. He denied being the murderer, but I felt he was uncomfortable because by saying he hadn't done it, he might be incriminating his friend.

"The last to be interviewed was Huggins, the staff member who had found Cullen. He was a virtual giant of a man, and I had to remind myself that the idea that big strong men were lacking in intellect was a dangerous cliche. Huggins's face displayed little emotion, but there was intelligence in those brown eyes.

"He stated that he had been working at the club for seven years. He was a little reluctant at first to give his opinion of Cullen, but when pressed described him as 'a bad'un', and said they should've kicked him out when he tried it on with Sarah – that was the waitress he had insulted – and would have been, if it wasn't for the National Championships and "their precious Olympics". He had joined the rest of the staff when they boycotted Cullen. According to Mr. McNeil, one of the staff was supplying him with drinks in the reception room for an inflated price. I asked Huggins if he had any idea who that might be.

"Huggins squirmed in his chair, a strange movement for so large a man, and admitted that it was him.

"'Money is money, sir,' he said. 'A bit extra always comes in handy. Please don't tell the committee, sir. I won't do it again. I mean, I can't do it again now, can I? Not now he's dead.'

"'All right, we'll pass over that,' I said. 'Just tell me what happened.'

"There wasn't much to tell. Cullen came in and rang the reception bell. Huggins went and answered it, and when Cullen saw it was him, he ordered a drink. Huggins went to get it, and when he came back, there Cullen was, dead, with that arrow sticking out of his neck. Huggins went for Mr. Harris, and the rest is as I have said."

"What do you make of it, then, Hopkins?" Holmes asked.

"Well, sir, it has to be either Edginton or McNeil, doesn't it? Both were excellent with the bow, and both hated Cullen. Ezdginton could have shot him through the open window, and McNeil could have stood at the open door and shot an arrow along the length of the hall into the reception room. It's a question of deciding which one. Edginton seems too nervous and sensitive to have done it, and McNeil seems too amiable – at first glance, anyway. We all know from experience that everyone has hidden depths, and that murder can find a home in what seems the softest of hearts."

"True," I said.

"It doesn't seem premeditated," Hopkins continued. "Edginton could have simply given in to a sudden impulse, and what we saw wasn't simply shock, but genuine remorse, and maybe horror at discovering that he was capable of murder. He doesn't seem the type who can live with guilt for any length of time. As to McNeil, Harris told us that McNeil uncharacteristically threatened Cullen when Cullen insulted Edginton. Was his friendship for Edginton so great that he'd kill to get Cullen off his friend's back?"

"You could look at it from a different angle," I said. "From what you've told us, McNeil and Cullen were polar opposites. They were bound to come into conflict."

"To the point of murder? And again, it seems unpremeditated, so we fall back on the idea that it was the result of a momentary impulse. McNeil saw Cullen, he had the weapons to hand, and *Whoosh!* Cullen's dead. McNeil then acted with fantastic coolness, went to his locker, got changed, and strolled into the restaurant, ordered a meal, and showed no sign of stress when Harris asked him to stay after the club closed."

"While these speculations are interesting, and no doubt of importance," said Holmes, "let us look first at what facts we have. Was the type of the arrow that killed Cullen the same as those used by Edginton or McNeil?"

"That was one of the first things I thought of, Mr. Holmes. Unfortunately, it is of the most common make, which is used by virtually everyone in the club."

"What was the exact position of the body when it was found?"

Hopkins reached into a small briefcase he had brought with him and produced a manila folder.

"These are the photographs of the murder scene, taken by our man, Atkinson. He's very thorough, and took them from every possible point of view."

The pictures showed a tall, dark-haired man of middle height, in his early thirties, dressed in archery gear, on his face on the floor with his head pointing in the direction of the door and the fatal arrow protruding from his neck. His bow and quiver of arrows lay on a chair.

"What do you make of them, Watson?" asked Holmes.

"I'm afraid these give no indication of the direction the arrow came from. As Cardew said, death would have been virtually instantaneous, but that doesn't mean that in his last moment Cullen's body might not have twisted, either in agony or from the force of the blow."

Holmes leafed through the photographs and after a minute or so gave a little smile of triumph.

"Nevertheless, gentlemen, these give us clear pointers as to the identity of the murderer."

"Then who should I arrest – Edginton or McNeil?"

"Neither. Your culprit, Inspector, is Huggins."

"Huggins? But he reported the crime!"

"Of course he reported it. Suspicion would have instantly fallen on him if he hadn't. As an intelligent man, he would have realized that."

"But the murder must have been committed by an archer, and Huggins was a member of the staff, not of the club."

"Really, my friend, you must learn to look at the facts, and not rely upon your assumptions. Just because the man was killed by arrow, that doesn't necessarily mean that it was shot from a bow."

Holmes spread the photographs across the small table around which we were sitting. I picked up each one and scrutinised it, but could find nothing to support Holmes's assertions.

"Our first indication that Huggins was lying can be clearly seen," began Holmes. "Or rather, clearly *not* seen. No?" he continued after a few seconds. "You still don't understand? According to Huggins, Cullen ordered a drink. Huggins went to fetch it, and when he returned, found Cullen dead and instantly went to inform Harris, who had the door closed. Where, then, is the drink? Had Huggins really brought one in, he would have put it down somewhere before going to tell Harris. But it is nowhere to be seen.

"Our second and third points may both be inferred from the arrow wound. Any arrow fired from a bow would have had sufficient force to not merely enter the back of the neck, but to go right through it. Then there is the angle of the wound. Again, if fired from a bow, it would enter at an angle of ninety degrees. The angle here is closer to forty-five degrees, which is consistent with the arrow being stabbed down *into* the neck by someone somewhat taller than the victim, and possessed of considerable strength.

"So, Cullen comes into the reception area, puts his bow and quiver on the nearest chair and rings the reception bell. When Huggins appears, he orders a drink and then turns his back, Huggins takes one of the arrows from the quiver and stabs it downwards into Cullen's neck."

"That's all very neat and logical, Mr. Holmes, but why did Huggins do it? He needed the extra money he made from supplying Cullen with drinks."

"From what you've said, Huggins is a large, powerful man. In my experience, such men may be divided into two broad categories. There are those who use their strength unscrupulously to gain whatever may be achieved by it, and those who have been taught from an early age, usually by their mothers, that their strength must be used carefully and responsibly, particularly where the weak are concerned. As the weaker sex, women are especially to be protected. As a manifestation of this tendency, consider how often one sees large men married to much smaller women.

"Yes, Huggins was dependent on Cullen for extra money. But he was also aware that Cullen had mistreated Sarah, for whom it is possible that Huggins has paternal, or even romantic, feelings. He may have loathed himself for accepting payment from such a man. These passions warred within him until – in one moment – he snapped. Casting self-restraint aside, he seized the nearest weapon to hand and dealt the fatal blow. I also think it entirely possible that had you arrested either Edginton or McNeil, Huggins would have come forward and confessed."

Hopkins stood up.

"Well, I shall certainly arrest him, and we shall see whether your speculations are correct. Thank you, Mr. Holmes. A very nice piece of work."

Huggins was tried at the Old Bailey some weeks later, and Holmes's theories turned out to be true in every particular. Among the witnesses was Sarah Crowden, a petite young woman who testified that she was sure that Huggins was in love with her, but hadn't spoken due to the twenty-five-year difference in age between them.

The jury found Huggins guilty after a very brief consultation, but submitted a recommendation for mercy, the mitigating circumstances being Huggins' previous good character, the bad character of the victim, exemplified by his mistreatment of the girl, and the fact that the act hadn't been premeditated. The judge concurred, and gave Huggins a custodial sentence with the possibility of parole, instead of sending him to the gallows.

The Adventure of the Long Arm

It was, I remember, towards the end of a particularly windy afternoon in late autumn when Holmes received a note from Inspector Lestrade of Scotland Yard. Through the windows of our rooms in Baker Street, one could see the fallen leaves and other items of urban detritus whirling along the darkening thoroughfare, while folk hurried along the pavement, clasping their outer garments to them against the rising cold. For my own part, I would have been perfectly content to remain by our fire, consulting my notebook, and composing the latest addition to my already copious collection of narratives concerning my experiences in the company of my celebrated fellow-lodger. The message from Lestrade, however, specifically requested my presence as well as that of Mr. Sherlock Holmes.

Of late, Holmes had become interested in the history of firearms, and as well as reading as many texts on the subject as he could accumulate. He was also experimenting with gunpowder, mixing it up from charcoal, sulfur, and saltpeter. This didn't make for a particularly pleasing atmosphere, but I was always happy to see him involved in any of his various interests, for while he was concentrated on these pursuits, he was distracted from any lack of cases, and therefore less likely to succumb to the temptation of resorting to any form of chemical stimulus. It was true that he had not used cocaine for many months, but the possibility that he might revert to its consumption was always there, an omnipresent spectre at the feast.

When he had read Lestrade's note, he rose from the seat at the acid-scarred deal table and strode towards the door. He took both our overcoats from their hooks and held mine out at arm's length.

"Come along," he said in a commanding tone. "The good inspector has summoned us both."

I reluctantly set my notebook and pencil to one side and pulled my coat from his bony hand.

"We'll miss dinner," I said somewhat petulantly.

"I'm sure Mrs. Hudson will gladly provide us with something when we return. Who knows – perhaps Lestrade will have a case for us which will be worthy of inclusion in your memoirs. You wouldn't want to miss that on account of your stomach, would you?"

I said nothing, but put on my overcoat with a sigh and followed his lithe figure as he eagerly hurried down the stairs and pulled open the front door. Fortunately we didn't have long to wait before the appearance of an empty hansom for hire.

When we arrived at Scotland Yard, the desk sergeant recognised us and informed us that Inspector Lestrade was waiting down in the police mortuary. We descended a set of metal steps and went along the familiar dingy corridor and through a set of double doors into a large room full of long tables whose walls were covered in cold, pale-green tiles.

A single body lay on one of the tables under a voluminous white sheet. Next to it was the familiar face and wiry little form of the Scotland Yarder.

"Good evening, gentlemen," he said. "I'm glad you could come."

"You've asked us here to look at a body?" I said. "Surely you have your own police surgeons for that."

"Of course, Doctor, and one of them will be taking a look at it. But once you've seen it, you'll understand why I've called on you and Mr. Holmes. But I warn you: It isn't a pretty sight."

"We've both seen plenty of the dead," Holmes remarked. "What makes this one so special?"

"See for yourself," said Lestrade, pulling away the sheet. It was a man's body, naked, though perhaps that was to be expected, given where it was. What was unexpected was that the head, hands, and feet had all been removed. Not only the spirit, or the life force, or whatever name one cared to give to the animating principle, was gone, but so too were the indicators of identity that preserved whatever remained of individuality, of personality, leaving only a slab of meat. It was, as Lestrade had indicated, unsettling.

"The only thing we can be sure of," the policeman said with a wry smile, "is his religion."

"Why, because he's circumcised?" said Holmes. "My dear Lestrade, you should know better than that. More than one religion practices circumcision, though I grant you that the balance of probability is against his being a Muslim. There aren't too many of them in London, and the paleness of his skin means he's less likely to be an Arab. And don't forget, some people have it done to their sons on medical grounds."

Holmes took his magnifying glass from the pocket of his Inverness and bent over to examine the organ in question. "I think he was, indeed, a recent convert to the Jewish religion," he said after a few seconds, straightening up, "and that he was engaged to be married. Do you concur, Watson?" he asked, handing me his glass.

"I agree with the first part," I said, when I had taken a look, "but I don't see how you arrive at the second."

"The scarring has not fully healed, which means the operation was carried out in the last six to eight weeks."

"That much is certainly correct."

"While the surgical process is perfectly safe, it is still not something most adult males would happily undergo. So he had a strong reason for wanting it performed. What is the strongest reason there could be? Love, the most common factor in religious conversions. He met a woman of the Jewish faith, fell in love with her, and demonstrated the seriousness of his intentions, and his conversion, by having his foreskin removed. At the same time, he would not have done so if he was not assured that she returned his feelings. So I infer that they were engaged, shortly before or shortly after."

"Engaged? How do you know he didn't have it done after they were married?" asked Lestrade.

"Intercourse isn't possible until after it's fully healed. Which, as Watson confirmed, takes about six to eight weeks. Now, while most people are prepared to wait out their engagement, few would be ready to go for that amount of time without being able to consummate their marriage."

"That sounds logical enough," said Lestrade.

"It's a working hypothesis, at least," said Holmes. "Was he found like this, without clothes?"

"Yes."

"That deprives us of one set of clues. Where was he found?"

"Morgan Street, a nasty little back-street in Whitechapel. A nine-year-old girl found him early this morning. Scared the living daylights out of her, poor little thing."

"Let us turn to the rest of his body. What do you make of it, Watson?"

The first thing that met my eye was a series of odd circular wounds that were scattered across the chest, belly, and legs of the victim. They could not be accidental. They must be intentional.

"This man has been tortured," I said.

"Burnt with a cigarette or cigar, " said Holmes. "Nothing else would produce such marks. He worked in the open air, either in short sleeves or with long sleeves rolled up. Though the tan has faded a little due to the time of year, it is still visible, extending from just above the elbow down to the wrists. Whatever labour he was engaged in, it was not hard physical labour. The body is generally fit, but the muscles in his arms are not particularly developed. He spent a lot of time kneeling."

Holmes pointed to the slight but noticeable callosities on the knees.

He pulled out his glass once more, this time looking at the neck, wrists, and ankles.

"At least two people carried out the amputations. The cuts that took off the hands and feet are clean, but the incisions on the neck are ragged. All were probably done with a heavy meat cleaver. A strong man might be able to cut through the wrists and ankles with one blow each. A skillful man might need two, but could still do it cleanly. Whoever cut the neck hacked at it with several blows before the head came off. I hope for this poor devil's sake that wasn't what actually killed him. If his head was in proportion to his body, he must have been about five feet six."

"One thing I don't see is why they cut his feet off," said Lestrade. "I mean, the head and hands I can understand, but you can't identify someone by their feet. Unless – unless he had some sort of deformity or birthmark on one of them. But then, why cut off both?"

"Well," said Holmes, "if you only cut off one, you draw attention to the fact that there may have been something distinctive about it. But I'm not entirely convinced that the purpose of the amputations was the concealment of this man's identity. In fact, I believe I can identify him. Has anything struck you, Watson?"

"I cannot say that it has."

"Let me help. Here we have a man who works in the open air, spends time on his knees, and rolls his sleeves up. That suggest that he is, or rather was, a gardener. He was engaged to be married to a Jewish woman . . . ."

I suddenly grasped who Holmes was describing.

"Good God!" I cried. " Luigi Manoli!"

We had first heard the name some two weeks before, when Hannah Goldman called on us one morning at Baker Street.

She was a petite young woman with a pale face, dominated by a pair of large and beautiful brown eyes. Little wisps of dark wavy hair had escaped from the blue silk shawl that covered her head, which was the only spot of colour in her clothes, the rest being plain black and clearly of poor quality.

The morning was chilly, and when Mrs. Hudson saw the young lady's pallor, she insisted on bringing her a hot bowl of beef broth, which Miss Goldman consumed gratefully. When she had set the bowl aside, Holmes inquired how we might be of service.

"It is my fiancé, Luigi Manoli, Mr. Holmes. We are due to be married soon, but he has vanished."

"How long have you known him, Miss Goldman?"

"About ten months. We have been engaged for three. I first met him when he was walking out with my friend, Sarah Wilkins, but when he saw me, and I saw him, there was an instant attraction, and before too long it had deepened into love."

She lowered her eyes and added, "The first love I have known."

Holmes pressed his hands together before him and said, "And how did Sarah Wilkins react to this development?"

"She was happy for me, happy for both of us. She liked Luigi, of course, but she had not been serious about him. She is my friend. She would not steal him from me, if that is what you were thinking."

As she spoke these words, I saw a hint of a fiery spirit within that slender body and behind that pale face.

"Are there any other young women in his life?"

"No. I have already said – He loves me."

"Then tell us about Luigi," said Holmes. "Does he have any enemies?"

"No, no. He is a good man, a gentle man. He is a gardener for the City of London, he loves to plant things, to watch them grow. He has no hatred in his heart for anyone."

"Was he born in London?"

"No, he came on the boat from Italy, about five years ago."

"From where in Italy, exactly?"

"I don't know. I have never asked. He has never told me anything about his life before he came to England."

"Are you not at least curious?" I interjected.

"Yes, but I am also in love. I know all I need to know – that he is a good man, that he truly loves me, and I him. If he wanted to tell me about his former life, I would listen, but if he does not want to, I will not pry."

Holmes stood.

"Miss Goldman, I am not without sympathy for your plight, but there is little I can do without more data. Do you have a photograph of your fiancée?"

"Yes, yes."

She reached into the pocket of her coat and pulled out a picture.

"Then I suggest you take it to Scotland Yard, or the police station nearest Mr. Manoli's residence, and ask them to deal with the matter."

Hannah Goldman pushed herself up from her chair and said, "So, I will get no help from the great Mr. Sherlock Holmes! I was told that you were willing to help poor people who came to you with their troubles, but it seems that is wrong."

Holmes remained calm.

"I assure you, Miss Goldman, that the wealth or poverty of those who come to consult me is of no importance. It is simply that in your particular case, there is little I can do on the basis of the information you have given me. In such a matter, the official force has more resources than I do. However, I will make a promise: If you leave your address, then should I gain any information at all about your fiancé, I will inform you of the fact. That really is, at the moment, the best I can do."

"Luigi Manoli!" echoed Lestrade. "I remember the name. He's on the missing list. His fiancée came and reported it. Rather pretty, she was. What was her name?"

"Hannah Goldman," I answered. "And yes, she's pretty. Beautiful, even."

I had seen the address on the piece of paper the young woman had handed Holmes. Like Morgan Street where the body was discovered, it was one of the poorest in the East End. If that was all she could afford, then she was doubtless working in one of the worst-paid jobs – as a match girl, perhaps, or as a seamstress in a garment factory. How long would that prettiness, and that spirit, survive the long hours of hard work, the years of poverty, and the childbearing that probably lay in her future? Childbearing, if – when she had recovered from the grief of losing Manoli – she was lucky enough to find another man who loved her. But of that, there could be no guarantee. Two lines from Chaucer floated into my mind:

O scatheful harm, condition of poverty,
With thirst, with cold, with hunger so confounded.

"Well," Lestrade was saying, "she must be told, though it's a task anyone on the Force would avoid if he could. Although thinking about it, we can't, in the absence of clear identifying factors, be one-hundred-per-cent sure that this is Manoli's body, can we?"

"I agree that the evidence isn't conclusive," said Holmes, "but the overwhelming probability is that the body is Manoli's. If it is not, and there is an innocent reason for Manoli's absence, he will return, and in her joy Miss Goldman will forgive the police for any grief you have brought her. If he is still alive, and has vanished because he's with another woman, or has fled after committing a crime, then she is well rid of him, and it is better that she thinks him dead."

"That's certainly one way of looking at it, I suppose," agreed Lestrade. "Well, thank you for coming, Mr. Holmes, Dr. Watson."

"Send us a copy of the Police Surgeon's report."

"Certainly. Good evening, gentlemen."

The solemnity of the experience had made me forget the state of my appetite, but, as Holmes had predicted, when we returned to Baker Street, Mrs. Hudson had already begun heating up some food in anticipation of our arrival. I gladly fell to it, but Holmes sat with his plate untouched, a faraway look in his keen grey eyes. He remained silent for the next two hours, and I went to bed, leaving him in his accustomed armchair with the smoke from his pipe curling above his head.

As Lestrade had promised, we received a copy of the medical report the following day. In a note at the bottom of the final page, the inspector added that no one else on the list of missing person resembled the description of the body, and he was therefore convinced that it must be Manoli.

The Police Surgeon confirmed that the amount of blood remaining in the body meant that the amputations had been carried out after death. Neither the contents of the stomach nor the blood contained any trace of poison. The surgeon concluded that death might have been caused by strangulation, whether by hand or by ligature, or the throat slit. The ragged state of the neck wounds would serve to conceal either of those methods. Another likely possibility was that the victim had died from a blow to the head.

Holmes summoned Billy, scribbled something on a page torn from one of his notebooks, and told the lad to take it to Scotland Yard. The boy returned in about three-quarters-of-an-hour with another piece of paper on which was written: "*No. 8*".

"*No. 8*?"

"The number of the house in Morgan Street in front of which the little girl found Manoli's corpse. That, Watson, is where we are going this evening. I trust that your old army revolver is in good working order."

"You saw me clean it only the other day."

"So I did. Well, need I add, load it and bring it with you tonight."

With that old familiar thrill of adventure coursing through my being, I joined Holmes as he summoned a cab. When were inside, he yelled to the driver, "Aldgate!"

I gave him a puzzled look.

“Aldgate? But Morgan Street is in Whitechapel, so why Aldgate?”

“As you know, my friend, I keep several rented rooms throughout the metropolis in which I can change both my clothes and my appearance. I keep one in Aldgate because, while it is close enough to the East End to be accessible on foot, it is also too far from there for any of the East End’s denizens to see me enter as my own self and leave as someone else. Believe me, if someone suspected that Sherlock Holmes was walking the streets of Whitechapel, and saw me depart in my disguise, my life would not have an hour’s purchase.”

“But I am with you, and while I’m not as easily recognized as you, it will surely give the game away if I’m at your side.”

Holmes gave a little chuckle.

“Really, Watson! What would you suggest?”

“You mean, I am also to be in disguise? But I have no talent for such play-acting. And – you don’t intend to have me shave off my moustache?”

“Certainly not. From the many times you have seen me in the guise of someone else, you must have realised that a mere change of clothing is often enough.”

“Well, perhaps, but I still say that to be truly effective, the man in disguise must be something of an actor.”

“All you need do is remain silent, and leave any talking that may need to be done to me.”

Never before had I been in one of Holmes’s secret rooms, so I was full of curiosity when we entered an unprepossessing building a street away from the Aldgate pump. Some of the windows were boarded over, and the paint of the front door was almost completely peeled away. Holmes took out a key and turned it in the lock, and as we entered the small hallway, I noticed a distinct, musty smell in the air. As we climbed the somewhat rickety stairs, I saw no sign that the place had any other inhabitants. Whoever owned it was probably glad that there was someone paying some rent, and Holmes was no doubt handing over more than the market price, which would not be difficult. We entered a room on the first floor. Holmes lit a gas lamp, illuminating a chamber that was purely functional, with no sign of any creature comforts. There was a bed, and if for any reason Holmes had to spend a night there, it would just about accommodate his long frame.

Holmes opened a large mahogany wardrobe. Inside was a variety of clothes, hats, and shoes, and on the floor of the cabinet there was a large wooden box full of wigs, false moustaches, and beards, and other less-immediately recognisable elements of disguise.

"We'll set you up first," said Holmes with a smile, and pulled out an off-white shirt that had seen better days, a thoroughly disreputable topcoat, dingy and threadbare, and a pair of brown trousers that were visibly thin at the knee. I divested myself of my respectable outfit and donned those uninviting garments, hoping as I did so that none of them were inhabited by fleas.

"Try on some of the shoes, " said Holmes, as began removing his own clothes. "There should be a pair there that will fit you."

At last, we stood facing each other. Holmes was clad in an old sailor's jacket, a pair of faded khaki trousers that must once have belonged to a soldier, and a collarless undershirt. He put a grubby knee-length coat over this ensemble and regarded me.

"You look splendid, Watson."

There was no mirror for me to look at myself in, but I strongly doubted that "splendid" was the *mot juste* for my appearance.

"Now, we just need a few finishing touches."

He rammed a dark curly wig on my head, then glued a pair of side-whiskers to his face and took out two hats, one a dusty bowler which he placed on his own head, the other, a battered cap, he handed to me.

"Left!" cried Holmes when we were once more out in the street. The weather was still somewhat chilly, though the wind had died down. I have never been a frequenter of the East End, and I was worried at first that Holmes had overdone our disguises. But as we made our way through Shoreditch and into Whitechapel, I became aware that many of the passers-by were dressed in clothes that were easily as down-at-heel and mismatched as those we were wearing. Nevertheless, I was happy that I could feel the weight of my old army revolver in the pocket of my shabby coat.

After about twenty minutes' walk we reached our destination in Morgan Street. It was an ill-lit, narrow street along which stretched a line of houses which were, by the area's standards, in reasonably good condition, but were identically dull and monotonous, built merely for use and function. Unlike the main streets along which we had passed, which were full of pedestrians in the middle of the evening, in this back alley there was no one to be seen.

"Now," said Holmes," we need to speak to the inhabitant of No. 8, but I rather suspect he will not open the door to us, not even a crack to see who we are."

"Why not?"

"Because he is in fear for his life. Unless I am much mistaken, he is a fugitive from his own land, and his whereabouts have been the subject of speculation in the European press.'"

"What should we do, then?"

"Observe, Watson, that there is only one light burning in the whole house, on the first floor. That must be where he is. Now, we shall go around to the back of the house, climb over the wall that runs along all the yards in the street, and effect an entry on the ground floor."

So once more, we were breaking the law. I had to trust, from my past experiences with Holmes, that this departure from the straight-and-narrow would have an outcome that would justify our transgression.

Within minutes we were over the wall and standing before a ground floor window. From his shabby coat, my companion drew his glass-cutter and removed a half-circle from the window, next to the handle, then reached inside and turned it. As silently as we could, we crept through the house and up the stairs, and along a short corridor until we saw a light under one of the doors.

Holmes signalled that I should stand by the wall on the right of the door, while he took the left side.

"Count Ridolfi!" he cried. "We have come to help you!"

"So you come for me at last!" came the answer in perfect English, spoken with a recognisably Italian accent. Then there were two loud bursts of gunfire, and the air sang with shattered shards of wood as two bullets ripped through the wooden door.

"I am Sherlock Holmes, and you have surely heard of me. My friend, Doctor Watson, and I mean you no harm. Please allow us to come in."

He pulled off the false side-whiskers and gestured that I should remove the dark curly wig.

"Yes, I have heard of Holmes, but how do I know you are truly he?" the Count responded.

"Have you seen my picture?"

"Yes, but that means nothing."

"Let me open the door."

"Very well, but I warn you, if you or your friend make one false move, I will shoot you without mercy."

Holmes opened the door to reveal a man of about sixty, seated in an old wooden chair, his long legs stretched out before him. His whitening hair was brushed back from his broad, intellectual forehead, and his blue eyes, filled with suspicion, were nevertheless clear and bright. But his complexion was pallid, and his face bore clear signs of illness or stress.

"Are you armed?" he demanded. "Tell me the truth, and remember: There are still four bullets in my revolver."

"Yes," said Holmes.

"Then take out your guns, slowly, and drop them on the floor."

We complied.

Count Ridolfi's weapon remained trained on us.

"Now", he said. "Prove you are who you say you are."

"You are Count Giuseppe Ridolfi, former governor of the Italian province of Frascillata. You are a just and honourable man, and you ruled that backward part of the country as well as any man has. But your justice, and your fair dealings, made you a target for the *Vecchia Fratellanza* – in English, 'The Old Brotherhood'."

"Who are they?" I could not help asking.

"Well, Dr. Watson – if that is truly who you are – you have no doubt heard of the *Mafia*, from Sicily – "

"Yes."

" – and perhaps even the *Ndrangheta* of Calabria, and the *Camorra* of Naples."

"No, never."

"The southern part of Italy, along with the island of Sicily, has a long history of brigandage, of secret societies and social unrest. It is not surprising. It is a poor, agricultural area, and its economic weakness and political instability have often been exploited, both by foreign states and by the rest of the country. It is entirely understandable that in the past, before the unification, poor men banded together in their own interest, and that, when they had no access to justice and the law was loaded against them, they broke the law in the cause of justice. That they came together in secrecy, swore oaths of allegiance, and brought vengeance down on those who betrayed them. Inevitably, the original ideals gradually fell away and were replaced by the baser desires of tyranny and greed. And so it was with the *Vecchia Fratellanza*."

"And now," said Holmes, "you are threatened by the *Bracchio Lungo* – 'The Long Arm' – an elite band of assassins, chosen by the council of the Old Brotherhood for their skill in murder. Have you ever known them to employ Englishmen to carry out their work?"

"No, they would never do that. It would be a slur on what they are pleased to call their "honour". Very well, I shall trust you, and I hope it is not the last decision I make in my life."

He laid the revolver in his lap.

"Tell me, Mr. Holmes, how you came to know of this."

"A man was found outside this house. His head, his hands, and his feet had been cut off. Now, although my dealings with them have been few, I have made a study of the practices of these secret societies. I recognised the condition of the dead as a kind of message – a warning to a man pursued by the *Bracchio Lungo* that they know where he is and will soon wreak vengeance on him."

"And this is how they carry out the sentence," said Ridolfi. "The victim is held down and his head beaten to a bloody pulp. Then the head is cut off, along with the hands and feet. The purpose of these mutilations is to send a message – that he who betrays the brotherhood, or leaves it, or stands in its way, is not merely dead, but stripped of all identity, as if he never was. These animals call themselves *Christians*, but this is part of an ancient belief, from centuries before the word of God came to Italy, that if any part of a man's body cannot be found when he is buried, then he cannot attain the afterlife."

"The man who was murdered was Luigi Manoli," I said. "Did you know him?"

The Count passed one of his slender hands before his eyes.

"Mio Dio!" he exclaimed. *"Manoli!"*

"Who was he?"

"His father was high up in the Brotherhood, but his mother left him shortly after Luigi was born, and, repelled by his ways, took the boy to the far north of Italy, where she hoped to raise him free from his father's influence. But the older Manoli set the Long Arm upon her, and though it took them seven years, eventually they found Luigi and his mother in the small village near Lake Maggiore, where they had taken refuge. The mother was murdered while the boy was sleeping, and they took him back to Frascillata and handed him over to his father.

"As the son of a member of the high council, he might have risen high in the Brotherhood, but his mother, though long dead, had done her work well, and at the age of twenty he came to me and gave me all the information he thought I needed to bring down the Brotherhood. Though we were able to eliminate many of their cells, it became clear that we had not succeeded in wiping them out completely. It was then that I realised that Luigi was in great danger, and I had him carefully guarded until I could send him to England, where I believed he would be safe."

He cast down his eyes and murmured, "But I see I was wrong. The Long Arm pursued him, even as it pursues me."

He looked up.

"Do you know what some call me in *Frascillata*? They call me *Guiseppe Fortunato* – 'Lucky Giuseppe' – because I survived four of the Brotherhood's assassination attempts."

He smiled bitterly.

"In the first of those attempts, my son died from a bullet that was aimed at me, and in the third my wife was killed by a bomb they planted on our *terrazza*. How then, am I 'Lucky Giuseppe'? It is true, I escaped to London. I changed my appearance, shaving off my beard and moustache. My English is good enough to get by, but I have kept myself to myself and been as inconspicuous as I could. But still they have found me, and I ask myself: What do I have to live for, now that I have lost my family? The only answer I have is that when they finally come for me, I will take as many of them with me as I can."

I was dumbstruck by the sheer tragedy of this narration, but Holmes, as usual, was all business.

"Count Ridolfi, we are here because I know from my studies that the dumping of Manoli's body on your doorstep means that you have three days grace before they come for you. That is why we are here: To stand with you when that moment comes. Are you with me, Watson?"

Stirred as I was by the old count's story, and knowing that I would never leave Holmes's side when he was in danger, I could only answer, "Yes."

"Please leave, gentlemen. I cannot ask you to die on my behalf."

"They will not be expecting three of us to be here instead of only one", said Holmes. "That will give us an advantage."

"They usually operate in cells of six," said the Count, "so they will outnumber us two to one."

"I would also suggest that you turn off the gas light and burn a single candle, so that it will not be so obvious, at least from the street, which room we are occupying."

This was not the first time I had sat in a darkened room with Holmes, my revolver in my hand, awaiting the arrival of a man of violence. Or *men* of violence, in this case.

The crisis came in the early hours of the morning, when the sky was at its darkest and the world at its stillest. All sensible men were long abed. I counted myself a sensible man, yet here I was, awake, with every fibre of my being taut with anticipation of the conflict to come.

From the floor below us we heard the sound of a window being smashed.

"Their entry was somewhat less subtle than yours," the Count said wryly.

There came the sound of doors being slammed one by one, and I realised that the assassins were checking each room. My grip tightened on my revolver as I heard them climbing the stairs. Again, we heard them opening and closing doors, until I realised that the room in which we sat was the only one remaining unchecked. There was no light in the corridor, or they might have noticed the bullet holes in the door. They must have realised that they had reached their goal, but instead of them bursting into the room, guns blazing, there came through the door the sound of low muttering, too low for even the Italian count to make out what they were saying. For long moments nothing happened, and then, finally, the door was kicked open and by the flickering light of the candle I saw three of the ruffians enter.

Holmes and the Count instantly fired, taking two of them down, but I was distracted by a movement at the window. I whirled and saw the other three men in the act of raising their guns to fire at us through the pane. They must have brought some kind of ladder with them. Two bullets whizzed past either side of my head, but I stood my ground and fired off four rounds in rapid succession. I had clearly hit at least one of them, for he fell back with a cry, knocking one of his fellows down to the ground beside him. The last, taking in the situation at a glance, fired off a shot at the Count, who gave a sharp cry as the bullet penetrated his shoulder and fell to the floor.

I discharged my remaining two rounds at the assassin and was gladdened to see him fall back as had his fellows. I then turned to see to the Count. Holmes was on the floor, struggling with the last man, whom he had somehow managed to disarm in the dim light, but they were now fighting for the possession of Holmes's firearm. I turned away from the Count and, seizing my revolver by its barrel, brought the heavy handle down on the would-be assassin's head, knocking him instantly unconscious.

Holmes scrambled to his feet.

"Once more, Watson, I owe you my life."

Holmes's praise was always welcome to me, but at that moment I had more important considerations on my mind.

As he grimaced in pain, I removed the Count's jacket and ripped open his shirt to examine the wound he had sustained. It was serious, but not fatal. The bullet had come out through his upper back, so there was much blood, but less danger of infection. I went down to the kitchen and boiled a kettle of water. In the bathroom I found an old but clean sheet which I ripped into strips. Entering the room once more, I cleaned the wound and bandaged it as best I could.

"You're wasting your time, Doctor, " the Count croaked. "In the end, they got what they wanted. I am dying."

“Nonsense”, I retorted. “You’ll be in the hospital for some time, true, but there’s no reason why you shouldn’t recover. You’ll have a nasty pair of scars – but that’s better than the alternative. I’ll send Holmes for an ambulance.”

I looked around. The man whose head I had cracked was nowhere to be seen – and where was my fellow lodger?

I later learned that while I had been preparing my makeshift bandages, Holmes had dragged his unconscious assailant down to the ground floor and bound his arms and legs with the sashes of the broken window. He then went into the street and ascertained that all three of the assassins who had climbed to the window were dead, two killed by gunshot and the other by a broken neck, sustained in his fall. The other two men who had come in by the door were likewise gone to meet their maker.

The gunshots had finally aroused the attention of the local constable on his beat, who blew his whistle to summon his nearest colleagues. They were, Holmes told me, at first reluctant to believe that this shabbily-dressed figure could be the renowned detective, but then a policeman with whom he had previously worked arrived on the scene and confirmed his identity. The surviving member of the Long Arm was bundled onto a police cart, and an ambulance summoned.

I have said before that often, when he had come to the conclusion of a demanding case, Holmes might be limp and listless, perhaps staying in his bed for several days. I must say that after the case of the Long Arm I had a somewhat similar reaction. I hadn’t seen so much action in many years, nor did I take it lightly that I was responsible for the deaths of three men, however much they may have deserved to die. So it wasn’t until some days later that I was ready to discuss it with Holmes.

I need not end this chronicle on such a sad note, for there was at least something of a happy ending. I never learned what became of Hannah Goldman, but Count Ridolfi made a full recovery and returned at last to his native land. Holmes's brother Mycroft had a word in the ear of a certain Gracious Lady, who communicated with her fellow-monarch, King Umberto I of Italy, to suggest that in consideration of his sterling work as Governor of Frascillata, Count Ridolfi should be given a pension and a suite of rooms in the palace, where the Royal Guard would keep him safe from any more attempts on his life.

The Adventure of the Rainsford Inheritance

During my long acquaintance with the world's first consulting detective, Mr. Sherlock Holmes, we encountered a wide variety of both clients and criminals. Sometimes Holmes was able to anticipate and prevent the commission of a crime, while in other instances it fell to us to ensure that the perpetrators of such misdeeds did not escape the consequences of their actions. We saw human nature at its worst, and at its best. The results of our efforts might be the prevention of an international catastrophe, or merely the survival or happiness of one or two individuals. Some cases – most of which, I confess, I have refrained from laying before the general public – revolved around murders of a particularly gruesome kind, but at the other end of the spectrum there were cases which, though they presented Holmes with an opportunity to exercise his powers, provided us with a welcome respite from the darker kind.

One such exploit was the matter of the Rainsford Inheritance, and while the happiness of a young woman depended upon its successful solution, I am sure my readers will concur that it is, in essence, a light-hearted tale.

It was a fine spring afternoon in early May. The sun was pouring through the windows of our sitting room, and we had just finished one of Mrs. Hudson's fine lunches. I sat back in my usual chair and smoked a post-prandial cigar. Holmes had concluded a difficult and important case, the affair of the Balkan Miniatures, only the day before, and I had expected to see little or nothing of him until the following day, for on many such occasions he took to his bed in a state of nervous and physical exhaustion and remained there for long hours. It seemed, however, that the freshness and beauty of the morning had had the effect of invigorating him, for he joined me at breakfast in a cheery mood, then spent some time on a chemical experiment which, so far as I knew, had no connection with any criminal investigation he might be conducting. He then turned to answering some correspondence, which couldn't have been urgent as he waited until Mrs. Hudson brought up our midday meal before he handed the replies over to her to post. Knowing his mercurial nature, I had no idea how long this congeniality would last, or how long it would be before he demanded an intellectual challenge to prevent him from sliding into the slough of despondency.

Fortunately for my nerves, the question did not arise. About an hour after lunch, our doorbell rang, and shortly thereafter Mrs. Hudson showed a young woman of about twenty-two into our quarters. I stood up when the lady entered the room, and though I am only average height, the top of her head barely came up to the level of my shoulders. This, combined with her pale face, delicate features, and light blue eyes, and the neatness and simplicity of her attire, an ensemble of light green satin, gave the impression of a figurine of Dresden china come to life.

"Good afternoon, gentlemen," she said. "Which of you is Mr. Holmes?"

"I am Sherlock Holmes, and this – "

"Must be Dr. Watson."

"Your servant, Madam."

"Pray take a seat," said Holmes. "And you are?"

"My name is Anna Wheatley," she replied. "I hope that you will not find my problem too obvious or trivial to be of interest. I can, of course, recompense you for your time and trouble."

"That is something we may discuss later, though I perceive that money is in some manner at the heart of the question you intend to put in our hands."

Miss Wheatley lowered her eyes and a blush suffused her face.

"You are correct," she said, "though I cannot see how you could know it."

"Your outfit was fashionable two years ago, but it has gone out of style since then. The seam of the right sleeve has been resewn at least twice, probably by yourself, since the mends are visible. Moreover, the dress shows signs of having been taken in. Since your form is slim, I can only assume that this weight loss is attributable to a long-standing worry. And your hands," Holmes concluded, reaching over and gently turning one of them, "show signs that you have been doing work to which they aren't accustomed."

It being spring, Miss Wheatley wasn't wearing gloves, and I saw that her palms were red, and that in places the top layer of skin had been rubbed away.

"It's true," she said. "I had hoped that I could present you with this problem without revealing the reason why I need the matter solved so urgently, but I see that nothing can be hidden from you. Very well, I shall give you the whole story."

"That would be the best course of action," I interjected soothingly.

"Since my mother died some years ago, my father, John Wheatley, has spiraled deeper and deeper into despair. His business – he inherited a bicycle factory from my grandfather – was making less and less with the decreasing amount of attention he paid to it, until I finally convinced him to sell it while there were still buyers who would give him a reasonable price. When the money from the sale came into his hands, he didn't invest it sensibly, as I suggested, but tried to increase it by gambling, for which he has no aptitude. He then turned to drink. Eventually I was forced to give the servants notice and take on the entire responsibility for the maintenance of the household. Now there has come a ray of hope, a light at the end of the tunnel, but a curious condition is attached to it."

"Ah," said Holmes.

"I had an uncle named Alistair Rainsford, my mother's older brother, Rainsford being her maiden name. I was very fond of him, and spent a lot of time with him as a child. I hadn't seen him for some years, as there seems to have been some quarrel between him and my father at some point. Uncle Alistair made some very successful investments and became a wealthy man, but my father would never have gone to him for help. Uncle Alistair was, to say the least, somewhat eccentric."

"You speak of him in the past tense," said Holmes. "I take it he has passed away."

"Yes, a couple of weeks ago. Shortly after he died, I received a letter from his lawyers informing me that as his only living relative, I was the sole beneficiary of his will, but there was a strange condition attached to it. He had hidden the will somewhere in his house – not even his lawyers know where – and that, in order to benefit from it, I had to find it. I'm not allowed to go in there and search thoroughly everywhere in the hope that I might discover it. No, I must work out exactly where it is, and then be able to go straight there and retrieve it. Accompanying the letter was a sheet of paper which is meant to help me find it – but of course, Uncle Alastair put it in code. I recall from my childhood that he was very fond of such tricks."

She reached into her reticule and pulled out a page covered with typed numbers and spaces.

"You said you were very fond of your uncle. Was the feeling mutual?"

"Oh, certainly. I spent a lot of time with him when my father was away on business. Why do you ask?"

"It means that he wanted you to find the answer. It isn't insoluble. He isn't torturing you. Rather, he is playing a game with you from beyond the grave." Miss Wheatley gave a rueful little smile.

"He loved playing all sorts of games during his lifetime, Mr. Holmes. In fact, he tried to teach me a little about codes, but I wasn't old enough to understand any but the most simple."

"Was your uncle married?"

"No, he was a lifelong bachelor."

"Did he have any romantic attachments of any kind?"

"I believe he was engaged to a girl called Claire as a young man, but she died of pneumonia before they could marry. I expect that's why he remained single. I'm afraid I can't recall her surname."

"Did he have a dog or a cat?"

"He had a dog at one stage."

"Its name?"

"Piper, I believe."

"One last question: Was any time limit placed on the solution? Must you find the will before a particular date?"

"No, Mr. Holmes, but you can surely tell from my story that I should like to have the answer as soon as possible, to save my father and myself from ruin."

"Of course. I have many calls on my time, but I assure you that I shall spend my every free moment on the solution. If you care to leave your card, I will send you a telegram when I have found it."

"Thank you, Mr. Holmes. I place my future in your hands."

“Well, Watson,” said Holmes when Mrs. Hudson had closed the front door behind our visitor, “while I have no doubt that that young woman’s plight has touched that chivalrous heart of yours, I fear that you can be of little help. A case for pure cerebration.”

“I should still like to know how you arrived at the solution, when you do.”

“Of course, old friend. Now, it is still early, and there may yet be another client to call on us with a more urgent case, but unless and until that happens, I shall concentrate on Miss Wheatley’s problem.”

I went over to that small section of our shelves that contained my books and selected a collection of the short stories of Guy de Maupassant. Then I poured myself a whisky, lit another cigar, and settled into my chair to read while Holmes worked on the code. I looked across at him twice where he sat at his desk: First when he lit a match and ran the flame under the page, and then when he took out several sheets of paper and began to cut them up along some folds he had made in them. Otherwise, I remained wholly absorbed in the French writer’s celebrated *Boule de Suif.*

No other client arrived to distract Holmes from his labours, and it was about an hour before our evening meal was due that the detective leaned back in his chair and gave a sigh of pleasure.

I looked up from my book.

“You have the solution, then.”

“Yes, I have the solution.”

“Well, what is it?”

“Patience, old friend, patience. You did say, did you not, that you wished to know how I arrived at it? I have been careful to keep a record of every step of the process. Let us see how long it takes you to come to the same conclusion. Here is the page with the code. Does anything strike you about the numbers?"

I took the paper from him and looked at it for a few moments.

24	14	25		11	9	11		5	20	
20	9	5		18	5	19		9	8	
24	8	19		5	1		8	9	23	
14	9	7	19	23	18		20	11		
9	9		19	9		5	20		2	14
14	6	14		4	5	7		5	9	
15	1		15	25	14	25	1	2		
5	8	22		15	20	1		20	16	

"The highest number here is twenty-five."

"What does that suggest to you?"

I thought for a second.

"The alphabet!"

"The alphabet. It was in any case hard to see what else it could be if any message was to be conveyed. So I replaced the numbers with letters, being careful to retain the original spacing, and this was the result."

He picked up another sheet of paper.

"One second, Holmes. Before we leave the original page – why did you run the flame of a match underneath it?"

"I was trying to ascertain the meaning of the irregular spacing, and it struck me that there might be invisible writing in the spaces."

"Invisible writing?"

"Yes. Lemon juice is the most commonly used, though there are other liquids that will serve the same turn. If you apply heat to it, it turns brown and can be easily read. But there was no invisible writing in the spaces."

I took the second sheet from him.

X	N	Y		L	I	L		E	T	
T	I	E		R	E	S		I	H	
X	H	S		E	A		H	I	W	
N	I	G	S	W	R		T	L		
I	I		S	I		E	T		B	N
N	F	N		D	E	G		E	I	
O	A		O	Y	N	Y	A	B		
E	H	V		E	T	A		T	P	

Recalling the tragic affair of the Dancing Men, I began to count the number of times each letter occurred in the hope of determining which stood for *E*, *T*, and *A*, but Holmes divined what I was at and shook his head.

"This is too short an example – only sixty-four letters – for us to be sure of any letters other than *E*, and if you continue to count, you will see that *E* is itself the most frequently occurring letter, which tells against the idea that it is a simple substitution code of the kind Abe Slaney used to persecute the unfortunate Mrs. Cubitt."

"Why did you ask Miss Wheatley about Rainsford's fiancée? And his dog?"

"Because I thought at first that what we might have here was encoded by the use of what is sometimes called a *keyword*, and sometimes a *headword*. It is quite common when using this method for the compiler to use a familiar name or word as the keyword. If the word used was picked at random, or had a significance unknown to Miss Wheatley, then decipherment would be impossible. For reasons I shall demonstrate, the key word cannot contain any repeated letters. *Claire* does not, but given her tragic loss to illness, I thought it unlikely that Rainsford would use it in a frivolous manner. So I asked about the dog, but of course, the name *Piper* contains the letter *P* twice. Now, I anticipated that you would ask this question, so I have prepared an example. You will recall that, during the last round of Fenian attacks on the capital, Scotland Yard asked for my assistance in decoding some secret messages that passed between the conspirators. At one point, the Yard had a coded letter they found in the house of one suspect, and a short message which merely read, *Brighton-on-Sea*."

"But no one ever calls it that," I objected.

"No indeed, and for that reason, and the fact that the seaside town was never the victim of an attack, I was led to the conclusion that it was the key to the decipherment of the letter. *Brighton-on-Sea*, the word, was really *Brighton on C*, the letter, and so I was able to compile this."

He handed me another paper, on which was written:

B R I G H T O N A C D E F J K L M P Q S U V W X Y Z
C D E F G H I J K L M N O P Q R S T U V W X Y Z A B

"And of the basis of this, you were able to prevent further atrocities and send an entire chapter of the organization to prison or the gallows."

"Just so. However, as I said, I came to the conclusion that it was not a substitution code of any kind. I wrestled with the significance of the spacing, and while I am one-hundred-percent sure that I have deciphered the message correctly, I confess that I am still unsure why it is laid out in that manner. In any event, after toying briefly with several other methods, I sat back and took a few moments to see if I could think of another way of tackling the problem. I hit on the possibility that rather than being encoded, the entire message was an anagram. A complex one, granted, but I was convinced that it was soluble by the application of logic, and so it proved to be. You saw me fold several pieces of paper and cut them into smaller pieces. One, in fact, for each of the sixty-four letters on the page. When I had finished the laborious task of writing a letter on each of the pieces, I considered the rest of the information the young lady had given us.

"If the will were hidden somewhere in the house, then the obvious thing to do was to see if the names of individual rooms were obtainable from the letters. Fortunately, the letters did not contain the word *room* itself, which enabled me to discard *bedroom*, *bathroom*, *dining room*, *living room*, *box room*, *spare room*, and so on. Three words which were obtainable were *hall*, *pantry*, and *library*. Of these three, I considered that the library was the most likely and decided to proceed on that supposition. So I took out the letters for *library*. I considered it likely that the message also contained the words, *the will* so I discarded the letters of those words as well, This left me with:

X N Y I T I E E S I H X S E H N I G S W T I S I E T N N F N D E G E I O A O Y N A B E H V E T A T P

"I mentally reviewed a list of words appertaining to the contents of libraries. I could not get the word *book*, as there was no *K*, but the word *page* was there, so perhaps the will was stuck to a particular page in a particular book. If that were so, the name of the book would be there too, but obviously, that would come near the end, because at this point it would be impossible to deduce it. I removed the word *page*, so what remained was:

X N Y I T I E E S I H X S H N I S W T I S I E T N N F N D E G E I O A O Y N A B E H V E T T

"I been worried about those *X*'s, but now I realized that if I had *page*, then it had to have a number, which might be six, sixteen or sixty, or sixty-something. Sixty-six would use both *X*'s. Then it occurred to me that if someone respected books enough to have a library, they were unlikely to paste anything to the page of a book, because its removal could damage the book. But they might put it between two pages, and I had the word *between*, so I took it out.

X N Y I T I S I H X S H N I S T I S I E T N F N D E G E I O A O Y N A H V E T

"Now I needed two consecutive numbers. I could get *five* and *six*, *six* and *seven*, *seven* and *eight*, *eight* and *nine*, and *nine* and *ten*, but I thought the other *X* was probably part of a number, too. I had two *Y*'s, so I took *sixty* out twice. Then I realised that I needed *pages*, instead of *page*. I had to take another *S* out.

"I could make *sixty-seven* and *sixty-eight*, or *sixty-eight* and *sixty-nine*, but I had no basis upon to decide which, so I went back and looked over what I had already done. Assuming Rainsford had made a grammatical sentence, which as a literate person I imagined he had, I would need a *the* before the word *library*, and *and* between the two numbers, whatever they were. Out they came.

N I H N I I S I N F N E G E I O A O H V E T

"That was of no immediate help, because I could still make *seven*, *eight*, and *nine*. Then I thought, there is a strong possibility that we need the word *is*. *The will is*. I couldn't do anything like *the will can be found*, or *the will has been hidden*. If I used *is*, then the number couldn't contain *seven*, because there was only one *S*. I took out *is*, *eight*, and *nine*. And of course, you will understand, that for the will to be between them, the first number must be even and the second odd. That left:

N I H I F N O A O V E

"I was beginning to have my suspicions about the name of the book, and when I took it out I was left with *of* and *in* which confirmed that my deduction was correct. Perhaps you would care to see if you can work it out for yourself."

And he handed me another paper on which was written:

H I N A O V E

"All one word?"

"All one word."

I gazed at it, prepared to be baffled as I so often was by Holmes's feats of intellect, but then I suddenly saw what it must be, and said, with a laugh of triumph, "*Ivanhoe*!"

"Yes, Watson – *Ivanhoe*. Now I had all the pieces before me, and all that remained was to arrange them into a coherent sentence."

And he passed me one final piece of paper, on which I read:

THE WILL IS IN THE LIBRARY BETWEEN PAGES SIXTY-EIGHT AND SIXTY-NINE OF IVANHOE

"Bravo!" I cried.

"Thank you, Watson. And now it only remains to inform Miss Wheatley of her good fortune. But that, I fear, must wait until the morning – ” He glanced over at the clock upon the mantelpiece. “ – as it is too late to send a telegram now. Pray ring for Mrs. Hudson, and see if dinner is ready, as I find I suddenly have quite an appetite.”

After we had finished our dinner – veal and ham pie with haricot beans and glazed carrots, followed by apple pie and custard, all washed down with a fine claret – I picked up the second piece of paper to see if I could find any reason for the inclusion of the odd spaces which had defeated even Holmes. On a whim I took a pencil and drew the following diagram in my notebook, eliminating the spaces altogether:

X	N	Y	L	I	L	E	T
T	I	E	R	E	S	I	H
X	H	S	E	A	H	I	W
N	I	G	S	W	R	T	L
I	I	S	I	E	T	B	N
N	F	N	D	E	G	E	I
O	A	O	Y	N	Y	A	B
E	H	V	E	T	A	T	P

After a few minutes contemplation, I cried, “Holmes! Holmes!”

The detective looked up from the book he had been reading.

“Yes?”

“I have discovered the reason for the spaces!”

“And what might that be?”

“They were there as a distraction, to divert any would-be solver from the fact that that without them, the message is a square of eight by eight.”

I stood and handed him the notebook.

“Look at the *T* in the top right-corner, then, go down to *H* and read each diagonal line from right to left.”

“*The will is in the* – Why, Watson, I should have handed you the paper straight away and saved myself an afternoon's labour!"

For all that Holmes had occasional bouts of vanity, he was, to do him justice, capable of taking a joke at himself, and he laughed in his quiet fashion for a minute or two.

"Well, well, I must console myself with the fact that no intellectual effort is ever truly wasted," he said, "and besides, it provided me with a few hours harmless entertainment. Bravo!"

Miss Wheatley returned the following day in response to Holmes's telegram, looking just as fragile and delicate as she had on her previous visit. When he handed her the paper, she fell into a chair and began to laugh so long and hard that Holmes and I exchanged glances. But before I could go over to my medical valise to obtain a sedative, her laughter subsided.

"Forgive me, gentlemen. It is just that my dear old uncle has played a last little joke upon me. He was a great admirer of Sir Walter Scott. The novels, the poems, the short stories, everything. He was always trying to encourage me to read him, so in the end I tried reading *Ivanhoe* and I absolutely hated it! Now he has made it crucial to my happiness. Mr. Holmes, Dr. Watson, I cannot thank you enough. My family's fortunes will be restored and I shall be able to concentrate on caring for my father. Rest assured that when I have full control of Uncle Alistair's estate, you will not find me ungenerous. But you can understand that I wish to be at my uncle's house as soon as possible, so please forgive me if I cut this interview short."

"Of course," "I replied. "We are most proud to have done you this service. "

The lady hurried down into Baker Street and hailed a cab.

Some weeks later, Holmes received, along with a letter of further thanks, a cheque from Miss Wheatley for the princely sum of £350.

"A young woman who is true to her word", Holmes remarked. "Now, Watson, Jacometti is appearing in *Cavalleria Rusticana* at Covent Garden this evening, and we can afford a box. There is time for a meal at L'Escargot d'Argent before the curtain goes up."

"Splendid," I said, and reached for my coat.

The Most Terrible Murderer

October 1903

My dear Watson,

Can you extricate yourself from the toils of domestic bliss long enough to join me for dinner at Baker Street on this coming Thursday evening at half-past seven?

Holmes

"Who is it from, John?"

I looked up from the brief note and across the breakfast table at my wife of eleven months. At times I still found it difficult to believe that this charming and sensitive woman had become a permanent fixture in my life, and was bound to me in holy matrimony.

"It's from Holmes, my dear. I'm invited to dinner on Thursday."

Emily put her coffee cup down into the saucer and smiled.

"Then you must go, John. You haven't seen each other for such a while."

It was true. Since the former Emily Manning had accepted my hand in marriage, and I had resumed my medical practice, this time in Queen Anne Street, the demands of work and domesticity had drastically reduced the amount of time I had to spare for my old friend and former fellow-lodger. I still retained my notes from the many investigations on which I had accompanied him, and had even given over some of my brief leisure time to casting one or two of them into narrative form. The last time I had been in contact with him had been to ask his permission to someday publish a story which we had previously decided should be suppressed for an indeterminate period.

"Well, I shall, then, if you don't object."

Emily took my hand and kissed it.

"Ah, my devoted husband! I think I can survive an evening without you, and you and he are such old friends, how could I object?"

Even as the cab turned into Baker Street that autumn evening, my mind was flooded with memories. Our first meeting in the laboratory at Barts. The sudden appearance of the giant rat of Sumatra. The awful revelation of the true identity of the Whitechapel killer. The crude stick figures of the dancing men. Merridew, who slit his own throat before our eyes, rather than face trial and an inevitable journey to the gallows. The odious Charles Augustus Milverton and his well-deserved end. And so much else – including, of course, Mary. It is a lucky man who knows such a love but once, and I have known it more often.

So familiar was the door of 221b Baker Street that I almost reached into my pocket for my key, but I caught myself, left the key where it was, and rang the bell.

The door was opened by a familiar figure.

"Mrs. Hudson! How are you?"

"Oh, I'm well enough," replied the housekeeper. "And I can see Mrs. Watson has been taking good care of you!"

"She has indeed. And Holmes?"

"Oh, you know him. The only time he's ever ill is when he's run himself into the ground over some case he's been investigating. He'll be pleased to see you. He has a little surprise for you."

"A surprise?"

"Yes."

She took my hat and coat.

"Go straight up. Dinner will be served in five minutes."

I climbed the steps to our old rooms. As I opened the door, I saw Holmes sitting in his accustomed chair, still his old self, clad in his disreputable dressing gown, his clay pipe clenched between his teeth and his hands steepled in front of him. He was not alone, however. A prosperous-looking man in his mid-forties, with a head of curly brown hair and a full beard speckled with grey, was seated in my old armchair. My first thought was that the man was a client, and about to leave, but he sprang from the chair and seized me by the hand.

"Dr. Watson! It's wonderful to see you once more!"

"Good Heavens!" I cried, in sudden recognition. "It's Murray!"

"How long has it been, Doctor? Twenty-two years? Twenty-three?"

"Since you came to see me in the base hospital in Peshawar. Holmes, you know this man saved my life?"

"I had heard something of the kind."

It was Murray who, after I had been wounded by a Jezail bullet at the Battle of Maiwand, had thrown me across a pack-horse and got me back to the British lines, at no small danger to himself.

"This is indeed a pleasant surprise, "I said. What have you been doing with yourself, old chap? You look as if you've come a good way in this world."

"After I left the army, I stayed in India and got a position managing a tea plantation in Assam. Well, I made a good job of it, if I do say so myself, and pretty soon I was managing a larger one, and made some sound investments with the money I earned."

"What brings you back to England?"

"My wife passed away – "

"My dear fellow, I'm sorry to hear it!"

" – and so I thought I'd come back to the old country. I could have obtained your address from your publisher, but I confess I was eager to meet Mr. Holmes as well as to see you again, so I came to Baker Street, and he was kind enough to arrange this meeting."

At this point, Mrs. Hudson brought up the first course of what proved to be a splendid dinner. Holmes said little while we ate, but smiled once or twice as Murray and I recalled our far-off days in the Jewel in the Crown of the Empire. When the meal was over, however, and we were smoking and taking a glass of brandy, Murray looked over to Holmes and said, "I'd like to ask you something, if I may."

Holmes drew on his cigar and said, "Please do, Mr. Murray."

"Well. I've read all of Dr. Watson's accounts of your cases, and enjoyed them all."

Here he turned to me and said, "I must say, I gained a little fame amongst the expatriate community by being the man who indirectly made your stories possible. But you often mention cases that remain untold. I'm not asking you to break any confidences, of course, but I am curious about them. For example, Mr. Holmes, who would you say was the worst murderer you ever had to deal with?"

"That very much depends on how you are defining 'worst'," said Holmes. "Dr. Grimesby Roylott only did away with one person, but his method of doing so was diabolical. Baron Adelbert Gruner more than once made an unsuspecting woman fall in love with him before it served his turn to kill her. Alfred Tarleton tortured his victims for some time before finally dispatching them, while Dr. Henry Staunton made a habit of killing his elderly patients after ensuring that they had remembered him in their will."

"Then there was Schofield, who murdered the whole Abernetty family," I said, "and Vigor, the so-called 'Hammersmith Wonder', a circus performer who used his powers of contortion to break into people's houses and rob and kill them in their sleep."

I was about to add the notorious Jack the Ripper, but I recalled just in time that we had agreed never to mention our connection to the case, let alone the true identity of the killer.

"And yet, Watson, I think you will agree that the most, shall we say, unsettling murderer we have ever encountered was Bert Stevens."

"Yes, indeed."

"What was it about him that set him apart?" asked Murray.

"It is an axiom of our profession, Mr. Murray, that one should not permit one's judgment to be biased by personal qualities. To do so is to depart from the road of clear reason, which is the only true path to the facts. Elspeth Carson, to give but one example, was a charming young woman, beloved by all who knew her, but she ended on the gallows for murdering three small children.

"Bert Stevens was perhaps the most extreme case of this dichotomy between appearance and reality that I have ever encountered. He was mild-mannered, soft-spoken and gentle in his ways. But beneath that placid surface lay a fiendish, calculating intelligence, untroubled by conscience. But if you would wish to hear the whole story – "

"Yes, I certainly would,"

" – then I hand you over to Watson. He, as you know, is the storyteller." He stood and went over to the bookcase.

"You may need this," he said, taking his casebook for the relevant year from its shelf. He opened it to the date in question, handed it to me, then returned to his seat.

"Thank you, Holmes."

"I shall only interject when I deem it necessary."

I took a moment to light a fresh cigar and gather my thoughts, then I began . . . .

The Events of June 1887

"Inspector Merivale, one of the better Scotland Yard men, and a friend to us both, called on us one evening in late June to discuss a rash of seemingly unconnected killings which had recently taken place in the metropolis. Now, it was unusual to have so many murders committed in such a short space of time – "

"Well," said Holmes, "that statement needs a little modification. It's unusual to have so many *unsolved* murders in such a short span of time. In most cases, it's obvious who the perpetrator is. A man kills his wife in a fit of jealous rage, another bludgeons his mate to death in an outburst of drunken anger – these stories are on the back pages of the newspapers, if they make it into the news at all. They'll be on the front page if the victims or the murderers are known to polite society, but otherwise – Well, there are murders being committed every day, but most of the public are unaware of the majority of them."

"Merivale asked if it were possible that they were all being committed by the same man, and Holmes replied that it was unlikely."

"Indeed," said Holmes. "It is actually quite rare for someone to kill more than one person, and when they do, the victims, if not known to the murderer, are at least usually members of the same profession or social class, and usually killed in the same way. The Polish murderer, Marek Wesolowski, or Thomas Kelly as he was known when he lived in London, killed four of his mistresses by the gradual administration of poison. Then there's the Whitechapel Killer, of course. He did away with at least five East End prostitutes. Perhaps he knew them, perhaps he didn't. He probably strangled them, then cut their throats and disembowelled them. He did more than that to his last victim, but then he killed her in her room, not out on the street."

"So," I continued, "we went through the victims with Merivale, one by one, as we shall now.

"First, Pierre Blanchard, twenty-four, a shopkeeper and a native of Dijon, found strangled in Eldon Street, Stepney, 11:30 p.m. He'd been dead for about two hours. From the marks on the neck, the strangulation appeared to have been carried out by the use of a broad ligature – a cummerbund, perhaps, or a scarf."

"Next was Robert Carver, draper, thirty-four, his wife Sophie, twenty-six, and draper's assistant Martin Ball, seventeen. They were all found in Carver's rooms above his shop in Putney at 7:30 a.m., 15th April. Their heads had been beaten to a pulp by some heavy instrument. They had all been dead between four-and-a-half and five hours. Then, let me see – yes, Jean Dawson, aged only sixteen, found in a dustbin behind Artillery Buildings, Victoria Street, 24th April, at six a.m. Her throat had been slit, her body was naked and completely drained of blood –"

"Oh, God!"

"Are you all right, Murray? Do you want to stop?"

"No, no, I'm fine, it's just – sixteen, for God's sake! And in a damned dustbin! What kind of monster could do such a thing?"

"Merivale suggested a vampire, and I of course said that there were no such things, but he pointed out that there had been killers who drank their victims' blood. Human vampires, you might say. What was the name of that man in Harrogate, in '84?"

"Walter Harvey," said Holmes, "and yes, he did drink some of his victims' blood after he'd killed them, but this would still be a problem: Jean Dawson must have been quite small if she could be stuffed in a dustbin, but even so, she must have had six or seven pints of blood in her body. The police medical examiner determined she'd been dead between two and three hours. The body was completely drained. The killer could have drunk six pints of water in that time, or even six pints of beer, but six pints of blood? He would feel ill after a pint, even if he were really determined to carry it through. No, I came to the conclusions that the body must have been hung upside down and drained somewhere else, then dumped where it was found."

I turned to the following page in the casebook.

"The next was Constable Ernest Romney, thirty-one. He was found in the Edgware Road at 10:25 p.m., May 2nd. He had a bullet wound to the chest, and he'd been dead between one and two hours. Only one of the other victims was shot, and that was in the head."

"Sad to say," observed Holmes, "policemen get killed on duty quite often, so while it certainly counts as an unsolved murder, it might have been even less likely to be connected to any of the others."

"Next we had Mehmed Kartal, secretary to the Turkish ambassador, twenty-seven. He was found in his rooms in Bayswater Road, at seven a.m. on the 15th May. He'd been dead five to six hours, and killed in a most bizarre fashion: A metal spike had been driven through his skull and into his brain."

"It does sound like an odd thing to kill someone with," said Murray.

"It does indeed," said Holmes. "Most murders are unpremeditated, with the killer using the first weapon that comes to hand. Even when a murder is planned, there is still a fairly narrow range of methods employed – poison, strangulation, a gun, a knife, or a blunt object."

"It was at this point, as I recall, Holmes, that you were beginning to suspect that there might, after all, be a connection between these killings, and there was but one perpetrator rather than several."

"Correct. I had, of course, been keeping a weather eye on the progress of the investigations, but it wasn't until we actually sat down with Merivale and began to discuss them together that that connection started to become clear. Now, Mr. Murray, I must tell you that in those little sketches of his, my good friend Watson here habitually exaggerates my abilities. While I own that I have brought the arts of observation and deduction, and of reasoning from cause to effect, to greater heights than any man living, I am still human, and so fall short of perfection. This is particularly true when one considers the fact that I have made it my business to study the crimes of the past, in order to see what light they may throw on the misdeeds of the present.

"The killer, whoever he was, was recreating some of those crimes of bygone days. Let us again take them one by one.

"Pierre Blanchard had been strangled using a ligature. Now, as someone who, like Watson, has served on the Indian sub-continent, you may have heard of the *Thugs*, or the *Phansigars*, as they are sometimes called."

"Yes, indeed."

"The British administration broke the cult in the 1830's. Their most prolific assassin was a man called Behram, who claimed to have had over nine-hundred victims. They worshipped Kali the Destroyer, and the story is that once Kali was fighting a demon, and every time she cut him with her sword, another demon sprang from each drop of blood that the demon shed, until she was fighting an army of them. She defeated them by strangling them, so that no more blood would fall. So her worshippers killed in the same way, using strips of cloth called *rumals*. They mainly killed travellers, and looked on their victims as sacrifices to appease the goddess, who would otherwise destroy the whole human race.

"Robert Carver and his wife, and Carver's unfortunate assistant, were killed in emulation of what are known as the Ratcliff Highway murders, in 1811. There were seven in all, the weapon in each case being a maul, a type of sledgehammer. The probable killer was a sailor called John Williams, who was staying near the Highway at a house in Wapping. He committed suicide before he could be put on trial.

"Now, Mr. Murray, have you heard of Countess Elizabeth Bathory?"

"The name is vaguely familiar."

"She is perhaps better known by her sobriquet, '*The Blood Countess*'. She was a sixteenth-century Hungarian noblewoman who became obsessed with the idea that bathing in the blood of young girls would restore her youth and beauty. She drained hundreds of teenaged girls of their blood over the course of two or three years. The highest estimate is over nine-hundred."

"Surely it would have obvious fairly soon that it wasn't working," said Murray.

"I'm sure you're right," said Holmes, "but it may have been a case of '*The Emperor's New Clothes*'. None of her servants had the courage to tell her that her youth and beauty were not returning, so the killings continued. It must be clear that it was her history which inspired the death of young Jean Dawson."

"What happened to this Bathory woman?"

"She was tried and sentenced to spend the rest of her life in one tiny room with no windows and only a small aperture to pass food and drink through to her. She died after a couple of years.

"The murder of Constable Romney was more difficult to place, because, as I said, policeman are killed with greater frequency than the bulk of the population. But working on the basis that our putative killer was modelling his crimes on those of well-known murderers, I surmised that in this instance he was following in the footsteps of Charles Peace, whose first victim was Constable Nicholas Cock of the Manchester Constabulary, in 1876."

"Which brings us to the case of Mehmed Kartal and the iron spike," I said.

"Yes," said Holmes, "and to explain that we must once again look back through time. In fifteenth-century Wallachia, now part of Romania, there was a *voivode*, or warlord, called Vlad Dracula."

"I've read that book," said Murray." Are we back with vampires?"

"I've met Bram Stoker – " I said.

"Yet another purveyor of fantastical tales."

"Thank you, Holmes. I was about to say, Stoker used the name, but his story has little or no connection to the historical character."

"Dracula was also known as *Vlad Tepes*, which means *Vlad the Impaler*. It was his habit to punish people by pushing long wooden spikes through various parts of their anatomy and leaving them to die a lingering and extremely painful death. Now it was unlikely that our killer, whoever he was, would be carrying a long wooden spike around, by day or by night, but his method fitted another story that was told of Dracula, and perhaps explained the choice of Mehmed Kartal as a victim: Dracula spent most of his life in conflict with the Turks, and on one occasion he was visited by three emissaries from the Turkish sultan, Murad II. He asked them to remove their turbans, and when they refused to do so, he had them nailed to their heads with iron spikes."

"So," I said, "Holmes had established the principle on which the murders were being committed, but how were we to know where the killer would strike next?"

"It seemed odd to me," said Holmes, "that someone who was copying the crimes of previous murderers should choose such an eclectic mix, from a wide range of places and times. We've had enough homegrown killers here in Britain over the last fifty years to supply a variety of motives and methods. This suggested to me either that the culprit was, like myself, a student of the history of crime, or had some other formula for choosing to emulate those particular criminals in that particular sequence. If the former were true, then the order might be completely random, which would make a solution virtually impossible. Clearly, it was not chronological, either backwards or forwards. What little we do know of multiple murderers suggests that their behaviour follows a pattern. We had to find out what that pattern was, and where it came from. I think you can stop there, Watson. There were more victims, but it was at this stage of our investigation that I began to formulate a theory as to what that pattern might be."

"Yes," I recalled, "Merivale left us at about half-past ten, and Holmes asked him to call again the following afternoon."

"I must say," said Murray, "this is just like one of your stories, Watson. Better, because it's straight from the horse's mouth. It's pretty grim, though, isn't it?"

"That's one reason why any account of it will stay unpublished for many years after we are gone. After Merivale arrived the following day, we walked together along Baker Street and into Marylebone Road. We visited a particular establishment there that you may have heard of: Madame Tussaud's Waxworks."

"I think I begin to see," said Murray.

"We made our way to the front of the queue, amidst much complaint from the assembled customers, and gained immediate admittance when Merivale displayed his identification. Once we were inside, Holmes led us to a particular part of the museum."

"The Chamber of Horrors!"

"Correct, Mr. Murray," said Holmes.

"We walked past wax *tableaux* of inquisitors torturing heretics, Jacobins guillotining aristocrats, Viking archers riddling Edward the Martyr with arrows, and Romans about to immolate bound Christians during the reign of the Emperor Domitian, until we came to a separate room devoted to representations of individual murderers.

"There were twenty main figures: Marek Wesolowski, Behram the Thug, John Williams, Elizabeth Bathory, Charles Peace, Vlad the Impaler, and the ones I haven't mentioned: Christopher Mills, whose charming habit was to shoot random people through the head, and who was caught when one of his victims unexpectedly survived and identified him – Guiseppe Cardoni, an Italian garrotter whom the Turks employed during the Greek War of Independence, Lu Mei Hua, who killed several of her rivals for the affections of the warlord Zhang Chang by stabbing them through the heart with a long pin, and Michael Bennett, a waterman who cudgelled and robbed some of his passengers and then threw them into the Thames to drown. Each of them, too, had had murders modelled on their crimes, and the killer no doubt intended to emulate the other miscreants represented in this grim tableau.

"'My God!" said Merivale, as we went slowly round the room at Holmes's instigation, weaving through the other visitors and looking at each exhibit.

"'They're all here, in that exact order,' I said.

"'Except for one," said Merivale, pointing to his left. 'Behram isn't the first.' The figure of Marek Wesolowski, alias Thomas Kelly, was standing closest to the entrance on that side.

"'I believe I have an explanation for that,' said Holmes.

"'Apart from Kelly, the murderer acted in accordance with the order of the wax figures,' said Merivale.

"'Holmes! There are twenty figures in here! Will there be eleven more murders?'

"'No, Watson, nine. And we can prevent them from happening.'

"He turned decisively, and Merivale and I followed him back out to the foyer.

"'We should like to speak to the curator,' Holmes said to the young woman at the cash desk. Having seen Merivale's police card, she left her position, led us down a corridor, and into an area cordoned off by ropes which bore a sign on the wall bearing the message, "*No Entry to the Public*". She indicated a door marked "*R. Pemberton, Curator*" and then left us to return to her position.

"'Best if you identify yourself first, Merivale,' said Holmes. 'The presence of an officer of the law tends to reassure those in a position of authority.'

"Pemberton recognised our names – "

"'Of course,' said Murray. 'Practically everyone has read your stories.'

I glanced across at Holmes, who made a mock grimace.

"Pemberton was a middle-aged man of about my height," he said. "Very dapper, his moustache waxed and teased into a point at either end, and he had a silver *pince-nez* perched on the end of the bridge of his long nose.

"'So, gentlemen,' he said, 'how may I be of use to you?'

"'How many attendants do you have working for you?' asked Holmes.

"Pemberton went behind his large mahogany writing desk, opened a drawer, and pulled out a brown folder.

"'About thirty,' he said with a smile. 'I try to be methodical. I have to be. I don't have a terribly good memory. They're all in here: Names, ages, pay, shift patterns, prev – '

"'Shift patterns?'

"'Oh, yes. We have to have guards here at night. Would you believe it, people have actually been known to break in and try and steal things from the figures – Napoleon's hat, the arrow in King Harold's eye, Queen Victoria's veil. I don't know if they think they're the real things, but anyway, we had to put a stop to it.'

"'Have any of your attendants been widowed recently?'

"'Yes, one has. What's his name? I told you my memory was bad. Ah, wait a minute – Stevens. Bertram Stevens, that's it.'

"'Can I see his records?'

"'Certainly.'

Pemberton opened the folder and leafed through it until he found Stevens' sheet, then handed it to Holmes.

"'You're on a case,' said Pemberton as Holmes ran his eyes down the page.

"'Well deduced, Mr. Pemberton.'

"'I hope you don't suspect Stevens of anything. I've never met anyone less like a criminal. He's a devout churchgoer. Man wouldn't hurt a fly. Meek and mild. Very quiet – even more so since he lost his wife.'

"'May I take this?'

"'If you bring it back.'

"'Of course.'

"Once we were back in the open air, Holmes suggested that we repair to the nearby Carpenter's Arms.

"'So, Mr. Holmes,' said Merivale as the bartender brought three foaming pints over to our table, 'may we take it that Bertram Stevens is your suspect?'

"'That's correct. Merivale, you pointed out that Kelly was the first of the wax figures, not Behram.'

"The Scotland Yarder took a sip of his beer. "'Yes, and you said you could explain it, that it didn't spoil your theory.'

"'And it doesn't. For what was Kelly executed?'

"'He poisoned four of his common-law wives,' said Merivale.

"'Four of them?" I said. 'How many did he have?'

"'He had a legal wife in Poland, and at least six mistresses in London – all of whom called themselves "Mrs. Kelly" at some point.'

"'All four died of antimony poisoning,' said Holmes, 'given in the form of tartar emetic, a means of inducing vomiting. They all had the same symptoms, but Wesolowski – or Kelly if you prefer – wasn't arrested, or even suspected, until the fourth one died. So, if Stevens killed his wife by tartar emetic, given in gradual doses, the same as Kelly, he might not have been suspected either, particularly since he didn't kill anyone else in that fashion.'

"'Well,' said Merivale, 'we can get an exhumation order for Mrs. Stevens" body, and we can make enquiries at the chemist's in Stevens" immediate area to see if he bought tartar emetic in any of them. It's a poison, so there should be a record.'

"I had been drinking silently, but now I said, 'I can see a couple of problems, Holmes.'

"'Go on."

"'Supposing Stevens had his wife cremated? And what if he didn't buy the poison in a chemist in his area? Are the police going to inquire at every chemist shop in London?'

"'Well, that's been done in the past, but I take your point. As for the cremation, that costs more than burial, and Stevens is not in a particularly well-paid job.'

"'Why did you take that sheet of Stevens' shift patterns?'

"'It may at least demonstrate that he was free to carry out the murders at the correct dates and times, though I concede that that is only corroborative if we have more evidence of his guilt.'

"A chemist in Bow Road testified that Stevens had purchased several packets of tartar emetic four months before his wife's death. On this basis, an exhumation order was granted on Mrs. Stevens' corpse in the Roman Catholic cemetery in Leytonstone, and it was found to contain a significant amount of antimony. Stevens was arrested and held in Pentonville Prison pending trial.

"Holmes and I were permitted to sit on the first interrogation carried out by Merivale at Scotland Yard, with a sergeant also in attendance. As soon as Stevens was brought into the room, I understood what Pemberton had said about the unlikelihood of his being a criminal.

"He was short, with wispy, wavy blond hair, a pale, pinched face, and behind wire-rimmed spectacles, large, china-blue eyes that seemed filled with a lasting sadness. His legs were slightly bowed, and I attributed this to rickets, which, along with the general frailty of his physique, suggested that he had suffered malnutrition as a child. Was it possible that this feeble creature had perpetrated such a string of atrocities?

"He sat down and looked from one to the other of us, with a seraphic smile.

"'Now, Stevens,' Merivale began, 'do you know why you are here?'

"'I am afraid I have no idea, but I put my trust in the Lord.'

"The sound of his voice was barely above a whisper, his demeanour modest and self-effacing.

"'Do you deny that you bought eight packets of tartar emetic at Boyson's in Bow Road four months before the death of your wife Sarah?'

"'Is that when it was? No, I don't deny it, if that's what the man at the chemist's says.'

"'Why did you purchase so much?'

"'Sarah had a tapeworm.'

"'But she didn't go to a doctor.'

"'She refused. Her mother died in hospital, which made her suspicious of the medical profession. I read that tartar emetic could be used against parasites, but I did not know how long it would take, so I bought a great deal of it. I talked to our vicar, and he advised me to pray, so I did, every night, but in the end it pleased God to take her.'

"'And that's how you explain the high levels of antimony in her body, is it?'

"Those blue eyes widened and tears welled up in them.

"'I – I don't like to say it, but I am rather afraid that she may have taken her own life. Please, please, don't say anything! I couldn't stand it if she were reburied in unconsecrated ground!'"

"Before Merivale could answer, Holmes interposed. 'You know, Stevens, there's one thing I don't understand.'

"'Wh – what's that?'

"'How someone as intelligent as you could make such a stupid mistake.'

"'I don't know what you mean.'

"'I imagine it was because you were just starting out. You were much more careful with the other killings. They were masterfully done.'

"A strange change gradually came over Stevens' face. The shy, childlike meekness began to recede. His expression held hints of both cunning and pride, but he repeated, though with less conviction, 'I don't know what you mean.'

"'I suppose killing Constable Romney must have been fairly easy, but I'm still trying to work out how you got Jean Dawson's body into that dustbin.'

"Stevens was now looking Holmes in the eye, as if to stare him down, but he said nothing.

"'And as for the iron spike in Kartal's skull – that was a stroke of genius. It took me some time to understand the reference.'

"Stevens' head pulled back until he was looking down his nose at my friend.

"'Do you know who I am?' said the detective. 'I'm Sherlock Holmes. You must have heard the name. And you baffled even me.'

"A self-satisfied smile spread across the murderer's face, which was now utterly transformed from a picture of uncomprehending innocence to one of arrogance, horribly tinged with a hint of glee at his crimes.

"'Even Sherlock Holmes,' he said. 'So, I shall have a special place in the annals of crime.'

"I shuddered. Twelve people had died at this man's hand, in a variety of grisly ways, and here he was, smiling.

"'Do you admit to these killings then, Stevens?' demanded Merivale.

"'My only regret is that I was unable to bring the work to a conclusion. Yes, yes, Mr. Whatever-your-name-is Policeman, I was the artist.'

"Once he had made his admission, Stevens waxed garrulous and began to go into the killings in detail. Holmes and I stood to leave.

"'As it says in *Proverbs*, "*Pride goeth before destruction, and an haughty spirit before a fall*,"'" Holmes remarked as we walked out into the open air . . . .

"That," said Murray, "was a remarkable tale."

"There's a little more," I said. "I see you kept the clipping from *The South London Sentinel*, Holmes. One of the radical newspapers," I explained to Murray. "Let me read it aloud:

> *The public has recently heard much about the shocking series of murders perpetrated by Bertram Stevens, and while it is not our business to condone these actions, we would argue that a little may be said in mitigation. We quote Sir Anthony Brocklebank, the noted alienist:*
>
> *"Bertram Stevens was found abandoned on the steps of the Sacred Heart and cared for by the nuns until the age of seven, when he was placed in the workhouse at Hunslet in the West Riding of Yorkshire. There he was provided with education, and just about learned to read and write, but was generally deemed ineducable and incapable of adopting a trade. He did show the beginnings of an aptitude for music, but this was not encouraged, and there were no instruments available on which he might develop an ability.*
>
> *"Around the age of twelve or thirteen he began to show signs of mental disturbance. He would go into trance states without warning, and when he recovered, earned the scorn of his fellow-inmates by claiming that he had visited far-*

distant and beautiful lands. He responded to their jibes with uncontrolled violence and invariably received a thorough beating in return. At other times he said that he was really the son of the King of France, or of Italy, and that very soon his father would send a coach for him to take him away, and again, no beating would shake this conviction, whether it was given by his fellows or by the adults in charge. At the age of fifteen, he was sent from the workhouse, devoid of prospects, with no-one in the world who cared a jot about him. He made his way to London.

"Somehow, Stevens learned to suppress the problematic aspects of his personality and appear 'normal', I would imagine as a survival mechanism. Indeed, those who encountered him described him as meek, soft-spoken, and deeply religious. This assumption of 'normality' is doubtless what enabled him to find a wife and get his job at the wax museum. All this I have gathered from conversations with him and what I have inferred from his records. What I am about to say is speculative, though there is little doubt in my mind that it is the truth: What we have here is a man who has no clear identity. What slender chances he had to form the beginnings of a healthy personality, such as his musical ability, were taken from him or not allowed to develop. He escaped, into oblivion or into fantasy, but these earned him scorn and violence.

"By the time he began work at the museum, he was what we might term a 'Jekyll and Hyde', or multiplex personality, a divided consciousness fitting in with the norms and conventions of society on the surface, but in the deeper

recesses of his psyche, full of a repressed need to express anger and violence. Now, the way he explained it to me is that he was 'possessed' – that was the word he used – by the spirits of these murderers, that they took him over one by one and sent him forth to do the same 'work' they had done. I have no doubt that that is what he believed to be the truth. My own interpretation is that on those nights when he was left alone with the wax figures, having few or no inner resources to distract him from brooding upon them, he would read the descriptive passages in front of each figure, and began to admire them – perhaps, for their defiance of the law and conventional human conduct.

"And so, working his way round the room, having no true identity of his own, he took on one persona after another, killing once in each identity, but each time finding it unsatisfying, and moving on to the next in the hope that another murder would bring balm to his soul. What he would have done had he managed to inhabit all twenty and remained unsatisfied, I don't know. Suicide, perhaps."

"Thank you, Watson. I say now, as I said then, that while I can feel compassion for the child he was, I have nothing but contempt for the man he became. To carry out those murders required meticulous planning and cold intelligence, and I have no doubt that what Brocklebank encountered was yet another false persona, geared to appeal to what Stevens must have sensed the alienist wanted to hear. In any event, the jury did not accept this in mitigation, and Stevens went to the gallows."

"I sometimes wonder," I said, "if killers like Stevens, and the Ripper, are not somehow harbingers of the nature of crimes to come."

"Watson! The evening is yet young, and you and Murray have, I fancy, much more to tell each other. Have another cigar, and I'll pour you both another brandy, and we shall forget for a while the dark and evil deeds of which humanity is capable."

Murray and I left at 11:30, and as he saw us to the door, Holmes said, "Let us not forget the words of *Havamal*."

"'*Havamal*'?"

"*The Words of the High One*, an ancient Viking poem: '*Do not let the grass grow on the paths between the houses of friends*.'"

Acknowledgements

Thanks must go first to David Marcum, editor of the MX Sherlock Holmes series, for his help and encouragement, which helped me extract more from Watson's tin dispatch box than I would have thought possible, and to Steve Emecz, publisher of the series.

Then to my friends both in the UK and the Czech Republic who have had kind words for my stories, both Holmesian and otherwise: Eva Zahradnickova, Jana Kubesova, Frantisek Holik, Martin Plant, Petra Pachlova, Alan Gray, Tomas Dubeda, Misa Cankova, and (in NZ) Ramsey Margolis. And lastly, to the late Michael Ballard, a good writer and a good friend.

MX Publishing brings the best in new Sherlock Holmes novels, biographies, graphic novels and short story collections every month. With over 500 books it's the largest catalogue of new Sherlock Holmes books in the world.

We have over one hundred and fifty Holmes authors. The majority of our authors write new Holmes fiction - in all genres from very traditional pastiches through to modern novels, fantasy, crossover, children's books and humour.

In Holmes biography we have award winning historians including Alistair Duncan. Brian Pugh and Maureen Whittaker who have all won the Sherlock Holmes Book of The Year Award.

MX Publishing also has one of the largest communities of Holmes fans on Facebook and Twitter under @mxpublishing.

MX is a social enterprise that has raised over $130,000 for good causes including Happy Life Mission (Kenya), Undershaw School for children with learning disabilities (UK) and the WFP (World Food Programme).

www.ingramcontent.com/pod-product-compliance
Lightning Source LLC
LaVergne TN
LVHW091643100826
845152LV00006B/144/J

* 9 7 8 1 8 0 4 2 4 7 2 2 8 *